LOVE DRUGGED

LOVE DRUGGED

James Klise

Woodbury, Minnesota

First Edition
First Printing, 2010

Cover design by Lisa Novak
Back cover image © iStockphoto.com/subjug
Front cover image © iStockphoto.com/Amanda Rohde

Flux, an imprint of Llewellyn Worldwide Ltd.

Library of Congress Cataloging-in-Publication Data
Klise, James, 1967–
    Love drugged / James Klise.—1st ed.
        p. cm.
    Summary: Fifteen-year-old Jamie is dismayed by his attraction to boys, and when a beautiful girl shows an interest in him, he is all the more intrigued by her father's work developing a drug called Rehomoline.
    ISBN 978-0-7387-2175-0
    [1. Homosexuality—Fiction. 2. Dating (Social customs)—Fiction. 3. Drugs—Fiction. 4. High schools—Fiction. 5. Schools—Fiction.]
I. Title.
    PZ7.K6837Lo 2010
    [Fic]—dc22
                                                    2010014228

Flux
Llewellyn Worldwide Ltd.
2143 Wooddale Drive
Woodbury, MN 55125-2989
www.fluxnow.com

Printed in the United States of America

For Mike

I now hasten to the more moving part of my story. I shall relate events that impressed me with feelings which, from what I had been, have made me what I am.

—*Frankenstein,* MARY SHELLEY

one

Judging by the angry mail we get, a lot of people consider me to be the villain of this story. The Chicago newspapers treat me like a public menace. They use the most biased headlines:

STRAIGHT CHARADE LEAVES READERS IRATE
NO MORE DATES FOR JAMIE BATES
WOULD YOU WANT HIM FOR YOUR DAUGHTER?

No, people, you would not want me for your daughter. That should be obvious.

It's true, I told a lot of lies. I lied to everyone, including myself. I took things that didn't belong to me. Valuable things. In the end, I resorted to violence, which I totally regret, and I set what I thought was a very responsible, very contained, tiny fire, which led to—well, massive destruction of private property.

But a villain?

My defense goes like this: Technically, in order to be considered a true villain, you've got to have a sinister plan. I suspect that a class called "Creating Your Sinister Plan" is taught during freshman year of Villain School.

Take, for example, the Disney movie *101 Dalmatians*. Cruella De Vil creates a plan: *I am going to steal these adorable puppies and kill them to make coats.* The crazy old people in *Rosemary's Baby* hatch a downright devilish plan: *Let's take this innocent young woman and use her body to give birth to Satan's immortal offspring.* In the *Friday the 13th* movies, the drowned teenager Jason Voorhees comes up with a truly ambitious, no-good, blood-splattered plan: *Maybe, if I avenge my young death by killing every teenager who comes to Camp Crystal Lake, over time I will find some measure of peace.*

Sure, these characters are all lunatics—certified, grade-A wack jobs—but they are bad guys nonetheless. They created evil plans; therefore, they are villains.

Let the record show, I never had a sinister plan. I never said to myself: *Let me trick a beautiful, intelligent female classmate into thinking I am heterosexual.* In our case, a relationship simply grew of its own accord. Opportunities presented themselves. It was the classic romantic scenario involving two young hearts, first kisses, exotic locales, and a stolen supply of untested pharmaceutical drugs designed to alter the sexual chemistry inside the brain.

I don't mean to excuse my crimes. These days I carry regrets with me like my grimy gray backpack, evident for the whole world to see.

People are complicated. Desire can be confusing. Not for you? Consider yourself lucky.

———————

Reporters hold their compact digital recorders up to my mouth. "Please, Jamie, talk about the drug," they say. "Tell us about specific changes to your mind and your body." They always ask me to describe the taste of the pills, and they always use the word "miracle."

Often they ask for a photograph, something for them to use instead of my freshman yearbook picture, which everybody's seen. Infamous me, sitting up too straight, with my shiny brown bowl cut. Toothy and too happy-looking—alarming glee, like someone just pinched my ass. Now when someone pulls out a camera, I slouch a little and push my bangs to the side. I cross my arms. I've learned how to stare at cameras with confidence, without needing to smile at all.

Chicago reporters like to include my background story. Here's my version: I'm an only child. For the past five years, my family has lived with my mother's parents in Rogers Park, north of Peterson Avenue. Before that—back when my dad had his quick-printing business—we lived on the city's west side. My grandparents' place is a brick two-flat, one apartment on top of the other, with a chain-link fence along the front sidewalk. It may not impress, but it doesn't embarrass, either. It fits in.

When we first moved in, I picked a bedroom downstairs, in my grandparents' apartment. I wanted to be in the middle of everything. In retrospect, my parents must have appreciated the chance to have the upstairs to themselves, where they had plenty of space for starting their endless chain of doomed businesses—discount magazine sales, website design, recipe subscription clubs. One half-baked venture after the next.

At first, my parents expected our stay would be short. "One year, tops," my father said. Of course he thought so. My dad wears his wavy brown hair exactly as he did the year he led his high school baseball team to historic wins. (Another headline: *SLUGGER BATES TAKES LAKERS TO STATE*.) I'll catch him paging through the old yearbooks we keep on the TV, next to the Bible, and even I'm struck by how much I resemble him at that age. Despite subsequent setbacks in my dad's life, he has always clung to the notion that the universe happens to favor certain people, like him, and that the universe is not fickle.

"Now remember, kiddo," he told me back then, as we carried my suitcases into the "temporary" bedroom, "we're guests in this home."

I looked around the room. The narrow window offered an unobstructed view of my grandparents' garage, squat and brick. On the bed lay an old toy, a small wooden carving of two painted ducks on a log. I reached for it. The ducks were at opposite ends of the log, but when I pulled a string at the bottom, the ducks moved to the center, flapping their speckled wings.

My father hung my clothes in the closet and continued to

give instructions in a low voice. "You're almost eleven, Jamie. Make yourself useful, and otherwise try to be invisible."

My mother came in, carting two rubber bins. She has always been freakishly strong. Unlike my dad and me, my mom is little, and she has straight ash-blond hair like her parents. "We're one floor up," she told me, pointing toward the ceiling with a sly smile, "like in a regular house. It won't be any different than before. Just bigger!"

It didn't take me long to realize that choosing the downstairs bedroom was a big mistake—the first in my noteworthy streak. Now and then, the phrase "suddenly an orphan" crossed my thoughts. My parents ate suppers on the first floor with us, but I got used to their early good-nights, quick kisses, and their departure through the front door. I would follow the sound of them climbing the stairs, then moving around the apartment above as they attended to business. Sometimes it sounded like ghosts.

I dreaded the quiet after they left. In the living room, an antique clock tolled ominously each hour. Every night after eating, I would rise from the table and say, "Thank you for the very nice supper," as I'd been trained to say.

"You're quite welcome," my grandmother answered. "Now go on, we'll get these dishes."

"Pleasure knowing you," my grandfather sometimes added, or "Nice doing business with you." It took some time before I understood he meant this to be funny. Then he'd reach for the TV remote.

For as long as I can remember, the rubber bins in my bedroom have stored all the things that brought light and sparkle to my life—toys and plastic superheroes when I was ten; books when I got older (I preferred books about explorers, astronomers, martyrs, events that changed the world, and people who took risky chances to improve their lives); and most recently, music and movies. In junior high, we took field trips downtown to see big musicals. We'd have lunch on State Street or Michigan Avenue, then race to get in line for the show. My favorites were *Wicked* and *Les Miz*, but I wasn't picky. Now I have a dozen recordings on CD. For eighth-grade graduation, my parents gave me a cheap TV/DVD combo for my bedroom, and I began buying used DVDs—classic titles that my dad recommended. I got them from the Korean video store for a couple of bucks each: *Rosemary's Baby, Strangers on a Train, Invasion of the Body Snatchers, I Know You're in the House Alone, Halloween.* I'd watch them by myself, with my bedroom door closed. Things are scarier when you're alone.

To be clear, I never felt unwelcome in my grandparents' apartment. They treated me with generous respect. "Jamie, we respect your privacy," they said, in order to explain why they never entered my bedroom. They smiled at me and patted my shoulder, but they had forgotten how to interact with a young person. Over time, their lack of communication intersected with my escalating need for privacy, and—*slam!* It was like the signing of the Magna Carta. We found an arrangement that worked for everyone.

"What I don't understand," reporters always say, "is why you didn't come out sooner."

Sooner. Simple as walking through a wide-open door into a perfect, sun-dappled day.

Give me a break, I was fifteen—a high school freshman.

"Gay" is the word my best friend Wesley used to describe the three-page essay on school spirit that we were assigned for English. "Damn, man, this project is *gay.*"

"That's gay," the girls remark, when a friend dares to tie a sweater around her shoulders as if posing for a magazine. *"You look totally gay."*

"No homo," boys say quickly in class, if they've expressed something bordering on sensitive and don't want to misrepresent themselves.

"Queer" is what they call the way-too-friendly guy who sells French fries in the cafeteria. *"Hands off, queer bait!"*

"Faggots!" This was the furious outcry directed toward the immature clowns who misbehaved in homeroom, making us lose our pizza party. *"Take a picture, faggot, it lasts longer."*

"Faggot," too, was the overweight, effeminate boy who showed up at school at the start of seventh grade and then silently endured a constant attack of projectiles aimed at his head—crumpled papers, rubber bands, even pencils. By November, he was gone. I imagined his life had become a series of sad switches, a long lonely search for a place to fit in. But I wouldn't be his friend, either. After all, I was getting by.

Recently, even a gay journalist asked me, "Jamie, why?"

Why put yourself through all this?" As if he had forgotten those harrowing years between ages ten and eighteen, when the meanest, most dreaded, completely acceptable, worst insult for any boy was to be called, simply, "fag."

two

The trouble started in January. I was sitting in the school cafeteria with Wesley. He had spent several lunch periods giving me grief about my decision not to try out for the baseball team. Conditioning had started over the winter break.

Wes gestured at me, as if his hands held magical powers of persuasion. "Dude, you played in sixth grade, you played in seventh grade, you were *good* last year—why not this year?"

"This is high school, Wes," I said. "Bigger pond, out of my league."

I'd gotten the same heat from my dad about not playing ball. But I knew that high school sports involved crowded locker rooms, with showers. In my mind, it meant a catastrophic boner disaster waiting to happen.

"It's worth a try," Wes said. "You can hit. Besides, the chickies love baseball players."

Chickies? Where had he learned to talk like that—*West Side Story?* Wes had grown about a foot taller since summer, and with the height, he'd developed a new appreciation for "the chickies." Obsessed, he let his eyes roam the cafeteria like a scanning device. His running commentary was remarkably comprehensive, almost scientific in scope, but his standards were pretty loose. One good feature on a girl was worthy of recognition, even if the rest of her was average. I prayed that his enthusiasm might rub off on me.

At the time, my strategy was to wait it out, get through high school. I once read an advice column in the local free weekly that said the best time to come out was when you had some independence, some resources of your own. The column said you needed a safety net. This made sense. Like my grandparents' brick building, I didn't stand out. I wasn't like the seventh-grade "sissy" who came and went. I thought if I kept my head low, I could fly under the radar all four years and make it out alive.

"Hey, now there you go, Mr. Picky," Wes said, facing me almost in challenge. "There's one worth your time. Over at the cash registers."

More like a waste of my time, I thought, but I turned to look.

There was no arguing this one. The girl was spectacular. Her shiny dark hair framed a face that was a wonder of genetic good fortune—small features, large brown eyes. She was tall and thin-waisted, with plenty of curves. When she saw us looking at her, she smiled and waved. Then she started coming our way.

Wes sputtered. "What the ... ?"

Funny thing was, I already knew this girl. She came straight to where we were sitting and perched her cafeteria tray on the edge of our table. "Hey, Jamie," she said. "Don't forget, Mr. Covici asked you to bring the treats next week."

I nodded. "He can count on me."

She grinned. "Hmmm, if you're bringing the treats, maybe I'll skip breakfast."

"Not recommended. I'll probably just stop at the gas station on the way to school."

"Well, I know you won't disappoint us." She patted my shoulder, turned on her heel, and walked away. The faint trace of her perfume lingered, exotic and expensive.

When she was out of earshot, Wes hissed, "*Who the hell is that?*"

"Celia Gamez," I said, pleased to impress him. "I'm in a club with her."

He seemed skeptical. "Which club?"

"The First Knights." This was a service club my parents had made me join—a small group, and not because it was selective. But even I knew that things like that would look good on college applications someday.

"Celia Gamez," Wes said. "I know that name. Yeah, my cousin Mimi went to junior high with her. That girl lives in, like, the biggest house on the North Side."

"Is that right?" I said, only half interested.

"She digs you."

"Sure she does, Wes. And those chicken fingers are made from the plump hands of *real chickens!*"

"But she does," he insisted. "Didn't you see her flirting? *'I know you won't disappoint us.'* Damn, maybe I should join one of these gay clubs." He turned and faced the wall, where a bulletin board advertised the Art Club, Book Club, Chess Club, Debate—a complete alphabet of school activities.

Celia moved across the cafeteria, and I tried to see her through Wesley's eyes. It was easy to appreciate how pretty she was. But below the belt, I felt nothing. Hopeless.

Wes reached up with one of his long skinny arms and tore down the Art Club flier. He scribbled something on it with a Sharpie. He smiled wickedly and asked, "Hey, Jamie, wanna join my new club?" He held up the flier, which now read: *FART CLUB. Every Monday. Come show off your special talent!*

———

Wes and I had been friends since the fifth grade. We were both transfer students that year, "the new kids," and the teacher parked our desks side by side in the back of the room like a package deal. On the first day, during class, Wes leaned across the aisle and reached for my new box of twelve Faber-Castell pastels. "Can I see those?" he whispered. I nodded and handed them over, unopened. The teacher was explaining fractions, how you broke numbers apart and piled them on top of each other to make a different kind of number. I followed along in my textbook, but after a minute I looked back to see what my new buddy was drawing. He wasn't drawing. All my pastels were broken into halves, and he'd spread them across the desk in mismatched pairs. Fleetingly I thought: *Are those...fractions?* Wes smiled at me, lifting his shoulders as if to say, *I have no idea how that happened.* I was too stunned to report him to the teacher. Later that day he broke a science lab window "by mistake" with a football.

What fascinated me about Wesley was his fearless energy. He was so confrontational, always on offense, unafraid of collisions. In the sixth grade, I tried to be like him. I stopped tucking in my shirt, ignored my comb, left shoelaces untied. If Wes playfully shoved me, I shoved back. I tried to imitate the effortless noise he made by being himself, the chaos he caused just crossing the room to sharpen a pencil.

Wes wasn't out of control every day, but the threat always lurked. Nobody ever knew what to expect from him. Then, during seventh grade, he changed. Almost overnight, he became calmer, more focused at school. He still called attention to himself, but it was more controlled and positive, more like regular confidence. The teachers liked him, and students learned to trust him. At the time I chalked it up to maturity and discipline; it wasn't until later that I learned the credit went to medicine—a twenty-milligram, time-release tablet after his breakfast each morning. Ritalin—the first miracle drug I knew by name.

———

I declined Wes' offer to be a founding member of his Fart Club.

I had a study hall after lunch, and my habit was to go to the school library to kill time. Maxwell Tech was a public school, one of the biggest in Chicago. Nearly one hundred years old, the school spread across a full city block like a fortress. It was crazy loud, too many students competing for limited space, calling out insults, filling the halls with squeaks as they scraped their tennis shoes along the polished floors. The teachers only added to the din, shouting for students to show respect, take off hats, return to class. Yet the teachers always smiled, a little strangely, like someone had pinched them in the ass, too.

The school library was relatively quiet. Plus, it offered thirty computers with excellent Internet access and a worthless filter. The first time I visited a site for gay teens, it was on a whim. It felt safe; everything was anonymous. Granted, my user name wasn't very creative: Chicagojamie. It didn't seem necessary to call myself Alex or Johnny or Pete; there were thousands of Jamies in Chicago. Besides, I only lurked in the chat rooms—never chatted. I never made plans to meet people or hook up. Everybody knew the horror stories about creepy adults pretending to be teenagers. I never visited these sites on my parents' computer at home or left traces for them to see.

Since October, I'd been following a thread about scary movies. People always listed recent slasher movies, the cheesy kind that went straight to video. Nobody seemed to have seen anything really excellent. One day, I boldly chimed in.

Chicagojamie: has anybody seen Rosemary's Baby? the best! esp the scene in the telephone booth. or the scene with the Scrabble pieces. u MUST rent if u haven't seen it.

I pressed *enter* and held my breath. It felt like crashing a party. I prepared myself for a flood of negative responses: *Who are you?! Who do you think you are?! Who asked you?!* To my surprise, nobody responded. The thread continued about the same stupid movies. I scrolled back again, to confirm I had, in fact, sent the message. There it was, sandwiched between all the others. My first comment—posted and ignored. I nearly logged off, when a private message appeared in the upper corner of my screen:

LaLaBoy15: Chicago, love that movie! Ruth Gordon rox! Have u seen Mia Farrow's other scary movie from that time—See No Evil? blind rich girl is in a big country house full of bloody corpses and she doesn't know it. Faaaaaaabulous.

My chest filled like a balloon with joy. Then another private message appeared:

Burtlovesernie: Ro's Baby is da bomb!! Good call. Scary movies were best BC—Before Carpenter— right? Try to find Let's Scare Jessica to Death from 1971—hippies versus vampires!

I disagreed about Carpenter (*Halloween* is a slice of perfection) but I responded to both of them, promising to rent these titles.

Just like that, I was hooked. My free period became the

one time of day when I could connect to guys who liked the same things as me. We chatted about actors we liked, usually the ones who looked good without shirts. We talked about our favorite movies—thrillers or romances that featured actors without shirts. I created an email account for ChicagoJamie, so we could exchange photos of shirtless actors and models. Shirtlessness was our religion, and we all said the same prayer: *Please Lord, send me someone with abs like those!*

We never chatted about sports. Sure, there were sites for guys who liked sports, but I didn't visit them. The kind of drama I liked best couldn't be summed up in a sports page headline.

I met a seventeen-year old guy online who had seen *Wicked* nine times on Broadway. This blew my mind. Besides *Oklahoma!*, I'd never seen a show more than once. The boys who lived near New York City couldn't believe I didn't see more shows in Chicago. I could be candid about a lot of things online, but I didn't know how to admit—in a clever or attractive way—that my family didn't have much money.

On these sites, we spent a lot of time joking about "the island." The island was where we'd all be forced to live once our families and friends shut the doors in our faces and told us we disgusted them. Weird, in retrospect, how we accepted this fate, as plainly as we expected that someday we'd move out of our parents' houses for college or jobs. Away from our families, we'd all gather together under the sun, the way the newspaper and CNN showed guys partying at the Pride parades each June. Muscular guys with their shirts off, drinking frozen drinks and dancing. Yes, sir, that was our island.

Offline, whenever I pictured the island, I didn't imagine sand, palm trees, coconuts, or laughter. I pictured only the vast water—deep and cold and blue—that would separate me from everything and everyone I knew.

three

The First Knights met before school, usually on Tuesdays. I arrived even before Mr. Covici, the librarian, who was also the club advisor. The library door was locked, lights off inside. It always felt weird to see the school hallways empty. My snowy shoes left puddles on the floor.

Soon Mr. Covici appeared, carrying a bundle of newspapers in each arm. Bespectacled and balding, with an outdated wardrobe and formal demeanor, Mr. Covici called to mind a bewildered time-traveler who had ventured far from home. He blinked at me groggily. "Please tell me you brought the treats."

I nodded, lifting up two plastic grocery bags as evidence.

I waited in the dark for him to turn on the lights, but only one came on, in the middle of the room. With the rest of the library dark, the lone fluorescent tube light shone down dramatically, the way, in movies, a bare bulb illuminates thugs during questioning.

I removed the contents of the bags and opened the containers. Earlier that morning, half awake at the deserted grocery store, I had agonized over what to buy. Popular brand names sure didn't convey a very masculine image: "Rainbow Chips" Deluxe, Sandies "Fruit Delights," Soft Batch Chocolate Chips. I bypassed the Lorna Doones and the "Double Stuffed" E.L. Fudgies and settled on something safe: Oreos, Chips Ahoy!, and a package of cheap napkins.

I sat and waited, staring up at the impressive beamed ceiling. The room was cavernous, elegant. From high dusty nooks, marble busts of philosophers, poets, and playwrights watched over the tables. Along one wall were a dozen arched windows; daybreak frost covered the panes in feathery white patterns.

The early morning silence impressed me, as always. During the day, the noise level was Mr. Covici's constant irritant, requiring his full attention. He tried everything to keep the room quiet, from gentle reminders to bursts of showy discipline, but nothing seemed to work. People liked to talk.

Last fall, Covici borrowed a ladder from the custodian. Although he didn't seem like the kind of man who climbed ladders frequently, he did so during my study hall, holding a can of black paint and a brush. We all went silent for once, watching as he painted words along the high wall above the bulletin board. He didn't even use a stencil. The letters were spindly but legible. It took him about an hour to paint the whole thing, moving the ladder as he went.

He wrote: *SILENCE IS A MANSION WHERE DWELL MY GREATEST NOTIONS.*

It sounded like something Thomas Jefferson might have said, or Ben Franklin, or Maya Angelou—one of those people who become famous for saying obvious things in interesting ways.

Like an effective ad jingle, the sentence echoed in my mind at unlikely moments ... looking out the window of the city bus at tree branches lined with snow; half awake in the shower, rinsing shampoo from my hair; in bed at night as I pulled the covers over my face.

Silence is a mansion where dwell my greatest notions.

Mr. Covici's message did not succeed in bringing lasting quiet to the library, but the phrase quickly made its way around the school like common knowledge. On the walls of the boys' bathroom stalls, quite a few tributes appeared:

Maxwell Tech is a toilet where dwell our greatest notions.
This toilet is the bottomless hole where dwell my greatest turds.
Pizza sausage is the motor that drives my greatest bowel movements.

Now, setting out the treats, I impulsively asked Mr. Covici, "Who said that quote, anyway?"

"Oh?" He glanced up from his monitor, then turned in the direction of my finger. "I did," he answered, before returning to his computer.

One by one, the other club members arrived and settled

silently into seats. Keenan was a sophomore, and so thin that he looked birdlike. Meeting after meeting, he rarely lifted his eyes from a hardcover copy of *The Giver*. Sophomore twins Mark and Maggie Mosinskey also kept to themselves. They showed up for meetings, where their twin votes held some influence, but they always had an airtight excuse when it came to actual volunteer work (future members of Congress, those two). Gwen, our only senior, had a round face and bleached yellow hair. She wore lipstick and carried a purse beaded with neon stars to match the stars on her jacket. Each time I saw her, Gwen gave the impression that she had stopped by school on her way to another event.

Anella, a tall, athletic-looking junior who I hadn't ever talked to, sat across from me with her friend Ivan, also a junior. I liked to sit facing Ivan. He was handsome, with dark blond hair that fell just past his ears. His eyes were a remarkable shade of blue. Our lockers were near each other, and I often noticed him around school. Once, I'd seen him remove a guitar—without a case—from the trunk of a car. Based on the little information I knew about him, I had decided he was tough and sensitive and funny and wonderful.

Celia Gamez finally arrived, looking rested, bored and very pretty as usual. Taking her seat, she surveyed the cookies. "Did you bring these, Jamie?"

"As promised," I said.

"Did you bring anything healthy?"

"Um, guess not."

Curses—foiled again by my useless gut instinct.

But then Celia smiled, showing off her perfect white

teeth as if she couldn't possibly carry a grudge. "No biggie." She reached into her bag and pulled out a yogurt and a white plastic spoon. She even ate with confidence, as if she enjoyed her breakfast in the library every morning.

There was silence among the group as Mr. Covici approached the head of the table. Notebooks folded shut, chairs squealed to attention.

Covici set his eyeglasses on the table; the lenses looked as if they hadn't been cleaned since Christmas. "Thanks, all of you, for participating in last week's Open House. And kudos to Ivan and Anella for helping the dean's office with envelope stuffing yesterday. We've certainly had a busy month of service to Maxwell."

I gave a private sigh. More envelope stuffing. Unlike the tennis team or the drama group, ours wasn't the kind of club that lent itself to dynamic yearbook photos.

Nobody, I realized, was eating my cookies—only me. I had eaten one, and had two others laid out on a napkin, like an old lady at a card game.

"And now it's that time of year again," Mr. Covici continued. "The time to start thinking about fundraising. It is the tradition of this club to make an annual gift to the school." He gazed at one of the far corners of the library, where the students went to fart. "For the past few years, we've held a Valentine's Day flower sale. Gwen, do you want to elaborate?"

Gwen sat up proudly. "My parents own a flower shop over on Clark Street, and they always get us a bunch of carnations wholesale. We sell them with private message tags attached."

Blue-eyed Ivan reached for a cookie, and I was insanely grateful. His hand went up. "Excuse me, what is the money for?" He spoke with the careful cadence of someone not born in this country.

"A gift," Gwen said sourly. "For the school. He already said that."

Ivan smiled, his dimples showing. "Yes, eh... but what are we going to purchase?"

"Hard to say, at this point," Mr. Covici answered. "Once we raise the money, we'll know how much we can spend this year."

I agreed with Ivan. This seemed like an ass-backwards way to go about things. But I was only a freshman, so what did I know?

"You'll work as teams," Covici said.

Celia quickly raised her hand. "I volunteer Jamie and me to design the flower tags."

"Fine," Covici said, writing it down. "But guys, do me a favor? Something more than a heart with an arrow through it? A *smidgen* of creativity, please."

As Covici assigned the other tasks, Celia smiled at me and mouthed, *Okay?*

I nodded, feeling my face go red. Maybe Wesley was right. Maybe this amazing girl really did have a crush on me. At least, a smidgen of a crush?

The first period bell rang and everybody rose to leave.

"Cake assignment," Celia said to me. "Designing the tags." Her eyes were so bright, her complexion perfect. I wondered if, over time, she would share her skin-care secrets with me.

I said, "So do you want to meet in the library after school, or what?"

"These PCs suck, in terms of graphics. Do you have a Mac at home?"

I only had access to my parents' ancient desktop; we called it "the relic." "No," I admitted.

"We can work at my house then. Let's meet in the Commons after school on Friday."

"Cool." I felt self-conscious, reduced to one-word answers. My face still felt warm. So this was what it felt like to be the object of someone's desire.

"I look forward to it." She studied my face, as if she was having difficulty reading my expression. "Okay then, Jamie ... Later."

"Later!" I called.

————

During my study hall, the library tables near me buzzed with conversation, gossip, and two students quizzing each other on Spanish vocab. One Asian boy with spiky hair sat by himself, reading aloud from the *Chicago Sun-Times* comics pages. I was always grateful for people who seemed more conspicuously crazy than me.

I logged on to a computer, eager to see who was online. Since the first of the year, I'd been chatting with a boy who said he lived in Chicago, too. His user name was CrazyforKFC—a reference to Kenny Francis Carter, the country singer, but his parents probably didn't know that. KFC was not my favorite person online. He asked too many dumb questions. He seemed a little too eager to be "buddies." But he often wrote questions specifically to me, and I answered to be polite. I figured that general friendliness was the rule of the game. I thought KFC was harmless.

> **CrazyforKFC:** hey, Chicago, do u ever go 2 Halsted Street?
> **Chicagojamie:** no, I live way north.

Halsted Street, between Belmont and Waveland, is the center of the gay universe in Chicago. I figured KFC wanted to meet and hang out. I wasn't ready for that.

> **CrazyforKFC:** u should come. it's awesome 2 watch all the guys.
> **Chicagojamie:** can't get over there, sorry. ☹
> **CrazyforKFC:** that's 2 bad. where do u go 2 school?

There are more than a hundred high schools in Chicago. The risk of knowing him seemed minuscule. Plus, I was distracted by a new friend in Minnesota who went by the name ScreamQueen. I wanted to answer KFC and be done with him, so I could respond to ScreamQueen. I typed my school name and pressed send. Within seconds, I had a response.

> **CrazyforKFC:** no shit, gurl, me 2!!

My fingers froze above the keyboard. I was a complete idiot. I didn't know what to write. Should I deny it? Say that I was kidding? His next message was like a punch in the gut.

> **CrazyforKFC:** r u in the library now?

Stupidly, I lifted my head. The gesture was automatic, a curious instinct. I sat up and looked around to see if anybody else was scanning the room.

By now the library had maybe twenty other students working at computers, their faces glued to their screens. But as I dreaded and expected, at the far end of the computer row, one pale boy slouched far back in his chair and looked straight at me. He grinned wildly, his narrow eyes like a laser on me. In retrospect, he was probably just friendly and excited. But to me it looked like the most villainous smile I'd ever seen.

You are a world-class dipshit, I told myself.

The boy's name was Paul Tremons. He was older than me, a skinny junior. His sister was a popular girl in my class, but Paul didn't seem to belong to any particular group. To compensate, he drew attention to himself in obnoxious ways—for example, wearing a pirate hat to school, or funny sunglasses, or bellowing loud fake laughter in the hallways. I couldn't believe I'd been chatting with him, of all people.

We both were staring. He gave a little upward tilt of his red, pimply chin, smiling, but I couldn't bring myself to smile back. I felt dizzy from exposure.

I thought of how gossip spreads, like water in a paper towel, absorbed quickly by large groups of people. Who knew if this jackass could keep a secret? Would I end up like the boy in seventh grade, under constant attack from all sides? One thing I knew for sure: I was not ready to go to any island *yet.*

The period ended and the bell rang. Everybody but me

got up and moved toward the doors. I took my time logging off, gathering my notebooks. I felt like I was moving in slow motion. Inside my head, I kept berating myself for being so careless. Most of the kids left, but Paul waited for me at the door.

He smiled, lifting his red chin. "Small world." His eyes were set too close together, giving him the look of a pathetic, red-faced dog. In any other circumstance I might have felt sorry for him.

"I don't want to be late for class," I said, almost whispering.

He leaned close. "Don't worry, I won't tell anyone. By the way, Jamie, I'm Paul."

I know who you are, CrazyforKFC.

I pushed through the door. "I have to go."

"Wait a sec," he said, but I didn't turn back. I imagined him watching me, studying my body, as I raced down the hallway. Did he think he had a chance with me? It felt too close, too real. It made me want to vomit.

I spent the rest of the day in a panic, my throat thick with emotion. It freaked me out to think that a boy at school knew my secret. If confronted, I couldn't deny it. I couldn't pretend I had visited that site by accident. We'd chatted for weeks. He mentioned hot actors and I responded with approval. He might have saved my messages. The worst part was not knowing if I could trust him. I worried about it constantly, the way my grandmother worried about leaving the iron on when we were at the grocery store. *Did I leave it on? Should we go back?* It was the kind of sharp anxiety that took over the mind, clouding out all other thoughts.

After school, I lingered in class with my math teacher, asking for extra help. I didn't need tutoring, but I had to kill time. I didn't want to risk running into KFC Paul again. But the effort was wasted. When I went to my locker, he was waiting for me, sitting on the floor in the empty hallway. He jumped up.

I faltered. "How'd... how did you know where my locker is?"

Smiling, he fluttered his fingers in the air like wings. "Oh, a bird told me."

I began to suspect that the "crazy" part of his user name was more significant than the KFC part. Maybe if I didn't speak, he'd get the hint. I opened my locker, trying to focus on homework.

"You look cute when you're stressing," he said. "But you have no reason to be. I said I wouldn't tell anyone."

Go away, I pleaded telepathically. I reached in and extracted two notebooks and my gigantic World History textbook.

"That book is a bitch, right? I may still have my notes from that class. I should give them to you and make your life a lot easier."

Go away... Go away... I dropped the textbook into my bag—*thud!* I took out my wool coat.

He leaned next to me, too close. I could feel his warm breath. "Dude, you need to chill," he said defensively. "I'm not a freak. Neither are you. Friends?" His smile was coy.

I picked up my backpack and slammed the locker shut. "Leave me *alone*," I hissed. I turned and raced for the exit.

The following days passed in a blur of paranoia and watchfulness. I stopped going to the library. Crazy Paul didn't approach me again. I ran into him one morning when we were both getting tardy slips from the main office. He stared me down but didn't say a word.

More than anything, I wondered if he had told someone. I tried to read the faces of random students in the halls. Did their eyes linger on me? Not as far as I could tell. Did they whisper my name like a horrible disease when I passed? Nope. Most people ignored me, as usual.

Still, I was convinced it was only a matter of time. Before long, people would know the big headline of my secret. Everyone—classmates, teachers, the creepy guy who sold French fries in the cafeteria—would start to see me through a pinkish gay lens: *There he is, the gay kid. That's the gay one there. You know Jamie—the gay kid?* I was not ready to go to the island. Maybe someday, but not yet.

I knew what I had to do.

I went back to the library. I logged on to my school account and erased my Internet history. It took only two minutes. I deleted my Favorites and cleaned out my Cookies. I went to ChicagoJamie's email account and blocked all the old names and addresses. It almost felt like murder—each click a little bullet aimed at a boy I didn't ever want to hear from again. *Click*, gone, *click*, gone, *click, click, click*, gone, gone, gone. The process was fast and scary and necessary.

I kept my eyes on the library door the whole time,

watching and dreading. When I was finished, I logged off, picked up my backpack, and fled.

I went to find Wesley at his locker. The contents seemed to have exploded around his feet.

"Cool, you're here," he said. "It's not too late for you to come to baseball conditioning if—"

I interrupted. "You told me your cousin knows that girl, Celia Gamez?"

He nodded. "Mimi went to junior high with her."

"I need to meet Mimi then. I want to know everything about Celia."

"Yeah?" He looked pleased. "So, this girl, she pushes your buttons?"

In this regard, Wesley had more buttons than a computer keyboard.

"Sure, yeah, she pushes my buttons."

He slapped me on the back like a comrade. "Finally! Dude, you were beginning to worry me."

"And your problem, Wes, is that you use the word *dude* without irony."

———

After supper that night, rather than hiding in my bedroom, I joined my grandparents in the living room. The TV was on, a loud, intense game show where contestants were made to answer a series of impossible trivia questions. My grandparents were sitting on opposite ends of the worn-out upholstered sofa. Hands on their laps, quiet as always. Both gray-blonds and small in stature, they could be mistaken for well-behaved children if it weren't for the wrinkles. I get my height from my dad's side.

Taking a seat in a chair next to my grandfather, I picked up the sports section of the *Tribune* and opened it, as if going over the scores was something I did every night.

My grandfather eyed me with suspicion. A semi-retired plumber, he'd spent his whole life scowling at problem pipes. He pointed to the newspaper spread open on my lap. "What do you plan to do with that?"

"Leave him alone," my grandmother said. Her eyes didn't stray from the TV screen. "He's just keeping warm."

"In fact, I'm going to *read* it." I gave the paper an impatient little shake, then bent closer to read. As much as I liked playing baseball with friends, pro sports did nothing for me. Every sports section was the same. Basketball players acting cocky. Football players looking mean. I scanned the columns until page five, which featured coverage of a tri-state college wrestling tournament. My eyes studied the winners—thick-necked boys with shoulders round as stones, heavy curving thighs. In one photo, two square-jawed members of the Wisconsin team displayed medals against their broad chests. They were perfect, muscular and athletic like the plastic superheroes stowed in the deep corners of my closet. When I was young, I looked at men like this with envy; I wanted so much to be like them. But now my feelings were complicated. I didn't want to *be like* them—I *liked* them.

I put down the paper, feeling angry. I had to swallow these feelings, bury them.

Leave me alone.

I'd always had a strong will. If I made a determined effort, maybe I could change.

Click, gone.

four

As requested, Wesley arranged lunch with his cousin Mimi. It turned out that this girl was the same Mimi who sat in the front row of my World History class, hogging all the airtime. She was little and loud, with tight brown curls that she wore in a single *poof* behind her head, like a poodle. She looked like a lot of girls in our school, always dressed in snug-fitting denim with tacky gold jewelry. In class she was outspoken and spirited, which I envied, but her opinions were fickle. It was always fascinating to watch her in debates, stating her passionate convictions in front of the group, only to jump to the other side when the opposing view prevailed.

As soon as we were settled with our food, Mimi started right in. "Wes tells me you're getting all cozy with Celia Gamez. I'm not sure I approve."

"I wouldn't say cozy," I said. "What's your beef with her?"

She hesitated, dragging her fork through her salad as if she were turning something over in her mind. "No reason. She's got a good story, I'll give her that."

Wes and I remained frozen at attention. "Please go on," I said.

"Okay. Where do I begin? I mean, look at her, she's gorgeous, she's richer than shit. But here's a less-than-glamorous factoid that you probably do *not* know. In seventh grade, her mom died. Totally out of the blue. Car crash on Lake Shore Drive."

Silence all around.

"Wow," I said. "That obviously sucks."

Mimi nodded. "Biggest news story of the year. And believe me, that was a year of big stories. First kisses, first tampons, all sorts of bra-snapping drama."

"Were you friends with her?" Wes asked.

"Not so much. No sleepovers in eight years, not one pillow fight."

Wesley sat up. "Ladies and gentlemen, speak of the devil."

"The angel," I corrected, and attempted a masculine leer.

We watched as Celia walked from the food line to a crowded lunch table across the room. She wore jeans and a tight orange T-shirt that read *PULP FREE, PURE PREMIUM*. She sat down without smiling or greeting her friends. Like anyone of superior beauty, there was something rare and isolated about her—an unattainable quality that could arouse a person's sympathy or their fear. Wasn't there always something a little frightening about really beautiful people?

Mimi filled us in on more of Celia's story. Her father was a doctor. He was born in Mexico, and Celia's mother was born in Argentina. Celia had one older brother who lived in Italy, and one older sister who lived in Los Angeles and was somehow connected to the film industry. Mimi repeated the fact that Wes had already told me regarding the Gamez mansion: "Biggest house on the North Side."

"Oh, one other item of interest," Mimi added. "I know for a fact that Celia was the first girl in our eighth-grade class to get her own birth-control pills."

I reached nervously for one of Wesley's French fries. "Is she, uh, slutty then?"

"Watch it, Mr. Judgmental," Mimi said. "I'm on the Pill, too."

"Ay, no!" Wes hooted. "Not my own cousin! My own flesh and blood!"

"Wes, my parents are practical. As much as they would prefer that I waited a long time to have sex, they don't want me to get pregnant in high school."

I nodded, hoping my shock didn't show. I never would have guessed this girl was sexually active. Wesley wasn't, as far as I knew. My fifteenth birthday had come and gone, and I was as close to kissing someone as winning the Kentucky Derby.

"Celia's dad must have the same practical attitude," Wes said.

"Dr. Gamez actually invents pills," Mimi said. "He has

this lab where he researches and creates new pills that he sells to pharmaceutical companies. No joke, shitloads of money."

"That explains the mansion," I said.

Mimi shrugged. "So maybe he's got a casual attitude toward the Pill—that old-fashioned granny pill."

Wes had been drinking milk, and the tiny straw poked through the side of his mouth. "Hey, I'm on a pill, too," he muttered. "My little Ritalin pill."

"Thank God you are!" we said in unison.

Then Mimi said, "If you like Celia so much, why don't you ask her out?"

I smiled, feeling the heat. "At this point, I prefer to admire from afar." If I told them about my invitation to Celia's house on Friday, Wes would apply the pressure. I wasn't ready to pursue a girl romantically.

Mimi had some sort of bug up her ass. "Hey, I've already got you figured out. Are you all talk? Maybe there's something stopping you."

I wondered, *What does she suspect?*

Rather than sparring with her, I described how Celia had snubbed my cookies. "Kind of bitchy, huh?" I said.

Now Wes frowned. "No excuses, dude. This is not about friggin' Chips Ahoy! You need to jump on this."

"Wes, give up on this guy." Mimi sneered in my direction.

"Seriously, man," Wes said. "When are you going to have the balls to spend time alone with a girl?"

Well, in one day, two hours, thirty minutes—that's when.

At supper that night, in the damp heat of my grandparents' kitchen, I wondered what it would be like to live in a mansion. Or to have a doctor-father who made important contributions to science and medicine.

My own parents preferred employment that allowed them to work from home, wearing what they called "jogging clothes." This attire ran the gamut from T-shirts and sweatpants to, some days, whatever they slept in. Recently they had embarked on yet another business venture—a package-mailing and receiving depot. They advertised in neighborhood coffee shops and in the local free paper: *We'll send it! We'll sign for it!* I assumed this venture would be another flop, but it turned out there were a lot of people who weren't home during the day to receive their UPS and FedEx packages. Now the rooms upstairs looked like a warehouse, with stacks of brown boxes, padded envelopes, poster tubes, and express mail everywhere. Each night between five and seven, the doorbell chimed nonstop as my parents greeted harried customers who wanted their packages. *Packages.* Wesley teased me mercilessly. "Just think," he said, "someday your family will be *famous* for its packages. I mean it. *Nobody* can service a package like your family can."

It was my brilliant inspiration for them to offer gift-wrapping on the side. Why not make an extra three bucks per customer? So the dining room upstairs had been transformed into a gift-wrapper's paradise—endless choices of papers, bows, ribbons, plastic novelties, stickers, raffia straw, feathers, anything to wrap gifts according to client whimsy.

After the rush, my parents sometimes tried to squeeze in dinner with my grandparents and me. This was a rare phenomenon, all five chairs filled. With my parents present for meals I felt more at home at my grandparents' table, not like a foreign dignitary.

"Things are going really well at school lately," I announced, reaching for Jell-O.

They all turned as if the pot roast had spoken.

My mother was chewing, but she smiled and raised her eyebrows to convey something along the lines of *Good for you, honey!* Usually she looks young for her age, unless she's tired.

"That's great to hear, kiddo," Dad said, "because to become the man colleges want, you have to start *now*. Listen to me, you hit the ball over the fence now, and you can take it easy going around the bases."

Whenever he used sports metaphors with me, I nodded to be polite. I really did not want to get into the baseball argument with him again.

"So did you get straight A's in high school?" I asked him.

His in-laws laughed softly into their teacups.

"Mostly A's?"

Now even Dad had to grin. "Buddy, look at your ole man. Hitting fouls and pop flies ever since college. But hey, I'm still swinging!"

"Did you get A's, Mom?" I asked.

When she hesitated, perhaps out of modesty, my grandmother said, "She did—absolutely she did."

My grandfather leaned toward me. "She was a superior student."

Mom folded her napkin next to her plate. "Jamie, here's the thing. The teachers told me what to do, and I did it. They said study, I studied. They said write a five-page paper, I wrote a five-page paper. They always gave me the information I needed. Teachers *tell* you and they *give* you. All you have to do is listen to the information and respond. I never understand these people who whine and say, 'Boo-hoo, poor me, school is so hard.' The truth is, there's never another time in your whole life when everything you need to succeed is handed right to you."

"Right on a silver platter," Dad said, nodding. "Meanwhile, me? I took that platter and scraped everything off so I could look at my goddamn reflection."

Everybody laughed, and my mother said to him, "The difference is, you had a baseball scholarship to count on when it came to college. Also, well, I have to admit, it *was* a handsome reflection." She smiled at me. "And now we see it in our beautiful son."

"No excuses, pretty boy," my grandfather said gently, resting his hand on the back of my chair. "You take what's given to you and you use it. Got it?"

I nodded to indicate my commitment to the plan.

My mother caught my dad's eye and tapped her wristwatch. Soon they would return upstairs to paperwork, leaving me with hours of quiet until bedtime.

My dad stood at the door with his arms folded. My mother began carrying dirty plates to the sink.

"One other thing," I said, sounding real casual about it. "There's a girl I like at school."

That got everybody's attention.

"Whoa there, Romeo," my mother said. "It's a little early for dating, isn't it? Romance can be expensive."

"But a crush is a wonderful thing," my dad said, grabbing a chair again. He sat down next to me. "Who is she?"

"A girl in my class named Celia," I said. "I barely know her."

"No shit," Dad said, grinning. "That's terrific, buddy!" He put his hand on my shoulder and studied me, as if maybe I was putting him on.

"Good for what ails you," my grandmother said, pointing at me with her bony finger. "That's what a crush is."

I looked away, wondering if she had any suspicion of what ailed me.

Would it break her heart?

An awkward silence settled over the room. I realized I had startled everybody with this news.

My mother stood with her back to me, scraping off plates. "No dating until you get your driver's license, next year," she said. "No girl wants to be picked up by her date *and* his parents."

"That's fair," I said.

"You've all got your mouths hanging open," my grandfather said sharply. "Fact is, a teenage boy without a crush isn't a teenage boy."

For once I had to agree with him. Ivan, my tough, sensitive, blue-eyed crush from the First Knights, flickered in my thoughts before I remembered we were talking about Celia.

Unused to this level of attention, I pushed my chair away from the table and stood. "Thank you for the very nice dinner."

I went straight to the bathroom so my abrupt exit would make sense. I closed the door, sat on the tub ledge, and took a few breaths. I wasn't used to lying to them so boldly. My heart was going *rat-a-tat-tat*.

Like the rest of my grandparents' apartment, the bathroom was pristinely clean. It looked like a pharmacy—cold white tiles, harsh lights, and dozens of brown plastic bottles lined up along the sink and the window ledge. I liked to examine the bottles one by one, studying their labels. For me, these prescriptions had always represented a mystery: Was sickness a secret? Were some illnesses so awful that they were not even discussed? Maybe these pills kept my grandparents from getting sick in the first place.

I took a pill bottle from the window ledge. Removing the white cap, I poured the colorful capsules into my palm—purple and green. Lighter than I expected, like cold cereal or sunflower seeds. They didn't tempt me, not really. I wanted a different medicine.

Five

On Friday afternoon, students rushed out through the main doors of the Commons. "The Commons" was Maxwell Tech's fancy name for the main lobby. The décor called to mind a medieval hall that had fallen on hard times. The walls were covered with green-brown tapestries depicting heroics from American history. Near the ceiling hung a row of drab silk flags edged with dusty fringe. Did these represent the noble crests of European royal families? No, they were the mascots of the other teams in our sports conference. In a corner, behind a useless velvet rope, stood a full-scale, not-very-shining suit of armor. Our mascot, of course, was a knight—impossible to draw on spirit posters, and unrecognizable on letterman jackets except to our own trained eyes.

I waited for Celia, rocking on my heels. I chewed gum like a maniac and tried to imagine things we could talk about. The situation made me think of that old wooden toy—the painted ducks on opposite ends of the log. I wondered what kind of string could pull Celia and me together.

This is not a date, I reminded myself. *This is only designing flower tags.*

If it were a date, what would she expect? Everything I knew about dating came from sitting alone in my bedroom watching movies like *Nightmare on Elm Street* and *Friday the 13th*. And those dates usually ended with a meat cleaver in somebody's neck.

Fortunately, this was not a date.

On top of everything else, I dreaded running into Crazy Paul, eager to avoid his beady eyes and pervy tongue. Was he out of my life for good, or would he reappear at regular intervals to torment me, the way, in the *Halloween* movies, Michael Myers kept returning to hunt down poor Laurie Strode?

Across the Commons, Celia came into view. When she saw me, her face brightened and she gave a little wave. There was no getting around her easy beauty. Here in the Commons she was like a bright comet in an otherwise dark sky.

"Howdy," I said, and remembered to smile.

"You okay?" she said. "You look like you swallowed a bug."

The air outside was freakishly warm for January, and I began to sweat under my heavy coat. Celia didn't wear a coat at all. To my surprise, she led me to the same bus stop where I waited every day. How had I never seen her there before? A crowded bus was waiting. We didn't find seats together, and I was grateful to have a few minutes to myself. We rode down Western Avenue for twenty minutes and finally got off the bus in the Lincoln Square neighborhood, a part of town I knew only from annual trips to see my dentist. Funny, I had the same jittery feeling now as when I saw Dr. Connor.

Celia stretched lazily. "I'm zonked. I need a major dose of caffeine."

"Right," I said, even though I tended to avoid caffeine. It made me lightheaded. But I knew the golden rule of new friendships: *When in doubt, simply agree.* "My treat," I added, in a way that seemed appropriately gallant.

We stopped in front of a sleek-looking storefront. A square painted sign next to the door said, *Bound & Ground.*

I peered uneasily through the glass. Not my usual kind of place. At first glance, it was a coffeehouse-bookstore combo that seemed to be lacking in both areas. Ten small tables, mostly empty; a few shelves of bestsellers and travel guides; a rack of luxury magazines. Behind the counter, an attractive older woman with shoulder-length gray hair sat on a stool reading a magazine, holding it in a way that showed off a full forearm of silver bracelets.

I said to Celia, "Look in, it's kind of hilarious. I imagine the wife of some investment banker telling her husband she wants to open up a little place, just because she's seen Julia Roberts do it in a movie. *Honey, can I please have my own adorable bookshop café?*"

"That's funny." Celia smiled. "You know what? You have seriously gorgeous eyes. Do people always tell you that?"

My ears burned. "Not really, thanks. You have amazing…hair." It was the first thing I thought to say. It seemed like a safe compliment. Would other boys have complimented her ass?

She crossed her eyes and twisted her mouth. "We're so pretty!" When she pushed through the door, I followed.

"Celia, my princess!" The woman stretched her arms toward Celia, silver bracelets sliding and colliding in a jangle.

"Aunt Rita, my queen!"

They hugged theatrically near the register.

I had just insulted her aunt. *Nice move, Casanova.*

Celia gestured toward me. "This is my friend Jamie, from school. He was telling me how much he likes your café."

"Nice to meet you." She shook my hand, looking me in the eye with a smile, then turned back to Celia. "Tell me, how is your father?"

"*Your brother* is the same," Celia smiled, shaking her head. "Hopeless."

"All work, that man," Rita said. "Like a burro with a plow."

Celia laughed. It was clear she adored this woman. "What do you want to drink?" she asked me.

Weakly, I scanned the chalkboard behind the counter. I didn't know lattes from lampshades. "Whatever you order is fine."

"Two small mochas, then," Celia said. "To go. We've got homework."

"Coming right up." Rita used the fancy stainless steel espresso machine with ease, as if she'd been doing it her whole life. She pulled the shiny knobs, which made a hissing sound, letting the coffee drip into our paper cups. Then she added whipped cream from a can. "On the house, *niños*," she said, setting the drinks on the counter. "Celia, say hello to your dad for me."

There was a bulletin board near the door filled with band and theater listings, art classes, and such. I hadn't noticed it when we came in, but on our way out I saw one of my parents' pale-green signs: *We'll send it! We'll sign for it!* I felt myself blush. Sloppily stapled and faded by the doorway sun...it was like encountering one of my own parents in public.

As we walked, I sipped through the lid of my cup. To my surprise, I liked the chocolaty taste of it, and the warmth. I hoped it would wake up my mouth so I could speak to Celia more easily.

We turned at Wilson Avenue and got to a street bridge over the Chicago River. The riverbank was lined with private docks. I had seen plenty of boats at marinas near the lake, closer to the Loop, but I hadn't known the river passed through neighborhoods on the North Side. We stopped so I could look at the view. Tall bare trees bent over the water from both sides of the riverbank, the branches nearly meeting in the center. Soon it would be dark, but to the south, we could see the tops of the tallest skyscrapers downtown, shimmering with sunlight from the west. I peered down at the brown water. A family of ducks swam in little zigzags across the surface. I thought again of the painted wooden toy.

Pull the string, dumb-ass.

"This is romantic." The word felt odd on my tongue. "I mean, cinematic."

"Actually," she said, "I'll tell you a secret. I've always wanted to stand here and kiss somebody, like people would in a movie."

Was this my cue? Or just friendly small talk? I wondered if I could perform the role of her boyfriend if I got cast in the part. Without a script, I didn't have a line.

"By the way," she said, "you're wrong about my aunt. Her husband didn't give her a dime to open that place. She divorced him ages ago."

"Your aunt seems awesome," I said. "I didn't mean to—"

"She rocks. The thing is, my dad pays to keep the café open. He pays her mortgage, too. So, in a way, you had the right idea."

"What does your dad do?" I asked, although I knew the answer. I wanted to hear Celia's own version of her life.

"He's a doctor." She didn't elaborate. "What does your dad do?"

This was the problem with asking too many questions. At some point, people began to ask questions back. "He's a... he's always tried... right now he's starting a new business with my mom. They're going nuts trying to get things off the ground."

"What kind of business?"

"Um, like, package shipping and receiving?" My tongue was in knots again. "For people who aren't around during the day?" It sounded too stupid to be true, like a high-school fundraising project.

"That's cool."

"Gift-wrapping, too," I added, without knowing why.

"Wow," she said generously.

I had never been ashamed of my parents before. Most families I knew were barely getting by. Wesley's dad worked at the same paper-goods factory as Mimi's.

Past the river, the houses were bigger. It was a contrast to my street, where the crowded houses all had dingy lawns, boring bland squares of grass. Here, even in winter, I could tell the gardens were complicated and interesting, designed by professionals, maybe, and maintained by laborers who probably lived close to me. We turned a corner and walked alongside a high rocky wall covered with brown ivy, like the ivy on the walls at school. We stopped at a fancy gate, black wrought iron molded into flowers. There was a security panel, and Celia entered a series of numbers before pushing open the gate. "Crazy warm out today, right?"

In response, I blurted, "Is it true you live in the biggest house on the North Side?"

"Complete horseshit. Who told you that?"

"I don't know," I lied. "I just heard it."

She hesitated. "Maybe it's the biggest house north of Fullerton Avenue. But there are way bigger places down in the Gold Coast."

We stepped through the gate and onto a flagstone path. Seeing the house, I stopped. I remembered what Mr. Covici had written on the library wall: *Silence is a mansion where dwell my greatest notions.* Well, here was a real mansion. Maybe now I'd understand what the hell he was talking about.

The house looked massive and old, three stories high, made of gray limestone. A green slate roof with two big chimneys. I counted eight windows along the ground floor, four on either side of the entrance, and matching ones above. All the windows reflected the dusk-blue sky.

Celia turned back to me. "What are you waiting for?"

"Okay, I just decided. You can *never* come to my house."

I was joking, but her eyes registered an insult. "It looks bigger than it is. It's wide, but it's only two rooms deep."

Far to the left, the driveway had been expanded into a parking lot. Five cars parked in a row.

"Are all those cars your dad's?"

"Are you high? My dad parks in the garage, which is, like, underground. Those clunkers belong to his assistants. They work for my dad in the lab on the ground floor."

"Do his patients park here?"

"You sure ask a lot of questions."

"Sorry."

"He's not that kind of doctor. No patients, I mean. He's more like a scientist, or an inventor. He develops drugs for pharmaceutical companies. Basically he's a drug pusher. That's what my brother and sister always tell him."

I realized we hadn't mentioned her mother yet. I hadn't asked if the cars belonged to her *parents*, plural, only her dad. Had I revealed that I already knew about her mother? I wondered when she would raise the subject herself.

"The thing is, the empty house next door is being rehabbed, so we've had bulldozers, dumpsters, tons of contractors hogging the whole block. The parking situation has been wacko the past few months."

"I'll bet."

"It makes my dad wig out a bit," she said. "He's super private. Because of his work, security is a big deal around here—lots of expensive formulas and stuff to protect. As you saw, even I have to punch numbers into a keypad to get in the house."

"That's not messing around."

The front door was painted glossy black and surrounded by a border of small square windows. Another security keypad. Celia punched more numbers, and the door unlocked with a short buzz. We walked into a large foyer. An open staircase with a carved banister, all made of earth-colored stone, wound in a giant arc toward the second floor. On the first floor, on either side of the staircase, were sets of double doors, each flanked with small trees in shiny blue pots. It was a place that someone in a musical would dance through, a story set in Morocco or Mexico or some other place I'd never been. Even the air smelled exotic and rich—floral, fruity, and clean. I wasn't sure if the etiquette called for outright gushing or silent awe.

"Let's go out back to work," Celia said.

"Uh huh," I responded, too overwhelmed to form a sentence.

She led me through the living room, solarium, and study. The furniture throughout the house looked heavy and ornate.

I had experienced envy before in my life, of course—the sting of not getting what everybody around me had. But this was different. Walking through this fantastic house, being allowed into Celia's world, I felt happy, as if being here was somehow a reflection of *me*. For once, it felt like something was opening to me rather than shutting me out. It was a nice change.

We passed a door that stood out from the rest, a white metal door with another security panel. It looked important and impassable. Without Celia saying so, I knew it led to her father's lab. Despite her claim, the house seemed every bit as gigantic on the inside as it did on the outside. It felt like too much space for only Celia and her dad. Maybe this explained the self-contained expression Celia often wore, as if she was used to moving through her life on her own, sitting in these large comfortable rooms by herself. I wondered if her home life was mostly quiet, like mine.

She led me into an enormous kitchen. The counter displayed photographs of Celia and her family, a cluster of black-haired, handsome people posed in outdoor settings—around a rose trellis, brandishing ski poles, waving from the prow of a yacht. I recalled Mimi telling us that Celia had two older siblings, and here they were, along with the mother. In each of the photos, the mother had a wide-open, full-lipped smile. She drew the eye, effortlessly stealing the attention from her children. She was the source of Celia's beauty. The father had a large head, handsome, with intelligent eyes. His gray hair, the color of steel, was combed back away from his face. He did not smile for photographs, which made him seem serious and intimidating.

We took our mochas and went through a set of French doors into the backyard. When Celia paused to flip a switch, floodlights suddenly revealed the garden, casting long shadows onto the brown winter grass. An evergreen hedge, high as my shoulder, circled a brick patio. There were two breaks in the hedge—one that made way for the brick path, the other to provide a view of the dark river passing by. Clay planters were set around, and I could imagine them spilling over with vines and flowers in summer. It was as if an artist had taken the amazing natural landscape and improved it.

In the center of the brick circle was an iron table and four chairs. Celia set down her coffee. "Can you draw?"

"Sure," I said, eager to impress. "As long as it's nothing too complicated."

She sank onto one of the metal chairs. "Trust me, I have no artistic talent whatsoever. Once you've got the design down, we'll use the scanner inside to make the flower tags."

I almost sat across from her. *Sit next to her, you first-grade Romeo.* Awkwardly, I moved to the closer chair. The metal seat felt cold through my blue jeans. I dug out a sheet of computer paper from my bag. "Should I draw a Valentine's heart?"

"Too obvious. Covici wants a *smidgen of creativity, please!*" Her eyes searched mine for inspiration. "How about using our mascot—the chivalrous knight holding a bouquet of flowers?"

I pounded on the table in mock protest. "Way too difficult!" But she had a point, since the medieval theme would please Covici. I recalled something I had learned in my English class. I said, "In the Middle Ages, they sometimes used pictures of a deer to represent love. The old word for a male deer is *hart.*"

She nodded. "And people still say *dear* to people they love."

"Right, it works both ways."

"Perfect. Draw a deer, and we'll be done with it."

"Okay." I tried to draw one. It looked like a squirrel with long legs. "Yikes, it's not so easy."

"Put antlers on its head," she said. "It'll be clear then."

I tried another one—shorter legs, but the thick neck made it look like a Frankenstein deer. I wasn't confident I could ever get the body right, but I kept at it. My fingers were cold, and I blamed the caffeine for making my hand tremble. "What about a caption?" I said. "People will want to write their own messages inside. But on the outside, beneath the deer, it should say something."

Celia smiled. "How about, *You're a deer!*"

We both groaned.

Then she said, "What about using two deer, gazing at each other lovingly, nose to nose? *From hart to hart.*"

My shoulders collapsed. "Who knows if I can even draw *one* deer?"

"I got it." She took one of the drawings I'd started and sketched something fast. "You'll have to redo it, but this could be easier." The shaky sketch showed the head of a deer, with enormous antlers, peering around a wide tree trunk. The tree concealed the deer's body. Underneath, Celia had written, *Don't hide your hart from me.* "What do you think? I think it's sweet."

The concept was perfect: clever and simple to draw. "I love it," I said. "I know I can get the head right. And the tree is easy."

"Let's knock this out. Get drawing, Picasso."

We hunched close, shoulders nearly touching, both of our faces hovering over my drawing hand. It felt suddenly as if we were on a stage, the floodlight shining down on us like a spotlight. I realized it would be easy to turn my head and kiss her. Her body language seemed receptive, but she hadn't yet broadcast a direct signal. Would I even get the signal if she sent it? I doubted that there was any boy in Maxwell Tech's freshman class less sexually experienced than me.

This is not a date!

I drew the deer/tree image three times, in a slow hand, stalling, trying to muster the courage to kiss her. I decided to count to five, and then go for it.

Five ... four ... three ... two ... one ...

Zero ... negative one ... negative two ...

Celia squealed and jumped out of her seat.

"Celia, I'm sorr—"

"Look!" she said, pointing. Maybe she hadn't been watching me draw after all. "Oh my grossness!"

I stood, my eyes following the direction of her finger. I searched the expanse of drab grass between the river and us until I saw it—a small, bright thing the floodlight had found. It glistened. It was a fish from the river maybe, or some sort of eel, a snake skin ...

We approached it. I said, "Oh my God, it's a ..." I hesitated to say the word out loud to a girl.

"Condom," she said. "A big ugly used condom."

I leaned closer to study it. I had not seen many condoms out of their packaging before. And never like this, unfurled and enormous, in the wild.

She jumped on one foot. "Crap, do you know what this means?" She pointed to the house next door, her eyes burning. "Some people from *there* jumped the fence to do it over *here*."

"Construction workers?" The words just fell out of my mouth.

"What?" She looked confused.

"Or anybody, I guess."

"Who cares who?" She was smiling. "Some people had *sex* right where I used to jump rope!"

As we stared at each other, I saw on Celia's face the same combination of surprise, revulsion, and curiosity that I was feeling—our first real moment of connection. I finally felt those wooden ducks coming together. Then I saw two more things in the grass, a silver bracelet and a plastic wallet. "Hey!" I reached down and scooped them up, thrilled to make a contribution to this discovery. The bracelet held a turquoise charm. The thin wallet contained eleven damp dollars and a student ID from DePaul University. We studied the photo—brown hair, a nervous mouth; dark eyes hidden behind round, John Lennon-style eyeglasses. I read the name out loud: "Amanda Lynn Hampton. What a funny name. Say it fast."

"*Amanda Lynn.*" She giggled. "Like naming your kid *Ann Accordion.*"

"Watch your step. There might be another used *condom* somewhere." Our shared discovery made me bold. "Yes ma'am, what we have here may be a whole *field* of condoms."

"Not likely. I'm telling you, my dad would freak at the thought of any strangers back here."

I handed her the bracelet and the ID. "Hard to believe they had sex outside this time of year. It's one way to keep warm, I guess."

She smiled insanely. "Let's call her!"

"Where's the phone book?" I gathered our school papers.

She led the way back into the house through the French doors. We entered the kitchen, but stopped.

Here was the intimidating man from the family photographs. He was shorter than me, not much taller than Celia. Thick gray hair. Intense eyes, shining and curious, but not unkind. He stood with his back to the window. Had he been watching us? Had he noticed me sitting close enough to kiss Celia, even if she hadn't—and even though I didn't?

"Hi, Daddy." Celia slipped the plastic wallet discreetly into her back pocket. "This is my friend Jamie, from school."

I had expected Dr. Gamez to be dressed like normal doctors, in a white coat, but he wore a navy business suit. His black shoes were glossy and expensive-looking.

"Pleased to meet you," he said stiffly.

We shook hands, and I felt self-conscious about my chewed-up fingernails. He wore stunning gem-studded rings on each manicured hand, like a rap singer or a fortune-teller. "Your hands are freezing," he said. Still no smile.

"Sorry," I said.

"Talented hands, too," Celia said. "We're making something for a club at school. Jamie drew these." She laid the drawings out on the kitchen table.

"They're not very good yet," I admitted. I wondered if I might have drawn them better if my hands were warm, or if I'd been less nervous.

Dr. Gamez nodded approvingly. "You have an observant eye. In my line of work, the talent to observe, the talent and the discipline—these are highly prized."

"He did it without even looking at a picture," Celia said. It felt nice to have her bragging on my behalf.

"Perhaps you have hunted deer," Dr. Gamez said to me.

I shook my head. "But one time we hit a deer with our car, up in Wisconsin."

"You didn't tell me that," Celia said.

It wasn't something I thought about much—just something that happened, between two more interesting stops on a vacation. But it seemed to spark some interest in Celia and her father, so I went on. "My dad was driving. I was in the back seat. But I watched it happen. Like slow motion. I'll never forget how the deer looked, waiting for our car to crash into it. His left eye never blinked, not once. Maybe that's how I remembered how to draw it."

"You are sensitive," Dr. Gamez said, his face finally softening. "Sensitivity and vision—both essential for an artist."

I felt myself blush. It flattered me that this man thought I could be an artist someday.

He patted his stomach. "Will we be eating soon, Celia? We like to dine out on Fridays, Jamie. You are welcome to join us."

I glanced at Celia, who looked as if she didn't care one way or the other. "Sure, if you want to," she said. She stared out the window into the sudden darkness, as if seeing something I couldn't.

The kitchen felt colder to me now; it was dinnertime but none of the fancy cooking appliances were turned on. A kitchen without a mother, I thought.

"I'd like to come," I said, "but my grandparents are expecting me." This was only half true. While my grandparents did expect me, they also wouldn't miss me. But I wanted to go home and process what I'd seen. Also, Celia's indifference had caught me off guard.

"We will drop you on our way," Dr. Gamez said. He looked at Celia. "If you are ready, then?"

She was reviewing the sketches, not smiling, as if her opinion of them had changed. "I'll scan this stuff into the computer later." She didn't consult with me.

Dr. Gamez opened a door off the kitchen, and we descended the stairs to the garage underground. Four cars, with room to spare. The car we climbed into was black with leather seats; the interior smelled like soap. Celia sat in the front with her father. We cruised up the cavernous driveway to the street level, glided through the tall iron gate, and moved into traffic.

I stared out the car window, feeling uncertain, wishing Celia had tried to convince me to join them for dinner. Wishing the two of us had more time alone to make a connection.

But Dr. Gamez's interest seemed genuine. He was a class act. It occurred to me, then, that true class included a good measure of warmth. I felt shy, as always, but we had only ten minutes and I wanted to make a good impression.

Prompted by Dr. Gamez's questions, I told them about our apartment. I made a joke about sharing a bathroom with "the Metamucil twins." I described my parents' new business; boldly, I even took credit for the gift-wrapping angle. When Dr. Gamez put in a CD of *Phantom of the Opera*, I announced that I only liked Andrew Lloyd Webber's early musicals and that all the rest were weak. "And," I added, "if you compare his really good stuff, like *Jesus Christ Superstar* and *Evita*, against shows like *Les Miz*, *Wicked*, or even, like, *Rent*, Andrew Lloyd Webber's don't really stack up. In my humble opinion." Suddenly my stupid mouth was running on overdrive.

Dr. Gamez smiled in a bemused way, and I wasn't sure if it was my words or my manner that struck him as funny.

We pulled up in front of my apartment building. Three other cars were double-parked, hazard-lights blinking, keeping my parents busy. Downstairs, my grandparents' windows were dark as usual, except for the flickering light of the TV.

"Let's talk tomorrow," I said to Celia.

She seemed to hesitate. "I'm busy this weekend, but call if you want to." She gave me a slip of paper with her number on it. "Oh, and I'll try to get in touch with Amanda."

I felt myself grinning, pleased to share that secret with her.

Dr. Gamez reached over the seat to shake my hand again. "Jamie, you are always welcome in our home."

"Thanks. And thanks for the ride!"

I ran from the car. Inside the hall, I dropped my backpack in a chair by the phone stand and heard the sound of my grandparents' TV. "I'm home!" I called, but didn't expect an answer.

My grandparents had to eat supper by five o'clock or they couldn't sleep. In the kitchen, a plate of baked fish, now cold and covered in plastic wrap, sat waiting for me on the countertop. I wasn't hungry. Instead I went to my room, closed the door, and put on a CD. I stretched out on my bed, imagining Celia and her father at a table in an elegant restaurant, reviewing the menu, talking about their day. Now that I was alone again, in my cramped bedroom in this stale and dark house, I felt that familiar pressure against my chest—envy.

I did not go upstairs to tell my parents about my day. I did not join my grandparents for an evening of boring television. I did not call Wesley to report on my progress with Celia.

Instead I lay on the bed with my eyes closed. I tried to picture the college girl, Amanda Lynn, with her lover on the dark lawn between the house and the riverbank. I wondered if sex was always like that, a frantic fumbling in the wild, a spontaneous reaching for warmth and connection. I felt light-years away from that kind of experience. Even the guys I had fantasized about kissing were never people I actually knew. They were on TV, in magazines, or on the Internet. Maybe that had been my problem all along. Maybe if I focused on real people—flesh-and-blood *girls*—things would change for me. Maybe I would change.

Was Celia Gamez the girl who could change me? Was she the one who could finally turn me on? Maybe I was like an expensive electronic device that required a very rare kind of battery.

SIX

Boys in high school were different from the boys I'd known before. They seemed older, tougher. Part of it was that I hadn't known them since the first grade. I hadn't watched them learn to read and tie their shoes. Plus, there were so many of them now, these tribes of scowling boys in the corridors between classes, punching each other. Arm jabs, titty twisters, whacking each other's balls from behind. They couldn't take their hands off each other. They never carried schoolbooks. They didn't smile at strangers. If they caught me looking, they stared me down until I looked away. *Take a picture, faggot, it lasts longer!* In sheer number, these boys were cuter than the boys at my old school. Sexier, more dangerous. As a safeguard, I wrote with a Sharpie on my binder: *Remember ... KFC.*

Leave me alone.

The best strategy, I decided, was to focus all my attention on Celia. It wasn't enough to *talk* about my crush with my parents and my friends. I needed to act.

On Monday morning, I went to the Commons before school because I knew Celia would pass by on the way to her locker. I would go every day if necessary, as if exercising a muscle I wanted to develop. I was in training.

A tap on my shoulder from behind, and Celia said, "You didn't call me this weekend." Not angry, just an observation.

"I didn't have time," I lied. The fact was, I had intended to call her. I'd wanted to call. But I couldn't dial the number. My nerve kept failing. I didn't want this thing to flame out before it began. "Did you track down Amanda Lynn?"

"No luck," she said as the first bell rang. "Now listen. We need to put our heads together and come up with a *plan*."

I liked the sound of that.

––––––––––

In the library, we saw Mr. Covici's ladder again, leaning against the circulation desk. The air in the room was laced with the smell of fresh paint. "Uh oh," Wesley said. "Michelangelo must be back at it." We dropped our backpacks and took seats while Mimi went to a computer to print out an essay for World History. Wesley opened a newspaper to the basketball scores.

I scanned the room, hoping like hell I wouldn't see Crazy Paul. I didn't like being there. I had quit the habit of going to the library during my free periods. Cold turkey. It only made sense; like a gambling addict who needs to stay away from the big bad casino, I didn't want to be tempted into repeating past mistakes.

Across the room, in shiny red letters on the wall above the photocopy machines, Mr. Covici's latest artwork broadcast a new message to the people: *KINDNESS OPENS MORE DOORS THAN THE VILLAGE LOCKSMITH.*

"Do you think he's got permission to be doing that?" I whispered to Wes. "Like from the administration?"

Wes lowered the newspaper and squinted to read the new quote. "Whoa. My uncle's a locksmith. He doesn't need this *kindness* crap to come in and steal his business."

Mimi returned from the printers, scowling at the world as usual. She flung her essay at the table as if the paper were a Frisbee. She was one gruff customer.

"Want me to proofread that for you?" I asked. It was always my goal to make Mimi smile.

She stuffed the pages into her folder. "Down boy," she said. "You're not opening *this* door, no matter what the damn wall says."

"Any progress with Señorita Gamez?" Wesley asked.

I shrugged. "Still laying the foundation."

"Yeah right," Mimi said. "My prediction? That's the only thing you'll be laying."

I wasn't ready to describe my afternoon with Celia to them—too much pressure. I could admit a little crush, but given this new access, Wes and Mimi might now expect a full-blown relationship.

Naturally, therefore, I didn't tell them about the folded-up note Celia slipped to me as we passed between lunch periods:

Help Wanted:
Investigator needed to track down criminal trespassers
and sexual outlaws. Part-time only, but the pay is
truly terrible. Applicants should inquire
at locker #3442 between lunch and fourth period.

At the appointed time, I made a beeline to her locker.

"Terrific, you're hired!" she said, shaking my hand.

After school, riding the bus across town toward Celia's neighborhood, a persistent thought dominated my head: *Would I see her bedroom this time?* This scenario seemed entirely possible, and yet the prospect amazed me. This was one of the miracles of high school—how quickly connections were made, relationships formed. Until a week ago, I knew Celia only from First Knights meetings; now we were spending time alone together, sharing an R-rated secret, and rushing toward her bedroom at twenty-five miles per hour along Western Avenue.

"I want to meet her," Celia said, studying the ID picture. "To give her stuff back. I've become obsessed with this chick."

"Understandable. I'm curious about anyone who's named after a musical instrument."

"Can you imagine somebody having *sex* in your backyard?"

"Celia, my backyard is surrounded by a chain-link fence.

The central feature is a knee-high statue of the Blessed Virgin."

"Hey," she said, "my dad has one of those in his office. Very sexy."

"For real? That's too weird. *And* a three-story apartment building across the alley looks down into our yard, so you'd probably have an audience."

"Hot, hot, hot," she said, laughing.

"Old people staring at you from behind their greasy window blinds."

"Stop, you're driving me wild!"

We got off the bus and walked along Wilson Avenue to the bridge. The sky was getting dark already. The river reflected white Christmas lights that lined private docks up and down the riverbank. The air smelled of wood smoke from a nearby chimney. We didn't stop this time, and minutes later we pushed through the fancy iron gate at Celia's. The immense house rose above us, dark except for an impressive spotlight on the front door. I felt thrilled to be back so soon.

At the front door, Celia punched in the code. Fleetingly I thought of Mr. Covici: *Kindness opens more doors than the village locksmith.* As if reading my mind, Celia joked, "Kindness may open some doors, but not ours."

"Nope. Kindness can just freeze its butt in the cold!"

She whispered, "I shouldn't tell you this, but … it's my birthday."

"Oh my God, Celia! Today is your birthday?"

"No, the *code* is my birthday. When I was young, I could

never remember the code. My parents changed it to my birthday so I would stop getting locked out."

"Wow," I said gently. "That's a little bit pathetic."

"I know, right? Trust me, I'm a lot smarter now."

Inside the main hallway, Celia slipped out of her coat and tossed it over the stone staircase banister, so I did the same. Underneath, she was wearing a sleeveless black T-shirt that drew attention to her chest. This girl wasn't afraid to show some skin.

I followed her down the hallway into the kitchen, which was four times the size of my grandparents' boxy kitchen. I noticed, this time, that the floor tiles were made of real tile, not plastic linoleum like at home. Matching tiles covered the vaulted ceiling, where a dozen copper pots hung from an elaborate iron rack. I looked again at the family photographs; Dr. Gamez watched us from multiple points of view.

"Is your dad around?"

"Somewhere, yeah," she said.

A glossy travel brochure lay on the black countertop. I opened it to a random spread, where the pictures showed beaches and palm trees, a romantic estate, pebble paths with peacocks. "What's this?"

"It's for Spring Break. We're going to Mexico—the Yucatán. I don't know why he has that brochure. We always rent the same *hacienda*. It's nowhere near the beach, but it's got a nice pool."

"It looks amazing."

"Have you ever been to Mexico?"

I shook my head. "We went to Florida once. That's about

it." My family's one big vacation had taken place years ago, before my dad lost his print shop. I'd been too young to appreciate it. All I remembered was chasing tiny lizards around the lava rocks in the motel parking lot.

"Florida's cool," she said. "Okay, Inspector, so where do we begin?"

"Internet?"

"I Googled her already—*nada*."

"Maybe we need to go through the university."

"I tried that, too. The switchboard said she doesn't live on campus."

"Let's try another department then. Do you have, like, a phone book?"

Celia pointed. "Center drawer." She leaned against the kitchen counter, her bare arms folded. "Are you hungry?"

I nodded. "Sure."

She opened the huge stainless steel refrigerator. "How about soup?"

"Soup is good." I found the university in the phone book—a long list of departments and offices—and reviewed the various options. My finger stopped on one that seemed promising.

Celia removed the lid from a plastic container. She dumped its contents into a saucepan, a solid block of shiny orange. She fired up the gas burner and then stood at the stove, stirring. "Ginger carrot," she said, as if I'd been looking at it funny. "My dad made it."

"Your dad cooks?"

"Yup, always. Even, you know, before my mom died."

The comment floated in the space between us. It seemed like an invitation to ask questions, but I didn't know what to say. So I picked up the phone and dialed.

Celia whispered, "He has a certificate thingy from the Chicago Culinary Institute. He worked as a chef when he was in medical school."

"Cool."

A woman's voice answered the phone. "University switchboard."

"Hi, can you please connect me with the Jobs Placement Office?"

"One moment please."

Celia gave me a doubtful look, and I held up a finger as if to say, *Just wait.*

"Jobs Office," a young male voice said.

"*Good afternoon,*" I said, dropping my voice an octave. "My name is Roger Johnson. I'm trying to contact one of your students. Amanda Lynn Hampton? I received a résumé from Amanda Lynn a while back—a very *strong* résumé—but when I called the number today, it said the line had been disconnected. Would you happen to have up-to-date contact information for Amanda Lynn?"

Celia's hands flew to her mouth. She leaned closer to listen.

"Who did you say you were?" asked the man on the phone.

"I'm Robert Johnson," I said firmly.

"Didn't you say *Roger* before?"

"Yes ... uh, well, Johnsonville Furniture," I said.

"You own the business?"

"That's correct, and I'm very, very busy. I'm just looking for Amanda Lynn's contact information."

"Have we placed students with you before, sir?"

I glanced at Celia. "It's possible. I ... couldn't say."

The man's breathing was steady and patient, as if he spent all day on the phone with boneheads like me. "Hold on a sec." There was a click at the end of the line, then music. Really bad, smooth jazz.

I covered the mouthpiece. "I'm on hold," I whispered.

"Mr. Johnson, I am impressed." She kept her eyes on me as she stirred the soup.

I swallowed. "I should have rehearsed."

"You do sound a little bit constipated."

I held my stomach. "I may be!"

The man on the phone returned. "Mr. Johnson?"

"Yes, this is *Roger* Johnson."

"Listen, sir, I can't give contact information about students over the phone."

"Really?" A moment ago, this had seemed like a done deal. "But as I told you, Amanda Lynn already sent me her résumé. I'm only following up."

"If she's interested, I'm sure she'll contact you again."

"But the job—"

"Sir, if you like, I can take *your* information, and when she comes in, I'll be glad to give it to her."

I stared at the receiver. "That won't be necessary. Thank you." I hung up.

The only sound was the soup bubbling on the stove.

"Damn," I said.

"You were *awesome*," Celia said, clapping her hands. "We were so close!"

"It's okay. We'll try another department." She poured the soup into white bowls with elegant gold rims. Then she set out heavy round spoons—real soup spoons, the kind you get in restaurants. The soup wasn't watery like my grandmother's potato soup. It was thick, like gravy.

"Ginger carrot," she said, setting a bowl in front of me.

"You said that already. Your dad made it."

Our faces were close and she was staring up at my eyes—again, not casually. For the first time since I'd known her, she didn't look confident or strong. She looked … *willing*. With her eyes cast upward, the difference in our heights became apparent, suddenly significant. The moment for our first kiss had arrived. She was waiting for me to make a move.

Something stopped me. "Where'd you say your dad was?"

Her eyes registered a sting as she looked away. "What does it matter?"

When I didn't say anything, she took a step away from me, then got out two coffee mugs and set them on the counter. "Thirsty?"

I nodded and tasted the soup. I had expected spicy, but it was sweet.

She opened the refrigerator door again. "Ah, here we go." She pulled out a half-full bottle of white wine. It might have been a bomb, the way it startled me. I must have flinched.

"Did you think I meant apple juice?" she asked.

"Well, no—it's just…"

"No pressure." But she had already removed the cork and held the bottle over the mugs.

"Wait!" I said, cringing. "You know what? I don't drink alcohol."

She lowered the bottle. "You don't?"

I shook my head. "My parents would, like, *murder* me if I drank."

"Okay." She returned the bottle to the refrigerator.

I leaned against the counter, breathing deeply. "Man, I feel stupid now."

"Forget about it." She shrugged, and her smile was guilty. "Okay, to be honest, I don't drink, either."

"You don't?"

"I saw it in there and thought I'd bring it out for us to try. It was a sudden impulse."

"Really?"

"Split-second impulse. A bad one. Sorry."

"No big deal."

"Gah!" she said, but not angrily. "Maybe I'm trying to be something I'm not. Weird. I swear I'm never like this."

Welcome to "Acting for Beginners."

"Celia, forget about it." I reached for her arm. "Just be yourself."

When I touched her, she groaned, almost laughing, and fell gently toward me. She'd learned her lesson once. She wasn't going to wait for me this time.

Here goes nothing.

She kissed me. Her lips were soft. When my eyes closed, my hands seemed instinctively to know where to go—roaming her sides, holding her, pulling her close. She rested her hands on my chest, north of center, in a place nobody in my life had ever put their hands before.

I observed the experience as much as participated in it. We were like characters performing on a teen TV show or in a movie. I braced myself for the meat cleaver, but then remembered to focus. I must have learned something somewhere along the way, because at one point Celia whispered, "You surprise me, Mr. Johnson, with your most excellent kissing."

"Come down to the furniture warehouse sometime," I said. "I'll find a job for you."

"Hmmm, really?"

We kissed again.

Maybe I am a natural. Who knows, maybe I'm not so gay after all?

Maybe what the old songs said was true: *Falling in love takes time.* Let the record show, I was willing to give it all the time it required.

Next to us, the soup cooled. We didn't make any more phone calls. Our exploration didn't go beyond kissing. As long as we stayed in the kitchen, standing in the safe zone at the counter, this was all fine with me.

I warned you at the beginning, it's a confusing story.

seven

In my defense, it can be difficult for almost *anyone* to tell the difference between a friendship and a romantic relationship. Especially in high school. In the case of Celia and me, after the spontaneous kisses in her kitchen, things developed as any new friendship might.

As a friend, I lent her my DVD copies of *Halloween* and *Nightmare on Elm Street*—eager to hear what she thought.

In return, Celia made me a dozen chocolate-chip cookies, just as any thoughtful friend would, and we ate them in the park after school, taking turns pretending we were Cookie Monster.

As a thank you for the cookies, I burned a CD for her called "Even Better Than Cookies," because I wanted my new friend to know that my taste in music was rock solid.

Within days, we developed the habit of meeting *as friends*

in the Commons each morning before the first bell. Celia picked up free coffees for us at the Bound & Ground, and I brought chewing gum to obliterate the bitter aftertaste. As the area filled with students, we sat alone in our favorite corner, partly hidden by the mascot knight, and finished our homework. At times, Celia was more easily affectionate than I felt comfortable with. She'd lean against my shoulder when she helped me with Algebra.

"Hey, I get it!" I said one morning. "You're like my *coefficient*. Up close next to me."

"Will you be my *variable*?" She fluttered her eyelids.

She let her fingers play in my hair and advised me about product and styling. Sometimes she'd close her eyes and then collapse dramatically onto my lap, pretending to sleep right on top of my textbook. When the first bell rang, we kissed each other's cheeks before going our separate ways.

Other kids may have noticed, of course. Our morning frolics had an unspoken aspect of performance. Was it important to Celia that people saw us as a couple? I did like the way being with her in public made me feel about myself. But when I gave it any real thought, I felt a hole growing in the pit of my stomach.

We are friends. We can never be more than just friends. And we both know this, right?

One morning, out of the blue, Celia presented me with a shopping bag. Inside was a pair of designer jeans.

"Celia! You shouldn't buy me clothes."

Her face beamed with a combination of anxiety and pride. "I wanted to."

How would I explain expensive new jeans to my parents? "Wow, this is beyond generous. Thank you." I kissed her on the cheek, and her smile widened.

I held up the jeans, feeling grateful but wary. They looked small.

"They're perfect for you," she said. "I promise. Enough with those baggie Levi's, old man. These are sexy. They were made for your ass."

At home I tried them on. The legs were narrow-cut and the back pockets hugged my butt like nothing I'd ever worn before. The waist felt too tight, but I had to admit, they did make me feel sexy. I decided to wear them to school.

The next morning, I tried to sneak out unnoticed. My mistake was to go to the kitchen to get a glass of orange juice. My grandmother and my mother were sitting at the kitchen table.

"Hey, Elvis Presley," my mother said. "Where'd you get those hip-huggers?"

I hesitated at the refrigerator with my back to them. Turning, I smiled. "And good morning to *you*, ladies."

"Answer the question." She blinked calmly over her coffee mug.

Not from my girlfriend, that's for sure.

I drank. Very slowly. "From Wesley. The jeans didn't fit him, so he gave them to me."

"They don't seem to fit you either," my grandmother said. "Too tight."

"They're designer. They're supposed to be tight."

She turned to my mom. "If he starts to feel light-headed, maybe he can undo the top button or something."

"Thanks for the tip," I said. I rinsed the glass and left it in the sink.

"Don't forget," my mother called. "Dentist appointment today after school."

"Crap," I said under my breath.

On the bus, the inseam on the jeans pressed uncomfortably against my balls. I wasn't sure sexy was worth it.

"They look awesome!" Celia said when I saw her in the Commons.

I turned in a circle so she could appreciate them before my digestive system shut down. "I feel like a different person in them."

"Oh, say, I have your DVDs." She pulled them out of her bag and handed them over. "Scary movies... turns out? Not my thing."

"Did you watch them both?"

"I started one, but turned it off."

"Celia, they're fun!"

"For you, maybe. But they're really misogynistic."

"What does that mean?"

"They're anti-women. The images they show... girls screaming and crying and running from a maniac with a knife? Not so cool."

I felt personally wounded, which made me defensive. "So that's it? You reject the whole genre? You dismiss acknowledged *masterpieces* of American cinema just because a *woman* is the main character?"

"If she's being victimized, pretty much yeah," she nodded. "Tell you what. Show me a scary movie where it's a *guy* who's getting into trouble that's not even his fault? And just when he's trying to escape, half his clothes start falling off his body? Maybe I'll watch that."

"OK, I'll keep my eyes open," I said.

"I said *maybe*," she added.

A cold winter rain fell all afternoon, streaking the windows of the dental office with oily gray squiggles.

Dr. Connor did his usual song and dance, stretching open my mouth for what seemed like an hour while he yammered on about his son, the "gifted" fullback who played college football in Wisconsin. Grateful I didn't have to respond, I closed my eyes and pictured Dr. Connor's son, who was displayed prominently in photographs in the waiting room. He had shiny, coppery hair that fell around his face, past his ears in long strands like a Roman soldier. The style reminded me of Ivan's hair. But Ivan's was lighter, golden, the color of buttered oatmeal. I imagined tough, sensitive Ivan as my dentist, delicately placing his big fingers into my mouth.

Quit it! I turned my attention to each painful scrape of Dr. Connor's instruments. I punished myself by focusing on the sharp tools cutting into my gums and forced myself to taste the blood. My hands clenched into fists.

You can stop thinking that way, and you will stop it.

Outside the window, another downpour. Minutes crept by while the office speakers emitted slow Beatles instrumentals.

After the oral agony, Dr. Connor's assistant handed me my backpack and I went downstairs and out onto the sidewalk. *Free!* Puddles spread across the pavement and water from the alleys flowed toward the street. I stayed close to the apartment buildings to keep dry. Rubbing my sore jaw, I decided to call Celia as soon as I got home. She said she wanted a grisly, terrifying tale with an innocent *male* victim? Now I could tell her one. This thought cheered me.

I found myself smiling whenever I thought of Celia— until I remembered that the relationship could never last. The whole thing was crazy. *How long could I fool this sharp girl into thinking I could be an ordinary boyfriend?* Sooner or later, things would escalate. Certain physical behavior would be expected. Sex would enter the picture. And just like that, I would lose her.

Even short-term success with Celia, I knew, depended on me avoiding any boy I might be attracted to. Including Ivan. At my locker, I faced the opposite direction whenever he was at his. I needed to transmit a key message to my brain: *This door is LOCKED to all blue-eyed locksmiths.*

The rain fell faster and harder as I walked toward the bus stop. I paused in front of the Bound & Ground. Now the windows were steam-filled, almost opaque. I pulled open the front door and went inside to wait out the downpour. The rest of the neighborhood must have had the same idea, because the place was packed. Standing room only.

I looked for Celia's aunt behind the counter, but didn't see her. A college girl in a shabby black cardigan worked the register.

"Decaf mocha," I said, when I got to the front of the line. "Smallest size, please." I had only a few dollars in my wallet but figured I could justify the expense if I used the time to get homework done. The thought of mucking up the dentist's hard work with chocolaty coffee made the drink even more decadent and delicious. I scanned the room for a free seat.

"Jamie?"

Celia's father waved at me from a table. In a dark suit and silk tie, he was the only formally dressed person in the café. His eyes and teeth had the conspicuous shine of a film actor. Smiling, half standing, he extended his hand in greeting. "This is a good surprise."

"Hi, Dr. Gamez. Taking a sick day?"

"Myself, I am never sick," he said. "And I love my work too much to waste an afternoon. No, sometimes I come here to get away from the lab and really *think*. Work through problems. It can be difficult to hold my concentration at the lab. Too many distractions." He had a stack of files on the table, which he pushed to the side. A white cup and saucer sat empty, long dry. "Will you join me?"

Kindness opens more doors than the village locksmith.

"I don't want to interrupt. You were just saying—"

"Please do. Look around, your options are limited. Take it before I offer it to someone else."

I sat, wondering what on earth we could talk about. It didn't seem polite to take out my Biology textbook. I took a long slow sip on my drink.

He said, "Celia has told me of your club's ambitions with the flower sale."

"Yeah, the goal is to raise a lot of money. Though we're not sure yet how we'll spend it once we have it."

"An unconventional approach." Dr. Gamez smiled. "Perhaps I should invent a pill and *then* try to discover new illnesses, so my innovative pill has a good use. Tell me something. How would you spend the money if it were up to you? Sports equipment?"

"No," I said quickly.

"Perhaps then something for the school theater? I recall that you have a real passion for theater and movies."

"Maybe." It impressed me that an important man like Dr. Gamez remembered random details about a kid he barely knew. I took another sip of my drink, embarrassed by his attention. "What are you working on?"

"Oh, many projects. Products that will transform society for the better. It's why my work is so exciting, so fulfilling. Through medication, it's possible to treat people for every kind of physical malady and psychological disorder. No exceptions. I believe that."

"Even cancer?" I said.

"Certainly, cancer," he said. "We know already that cancer is caused by a combination of inherited genetic factors, which can be tracked and treated, and *acquired* factors. One of the most important factors is stress. If a person can eliminate the stress through medication, he can virtually prevent the growth of cancer cells. I truly believe that in the future, the services of the physician will be obsolete, replaced by the services of the pharmacist."

"Hard to picture," I said.

"It is true! Already you must see how the lives of people even your own age are improved through prescribed medicines. Medications to make their skin clearer, to make their muscles bigger, to make them calmer and more focused throughout the day."

I nodded, thinking of Wesley and his Ritalin.

"You are not on any medications yourself?"

I shook my head.

"No anti-depressants or growth hormones? Stimulants?"

"Does caffeine count?"

"No," he said, smiling. "Not to me it doesn't."

"Then nothing. Guess I'm lucky."

"Lucky, yes. As well as healthy. A very rare thing." He paused, his gaze lost above my head for a moment as if he was considering what to say next. Then he lowered his eyes and studied my face intently. I could see what made him a successful scientist. There was a long moment between us, and I suspected it was my turn to toss out a topic for conversation—something about Celia or school, maybe—but then he leaned toward me, lowering his voice. "There is one new project in particular that excites me. Would you like to hear about it?"

"Sure."

"May I count on your discretion?"

"Absolutely."

Dr. Gamez glanced over his shoulder, as if to ensure that no one was eavesdropping. Then he began. "Over the past several years, my laboratory has been developing a line of behavior modification drugs. More specifically, Response

Inhibitor Drugs, or RIDs. At present, the FDA is reviewing them. This can take years. The wait can seem endless. But once these products are on the market, I feel certain that they will transform our society for the better." He leaned closer to me, almost whispering. "We will be remembered forever for the important work we are doing now."

"Wow," I said.

"Yes, well, you cannot imagine the *exhilaration* of such a secret."

Doctor, you have no idea.

I asked, "What are the RIDs used for?"

"To treat people who suffer from unwanted physical responses. Prototypes of such drugs already exist. For example, to treat people with panic attacks. Or with destructive, violent tendencies. Each RID suppresses a different response. Ours will be one of the most advanced, and initially, I suspect, the most controversial."

"Controversial in what way?"

Dr. Gamez surveyed the room again before reaching into his bag. He pulled out a plastic pill bottle with a white cap, similar to the ones above my grandparents' bathroom sink. Locking eyes with me once more, he kept his voice low. "This is one of the new drugs. We call it Rehomoline." He removed the cap and poured the pills onto a paper napkin on the table.

The pills were light blue, small, pretty. There were maybe twenty on the napkin, like a pile of semi-precious stones. Something a girl would make a necklace with.

"Your artistic eye no doubt appreciates the color. The color of the morning sky. A new day for these patients."

"What do they do?"

He hesitated. "Put simply, Jamie, Rehomoline suppresses the homosexual response in the male brain."

A tide of warmth rushed to my face. I had misheard him. "Excuse me?"

He repeated the words, quiet and slow. "The drug suppresses the male homosexual response."

He's talking about me. He's figured me out.

In a kind of shock, I sputtered, "The drug changes... sexual orientation? That seems impossible."

Celia and he probably discussed it during dinner. She's not fooled either.

"Lower your voice, please. In fact, it's no different from an allergy medication. Think of homosexuality as an allergy. During an allergic episode, the body responds to an external factor. Allergy medicines *inhibit* that negative response—for example, so that you can play with your kitty-cat without sneezing. The RIDs operate on the same principle. Rehomoline, used over time to treat homosexuality like a chronic condition, will inhibit the homosexual response. And at the same time, the drug will increase masculine characteristics by adding other agents as needed."

I'd need twice the recommended dosage.

I sat back in my chair, feeling weirdly embarrassed, overwhelmed. I was too dazed by the concept to listen to his details. All I knew was that I was finally hearing what I'd always wanted to hear—that there might be a solution after all. A way out.

"Wow," I finally said. "So gay men won't be attracted to other men? That's incredible."

A miracle, in my case.

"Yes, exactly that simple. We're also developing a lesbian counterpart. These products are going to change our society. Our world."

"I see what you mean about controversy."

"Well, there has been such debate about homosexuality. So much sadness. Families broken apart, communities divided, terrible hate crimes we read about in the newspapers. Our drugs will help to alleviate this. In the future, thanks to a simple pill, homosexuality will be a thing of the past. Something we read about only in books. Like leprosy."

"Huh," I said neutrally. "That does sound interesting."

I'll be changed. Me and all the other island boys like me.

I reached for my drink and took a sip. It was still three-quarters full. I drank it to avoid having to say something.

"In fact," he added, "our biggest challenge has been to find a proper test market. We've had to go overseas to find subjects willing to participate in the preliminary drug trials."

"Why overseas?"

Why am I so interested in this? Am I trying to broadcast?

"Many homosexuals in this country do not see their condition as a problem. They wave their flags, march in parades, fight for the right to marry. Many homosexuals treat their sexuality like it is the thing they are most proud of. I do not understand this pride over something they have nothing to do with—no more than we can take credit for the color of our eyes."

"Do you think homosexuality is wrong, then?"

Careful, my mask is slipping.

"Jamie, please, do not put words into my mouth. I feel the *divisiveness* is wrong. The hate and violence are very wrong, very bad for families and for our society. And all so unnecessary. Anyway, my role is not to judge. I'm a doctor, a scientist. My job is to provide medical solutions for people who want them."

He checked his wristwatch, then used the paper napkin to begin guiding the pills back into the vial. "I have a meeting in the far northern suburbs. I should be wise and use the men's room first. Please excuse me." He stood, pushed his chair in, and went through one of the doors at the back of the café.

I felt lightheaded, but I couldn't blame the caffeine this time. I couldn't move any part of my body except my eyes. My gaze darted around the café like a fly, touching on all the familiar things—granite countertops, customers reading, overfilled garbage bins.

Am I dreaming?

I glanced back at the table. Dr. Gamez had left his papers and file folders scattered. And the plastic pill bottle. The pills were as real as everything else.

Take some, dipshit.

I stared at the bottle. It appeared to be full. Would he miss some pills if I took them? He'd only been gone a minute. I had time.

He won't miss a few. He's probably got thousands back at the lab.

My hands lay on my lap, heavy as anchors. How did I know the pills were safe? Would taking them change my whole personality? Were they lethal?

Like a neon sign, my grandfather's advice flashed across in my mind: *Jamie, you take what's given to you, and you use it. Got it?*

Nobody was watching.

Take them!

With my head turned toward the bathroom door, I lifted my right hand to the table. I moved my fingers, sweeping frantically across until I touched the bottle. I closed my hand around it and brought it into my lap.

Again, I looked around. Nobody had seen me. It was like I was invisible.

Glancing back at the bathroom door, I removed the cap and poured some pills into my left hand. I replaced the cap and returned the bottle to the table in a fluid movement. My right hand came back to my lap just as Dr. Gamez emerged from the bathroom. Now he was talking on his cell phone.

Fool, quit breathing like a lunatic.

Approaching the table, Dr. Gamez ended his call. He slipped the phone into the pocket of his suit jacket. Then he stared at the table. "I might have known," he said sternly. "Something has happened in my absence."

I nearly fainted before realizing he meant at his laboratory.

"My assistants are some of the most talented researchers

in the field," he continued, gathering his papers. "But ask them to conduct a simple inventory of the supplies cabinet, and you would think I asked them to walk on the moon." He stowed the pills and the paperwork in his briefcase. He extended his hand. "A pleasure to see you again, Jamie."

"Absolutely," I said, glad the pills were in my left hand.

"Come by the house again, and let us see how you are."

"Yes, sir."

When he was gone, I opened my hand and looked at my palm.

Eleven little pills, that was all I'd gotten. Not enough to do me any harm, probably. But were they enough to do me any good? I couldn't believe my luck. Against my pink skin, the pills looked darker. Now they were the blue of Lake Michigan in the summer when swimming is good, the blue of my mother's best blouse. They were the blue of the three plastic bins that had housed all my childhood treasures. They were the blue of Ivan's eyes.

eight

I closed my bedroom door and stood in darkness, listening to myself breathe. My clothes were wet from the rain. I switched on the creaky metal reading lamp on my desk, then pushed aside the random magazines, school papers, and old CD cases. Now I faced a clean, flat surface. The pills rolled from my trembling hand onto this hard surface, spilling like tiny dice. A tiny roll of my future.

I corralled them into a cluster, observing them under the glare of the bulb. They looked damp. They would dry under the lamp, but I worried that I'd spoiled them with my sweating hand or in the rain-soaked pocket of my jeans. For the first time, I noticed a clear, elegant *R* stamped on the side of each pill. *Rehomoline.* To me, that R meant Redo me. Renew me. Realign me.

The eleven little pills sitting in front of me were the

simple solution to everything I'd worried about for as long as I could remember. They meant the end to all my secrets. The end of dealing with people like Crazy Paul. And a grand *adiós* to the faraway island! If Dr. Gamez was correct, and the pills actually worked, I would be a grateful, loyal Rehomoline user for the rest of my life.

"Jamie, come and eat!" my grandmother called from down the hallway.

"One minute!" I said.

What I didn't have were basic instructions. To begin with, would I take one pill or two? When I had a headache, I always took two of whatever we had in the kitchen cupboard. But with my grandparents' prescriptions, I noticed that they took one of each pill. In this case, one made more sense; if I didn't feel a difference with one, I could always try two. With eleven pills, that would guarantee at least five good doses.

Second question: When to take a dose? Wesley, I knew, took his Ritalin with breakfast, but my grandparents took most of their pills after dinner. If Rehomoline was truly like an allergy medicine, the way Dr. Gamez had said, maybe I only needed to take it as needed. *As needed*—as in, whenever I found myself among other people?

Third question: What about side effects? This was the scariest part. I knew from TV ads that many prescriptions could cause a range of side effects in patients. Headaches, drowsiness, rashes, insomnia, nausea (*ugh*), oily diarrhea (*gulp*), rectal bleeding (*whoa*) ... Not very appealing, but if the pills worked, any side effect would be worth it. Moreover, would taking the pills change my personality? This part freaked me out the most. Was it a risk I was willing to take?

"Supper's getting cold!" my grandmother called.

I jumped out of my chair, leaving the pills under the desk lamp to dry. One of the advantages of living with my grand-parents was the guaranteed privacy. Nobody would come pok-ing around my bedroom. I could have left the drugs on my desktop for weeks with a large handwritten sign that said "Sto-len Pills RIGHT HERE!" without anybody ever noticing.

My grandparents had begun to eat without me, cutting into their food with the grim faces of surgeons at work.

I slipped into my usual seat. "Mom and Dad coming down?"

"No, sir," my grandfather said.

"Cool beans, Jellybeans," I said. "I'll go up later and say hello."

The table offered familiar choices. Chicken baked in rice, peas, Jell-O. I filled my plate.

"Somebody's hungry for once," my grandmother said.

"Everything looks terrific." I leaned forward in my chair, taking quick bites. "Some rain we had today, right? Lucky it wasn't snow."

"Pretty gloomy all afternoon," she said.

"Water in the basement again," my grandfather reported.

We ate in silence for a minute, rain beating against the kitchen window.

"Dentist said no cavities," I said.

"At your age," my grandfather said, chewing, "I had so many silver fillings, the other kids called me Tinfoil Tony."

"Ouch," I said.

"I didn't mind. Hell, it was a point of pride. Every time I opened my mouth, it showed I wasn't afraid of pain."

"It wasn't attractive, I'll tell you that," my grandmother said. "I had to learn to look elsewhere."

"Over time," he said, "they got replaced, one by one, with fancy white porcelain ones. I have the mouth of a movie star now, but I miss looking tough."

"Well," I said, shrugging, "I'm taking care of mine. I guess I can celebrate."

My grandmother pointed at me with her fork. "You start to celebrate, that's when the cavities get a lucky break."

At the end of the meal, out came their pills, the nightly ritual. I watched with a renewed interest as they poured from the shiny plastic bottles. My grandparents' eyes never met as they swallowed.

I felt giddy and bold. "What are those pills for, anyway?"

"Heart and bones," she said.

"Blood and brain," he said.

"Sounds like you got your bases covered." Sports metaphor—already I was getting into the spirit of my new straight life. I jumped up and took a plastic sandwich bag from the cupboard and put it in my pocket. I wanted to keep my pills nice and fresh. There had to be a reason pharmacies distributed drugs in airtight plastic containers.

My grandmother remained at the table, but her eyes never left me. "What's the bag for?"

I hesitated. "School project. Do you want me to help with dishes?"

"No, but thank you for asking," she said, nodding. "You've got your homework."

I paused at the door. "Thank you for the very nice dinner."

"Pleasure doing business with you," my grandfather said.

In my bedroom, I discovered that the pills were dry. I slipped them into the plastic bag, then held the bag closer to the desk lamp to study the pills better. They fell into order along the bottom, lined up in a neat row. I wanted to kiss them through the plastic. I opened a desk drawer and stowed the stash there, among never-sharpened souvenir pencils and rusty batteries.

I went upstairs to check on my parents. They were taking turns organizing the UPS shipments and running individual packages down to customers. The apartment smelled like popcorn. I liked to help out with gift-wrapping during evenings, working alongside my parents even when we weren't talking. A combined effort for the family good, something farm families did in black-and-white movies. I stood at the buffet table in the dining room, where the to-be-wrapped orders waited. The first one in line was a medium-size package that needed to be gift-wrapped for a newborn girl.

I selected the pink wrapping with the yellow and red stars. For me, wrapping packages offered a reliable rush of pleasure—cutting the paper to the precise length, folding and taping it neatly at the sides. I chose a thick gold-threaded satin for the ribbon and tied it with a generous bow; as an extra I tucked a white plastic giraffe through the knot.

When my mother passed by, she said, "Excellent. The master is at work."

"My son," Dad said, "future manager of Bloomingdale's gift-wrap counter." He didn't mean it as an insult. He'd said it before, and we all laughed about it.

"They didn't pay for the giraffe," I said. "Is it okay anyway?"

"Fine," he said. "Little extras like that keep them coming back for more."

"Don't go overboard," my mother called from the living room.

I wrapped a wedding present, using the thickest gloss-white paper and the same gold-threaded ribbon, and then a retirement gift: golf-course paper with the green ribbon with little white balls on it. Standard.

Next was a large package to wrap, a birthday present for a high school boy. I searched through the paper, looking for something we'd used before. It should have been easy to choose—*I was a teenage boy myself*—but I always got stuck on these orders. My instincts were wrong. The papers I liked were, according to my parents, either too childish or too pretty for an older boy. In the past they had forced me to re-wrap some of the gifts for boys, and I got lectured about wasting paper.

Tonight nothing could spoil my mood. I wanted to sing.

> *Got me a smile on my face*
> *A desk drawer full of pills…*

I happily set the package aside and moved on to the next order, something easy—a house-warming gift: pale green paper with green ferns, navy blue silk ribbon. Classic and homey.

Romance, I knew, unlike friendship, required some money. I didn't have any. I'd never held a job besides household chores, which, in my parents' view, didn't merit anything more than the food and shelter they provided. In the past, whenever I wanted to buy something—games, books, or music—my parents simply considered the request and either paid for it or didn't. But in their view, I was too young to date.

He was too young to date
Too poor to care...

I finished with the house-warming gift and stepped away from the table. I glanced over my shoulder at the cash box. My parents were in and out of the door, attending to customers.

It was wrong to steal. I knew that. At the same time, I'd done so much work for my parents lately. Plus, the gift-wrapping angle was *my idea* to begin with. Didn't I deserve some compensation? Was I expected to go through life asking for payment? Weren't child labor laws designed to help hardworking kids like me?

Humming with nonchalance, I took three steps to the sideboard and lifted the metal lid of the cash box. I barely glanced at what was in there—just pulled out two ten-dollar bills, closed the lid without making a sound, and went back to the wrapping table. I folded the bills and slipped them into my pocket. Fifteen seconds total, from initial impulse to completion.

I was already acting like Wes, and I hadn't even taken a pill yet.

It would have been crazy to beat myself up about it. It was only twenty bucks. Still, my heart drummed under my T-shirt and I had to steady myself on the back of a chair.

Two petty thefts in one day. I was becoming a pro.

———

In my bedroom, the red light of my cell phone was flashing. Celia had left a message, asking me to call her right away. Her tone was cautious, all business. I wondered if Dr. Gamez had mentioned something to her about the stolen pills. What were the chances?

A little nervously, I dialed her number.

She answered in a fake voice: "*Good evening,* Ann Accordion speaking."

"Excuse me, Ann, I'm looking for Amanda Lynn."

"So," she said gamely. "You're having coffee with my dad now?"

"Don't be jealous. We talked about *you* the whole time. About Perfect Miss You."

She laughed. "What a delicious pleasure for you both."

"It was a pleasure."

"My dad likes you a lot. Funny, I don't see it."

"Really."

"Yeah, weird. We spent half our dinner tonight talking about you."

Not about missing pills, I hope.

I remained calm. "I...I like your dad. He's smart. Refined. I don't know any other men like him."

"Congratulations, he's your number one fan. Don't let it go to your head."

"Is this why you called? To let me know I have Dr. Dad's seal of approval?"

"Not really," she said, her voice almost shy. "I missed you, nerd. Do I need an excuse to call?"

"Nope. Call anytime."

"Great. And my dad said you can come hang out at the house anytime."

"Cool. He must trust you. And trust me."

And he hasn't missed the pills.

"I assured him that you and I are just friends."

Pause. Long pause.

"Right, just friends," I repeated, grateful for the clarification. "Okay..."

"What, are you saying you're not my friend?"

"Celia, I'm totally your friend! Even though you seem to have a very limited taste in movies."

"Yeah, well—when it comes to movies, there may be room for growth for both of us." She laughed, sounding like herself again. Not cautious, not shy.

I lay back on the bed and told her about my trip to the dentist. I exaggerated all the gory elements, the scraping and bloody gums, but left out the part about Dr. Connor's son, the football star. Charmingly, Celia expressed zero sympathy for my pain.

She likes me.

And I liked her. There is no one more attractive than a person who likes you. Mr. Covici should write that on the wall of the library.

Talking to Celia made me feel happy, relaxed. Maybe I didn't even need Dr. Gamez's magic pills to make me straight. Maybe being with Celia would be all it took.

Just in case, only five feet away, my desk drawer contained any backup I would ever need.

Twenty minutes later, I hung up and turned out the light. For the first time since I hit puberty, I fell into a deep, peaceful sleep.

nine

The night was endless, weightless, and suddenly I was dreaming. The dream didn't have a beginning. No context, no setting. It wasn't the kind of kiss I had ever experienced—no quick peck on the forehead or cheek. This was the real thing: a hot, wet, mouthy kiss. Hands on my face, pressure against my jaw. It felt amazing. I was so hungry for it, as if I'd been starving but didn't realize it. For the first time, I felt sexually ... *normal,* not like a freak. We rolled over, so that I was on top, and eager hands moved behind my head, pulling me down. I stayed right in it, full contact, no breathing required.

The alarm on my clock/radio would go off in a minute—a fact that my body somehow anticipated each day. I felt myself waking, growing aware that I was only dreaming. I wanted to say, *"No, Celia, keep going—I like this. Thank*

God…I like this!" But when I pulled my face away, I wasn't staring at Celia. Instead, I saw Ivan, the blue-eyed junior from the First Knights. He didn't speak, just half smiled, lifting his mouth again toward mine. It wasn't the first time I'd dreamed about him.

I sat up in bed as the alarm went off.

I reached for the pills, and then stopped myself.

Not yet. I couldn't waste them. I only had eleven.

An hour later, I was the last person to arrive at the club meeting. The one remaining free seat? Between Celia and Ivan, of course.

Relax. Focus on the treats.

Gwen, the yellow-haired senior, had laid out three glass platters covered in wax paper. Once the paper was removed, two of the platters revealed chocolate-chip cookies and brownies that Gwen had iced with yellow smiley-faces and pink butterflies. The third platter held sliced pears, apples and bananas. So many choices—some healthy, some decadent. It was all disturbingly perfect.

The goal for the meeting was to prepare for the Valentine's Day flower sale. Mr. Covici had already approved our message-tag design and caption: *Don't hide your hart from me!* He'd photocopied the design onto bright red cardstock paper.

Perfect Gwen's cookies may have been smiling, but she studied the message tags with a sour expression. "What's that poking its head around the tree? It looks like a big snake with antlers."

"It's a deer," Celia said in my defense. "Jamie drew it."

"Very clever," Mr. Covici said. "Poets in Shakespeare's time used the deer as a symbolic image of love's desire. I'm delighted with it."

"Well, you misspelled *heart*," Gwen said.

Covici explained the heart/hart pun to the group, and I worried it was too clever.

Ivan spoke up. "Anyway, Gwen, snakes don't have antlers—or ears. You should have learned that fact in your science classes." His pale blue eyes darted from Gwen to me, and he grinned.

No wonder I'd dreamed about him. I could smell his after-shave. Spicy, fruity. I wanted to bury my face in his neck.

What am I thinking?

I needed to curb these thoughts—these hopeless hopes. Seeing Ivan only reminded me of what I dreaded about myself. Maybe I would need to take the pills before seeing *Ivan* rather than before seeing *Celia*.

Mr. Covici divided the labor and put us into two teams. I was with Celia, Ivan, and Anella, who usually stayed quiet at meetings.

"We will work with the *leetle* freshmen," Anella said, with an accent identical to Ivan's. She smiled at me. "If we must."

It turned out that Ivan and Anella were born in the same town in Eastern Europe; their families were friends long before they came to the U.S.

Mr. Covici gave us everything we needed—a big cardboard box (the kind copy paper came in), a stack of old magazines, construction paper, scissors, and glue sticks. "All the Valentine's messages will go in this box," he told us. "Make a wide slot in the top and then decorate every inch of it with construction paper and pictures. Make it look romantic and special. People, it's Marketing 101."

Another cake assignment. We thumbed through the magazines, ripping out pictures of "love"—couples laughing, kissing, dancing; groups of friends with toothy smiles; newlyweds posed on a bridge. I showed this last one to Celia. "Look, here's a movie bridge for you."

Celia studied it. "They look like they're ready to jump."

Across the table, Anella used the construction paper to cut out the words "love," "friends," "kisses," and "hugs." She began gluing them to the sides of the box.

"Don't forget S-E-X," Ivan suggested, his sly grin directed at me.

Anella punched his arm, laughing.

Celia said, "Yeah, sure. Send a flower, a little action is part of the deal."

"I will send a lot of flowers then," Ivan said.

Anella reached to tap my hand. "Don't feel bad, *leetle* freshman. With your baby face, you may get a flower or two."

Celia glued a picture of two puppies to the box.

Ivan scowled. "What do dogs have to do with love?"

"Puppy love!" she said. "Look at them. Everybody loves puppies."

Anella held up a photo of two men sitting at a table in an elegant restaurant. Handsome men, wearing dark suits. It wasn't clear if they were a romantic couple or just buddies out on the town. "Okay if I put this picture on?"

I looked away, feeling nervous. *Is this question directed to me?*

"Hey," Ivan said, "if puppies can go on the box, we can put *anything* on."

"Sure," Celia said. "We want to sell these things to everybody. Besides, gay boys are so romantic. They'll buy lots of flowers."

Is this true? Are gay boys more romantic than straight boys? And how does Celia know?

Now Ivan addressed me. "What do you think?"

I shook my head, blinking. "What? I'm sorry, I wasn't paying attention." Then I whispered, "Gwen's smiley cookies are freaking me out."

Gwen may have heard me. "People, my parents are *donating* the carnations," she bragged loudly at the other table. "So I mean, it's all *profit* for the club."

"Okay," Mr. Covici said, "and thanks to the generosity of Gwen's parents, each club member can send five carnations for free. You can buy more, of course, but the first five are free, thanks to your hard work." He moved around the tables, giving red slips to each member. "Or, your *hart* work, in this case. We'll attach these to the flowers on Valentine's Day, when we attach the rest of the tags."

I took my five tags and moved to a far table to fill them out. Despite what Anella said, I was a little concerned that I wouldn't receive flowers from anyone. So the first message I wrote was addressed to me: *Hey Jamie, you rock! Love, Yourself*

Wesley and Mimi were my lunch posse, so I owed them each a flower. On Wesley's message, I wrote, *Hey slugger, sorry I won't be joining you on the field this spring. But I will be your best athletic supporter! Thanks for being an awesome friend. (Sorry this isn't from a chickie.) Jamie*

On Mimi's, I wrote, *I'm glad Wes introduced us. Keep on smiling! Jamie*

I hoped this subtle sarcasm might actually encourage her to smile for once.

Obviously, I needed to send one to Celia. I didn't want to say something romantic—too early in the game. On the other hand, I didn't want to write that I was satisfied being only her friend. In the end, I wrote, *Give me my wallet and bracelet back, you bitch! I know where you live. A.L.*

I had one message left. My pen stalled on the paper, waiting for instructions from my brain.

The first bell rang. Everyone jumped up and raced for the door.

I addressed the front, then opened the message tag and printed in strange, crude letters, *Hey, Blue Eyes, get out of my dreams. Thanks.*

I stuffed my messages into the big box and ran for class.

———

At lunch, Wesley reported that Mimi had stayed home. Ever since she began joining us for lunch, it was rare for Wes and me to get any time by ourselves. So we seized the opportunity and spent most of the lunch period as aliens transported to Earth, trying to make sense of the mysterious utensils on our trays. We cut sandwiches with spoons and sucked applesauce with a straw. Mimi would not have approved.

"This is nice," I said, breaking out of character.

Wes nodded. "Ever since I started baseball conditioning I feel like I never see you."

"I was thinking the same thing!"

"No homo," he said, "but we need to make some time … you know?"

"Totally."

He looked almost guilty, as if the situation had been weighing on his conscience.

I wanted to let him off the hook. "Don't feel bad, Wes. I've been busy, too."

"Yeah, what's up?"

"Our club is having its annual fundraiser this week. Flower sale for Valentine's Day."

"Flower sale, really?" He smiled, as if suppressing a laugh. He loved to tease me. "And, let's see, you're still doing the gift-wrapping thing at home?"

"Wes, don't say it."

"I'm not saying anything! Very manly activities—that's all I needed to say."

"If it makes you feel any better," I said, "I've also been hanging out a lot with Celia Gamez."

"Really?" He leaned back in his chair, as if stunned.

"Nearly every day before school. Sometimes after school."

"Dude, that is awesome!"

I smiled, feeling proud and embarrassed. I hadn't intended to tell anybody so soon. "Sorry I haven't mentioned anything. It's only been a couple of weeks."

"You are a *major stud*."

This made us both laugh.

"Let's be real," I said. "It could be over by Spring Break."

"Well, I'm excited for you."

"Thanks."

"I'm telling you, Mimi will be ... shocked."

"Of course."

"She will require photos as proof. Signed statements, DNA samples, and so on ..."

"We'll see what we can do."

"Listen, as long as we're in confession mode," he said softly, "I have some big news of my own."

"Excellent. Lay it on me."

"I'm thinking of giving up my pills."

"Your Ritalin? Why?"

He shrugged. "I'm tired of them. They suck the energy out of me and put me in a fog. At baseball conditioning, I feel like I'm slower than everybody else. I'm sick of not feeling like me."

I remembered what Wesley was like pre-pills—all the negative drama. It seemed like a lifetime ago. "This is huge. Congratulations."

"I'm old enough. I'm ready. Baseball tryouts start the day we get back from Spring Break. I'll stop taking them over break so I'm sharp when tryouts begin."

"What do your parents think?"

"Well, that's interesting." He hesitated, moving his tray back and forth. "They don't know, and I'm not telling them."

"Wesley, that's crazy! You need to tell them. And your doctor."

"Nope. No one needs to know. And FYI, I'm not even going to tell Mimi, because she's a loudmouth, in case you hadn't noticed."

"What if your body has some sort of freaky reaction to going off the pills? What if you start throwing punches again?"

"I know my own body. It's going to be fine. No punches, no broken glass. I promise, I won't break your fancy pastels into halves this time."

I couldn't help but smile at the memory. "Wes, your parents are going to notice if you stop taking the Ritalin."

"Duh, I'll still *pretend* to take it, every morning," he said. "I'll pop one in my mouth on my way out the door, and then I'll spit it out just as soon as I'm on the sidewalk. Maybe some hyper-ass squirrel will benefit from a calmer lifestyle. Miracle of modern science."

"I don't know. It seems risky." All I could think of was the old Wesley I'd known in middle school. The pastel-snapper, window-breaker, fist-thrower who'd been such a terror. But that was years ago. Maturity might have been all he needed. Plus, it didn't seem fair to argue with him when I had a stash of secret pills in a drawer at home.

The bell rang.

"Trust me, it'll be okay," he said, standing.

"It better be."

Walking to class, I kept picturing those broken pastels spread out across my desk—pastels as fractions. I wondered if that was what would happen to us as we moved through life. Would we become like fractions rather than whole numbers? Each time we started taking pills, and then stopped taking them, how different from our original selves would we become?

ten

The weather was as confused as everything else. After weeks of rain, the snow returned. In the grocery store parking lot, headlights passed through falling flakes. With my grandfather behind the wheel of his old Ford Taurus, we circled until we found a spot. I stretched out miserably in the back seat. There were few experiences I dreaded more than waiting in the grocery store parking lot. Pure torture. The only experience I disliked more than waiting was going in and actually helping.

"Neither of you coming in?" My grandmother was scowling. She opened the passenger side door. "Fine, but don't crab to me later."

My grandfather made a familiar sound deep in his chest— equal parts argument and apology. He opened a *Newsweek.*

My grandmother slammed the car door shut.

"Damn it," he said to the magazine, "no need to slam it."

I smiled at his geezer rap.

Resting my head against the window, I tried to picture Celia reading my flower message, laughing at the joke. I wondered if she had sent me a free flower, too.

My eyes remained locked on the store entrance, waiting. What would Ivan think when he read my stupid message? Would it freak him out? Would he be flattered? Did he have a girlfriend? He would never figure out who sent it. He'd probably get flowers from other people, too. Why had I sent him one? Idiotic move on my part. Ivan seemed like a nice-enough guy, but I did mean what I wrote. He was not welcome in my dreams.

Good riddance, adiós, and peace out, bro.

The car was hot, the windows cloudy. I cracked open the glass.

Why hadn't I dreamed I was kissing Celia? For weeks I'd been training my attention on her. I had the pills. I was ready to fall in love. Would it only be a matter of taking the pills?

On the floor of the car, my foot brushed against a dog-eared paperback. I reached for it. The book was called *One Hundred and Twenty Bible Miracles in Verse.* It belonged to my grandmother, and it had lived in the back seat of the Taurus for as long as I could remember. I opened to random pages:

The angel came and calmed the lions' rage
Devoutly Daniel praised God from the cage.

With only bread loaves five and fishes two
Jesus fed thousands and converted souls anew.

Some of the miracles made me smile—especially in Numbers, with the "speaking sass" of "Balaam's ass," or Aaron's "sturdy rod," which yielded a "good-sized almond wad." As poetry, it definitely sucked. But I had always wanted to believe in the magical world the book depicted: tales of walking staffs turned into serpents, bodies raised from the dead, and no shortage of miraculous healing cures for leprosy, lunacy, palsy, dropsy, withered limbs, impotence, mysterious "women's issues," blindness—a complete anatomy of life-changing miracles. Now, at home in a drawer, I had a miracle of my very own.

With a little blue pill and the approval of God
Overnight Jamie became as straight as a rod.

My grandfather made that sound again in his lungs.

I leaned forward and rested my head against the seat back. "Hey, Pop, do you believe in miracles?"

He set down the *Newsweek* and glanced at the store entrance. "I guess I do," he said.

"Like what? What kind of miracles have you ever seen?"

My grandmother came out of the store, walking slowly toward the car through the snowy parking lot. A bag of groceries dangled from each arm. She was still frowning.

"For one thing," my grandfather said, "it'll be a miracle if she doesn't poison us."

"Pop, I'm being serious."

"So am I. The fact that we all live in the world together, and most of us refrain from killing each other. That's got to be the biggest miracle there is."

"What about...love?" I asked. "Do you think love is sometimes a miracle?"

My grandfather leaned over and opened the car door for his wife, letting in the cold wet air. "Not sometimes, Jamie," he said. "Always."

Always.

This information filled me with hope.

———

We sold nearly five hundred message tags the week before Valentine's Day. Covici asked some of us to be at school at dawn on February 13th, to sort the tags into homerooms and attach them to flowers. The other club members would sort the next morning. At Maxwell Tech, Valentine's Day was a forty-eight-hour event.

Half awake, I faced a row of plastic buckets filled with pink and red carnations. The library was filled with a sharp leafy smell, like a greenhouse. We started hole-punching the messages and attaching them to the stems with twist ties. The process was fast and repetitive—it reminded me of gift-wrapping at home. For once, my parents had equipped me with a useful life skill.

Although I stood next to Celia, we worked without speaking. Her hair was hidden under an orange knitted hat, and her face looked different, somehow younger. Our elbows brushed once in the frenzy.

"Sorry."

"Sorry."

I wasn't sure if she was tired, or only trying to concentrate, or giving me the cold shoulder. Why were girls always so inscrutable?

Across the isle, Ivan and Anella worked more like a team. They'd divided the labor, one using the twist ties and the other sorting into homerooms. Side by side, they looked almost like siblings, with their dark-blond hair and rosy complexions. I wondered if they'd ever dated. They were so playful together. He marched two flowers across the table toward her and made them dance and sway, earning giggles. It was easy to be distracted by him.

My eyes searched for the message I'd written to him—in hindsight, a bonehead mistake. It was wrong of me to indulge in that negative behavior, even if it proved to be harmless. If I could spot it, maybe I could pocket it and throw it away.

I saw one message that seemed to be written in Chinese. I showed it to Celia. "What do you think this one says?"

She studied it, finally smiling. "It says, '*Why does the snake have antlers?*'"

"Ah, yes, the question that will be on everybody's lips this week."

"Kidding! Jamie, the drawing looks exactly like a deer."

"No time to read other people's notes," Covici advised. "Keep focused, so we'll be finished when the bell rings."

I couldn't find Ivan's message, but decided not to sweat it. He would never know who sent it. But I made a promise to myself: *Remember KFC. No more sending messages you can't unsend.*

When the message tags were attached and the flowers sorted, we moved them all to a corner, swept the floor, and wiped down the tabletops.

"Excellent work, guys," Mr. Covici said. "Ivan and Anella, you'll be selling again at lunch. But all four of you are off the hook for the next early-morning assembly line."

"Amen," Celia said, reaching for her books. "I woke up late and I'm a mess. I need to get ready before the bell."

"You look fine," I said, meaning it. "Better than fine."

"I look like I'm ten." She gave me a small, restrained smile. "It's weird, but sometimes I feel like I can't *think* without makeup."

"You wear makeup?"

She patted my arm. "Jesus, it must be sweet to be a boy. See you later."

"You look great!" I called, watching as she joined the flurry of students passing through the corridor. Within seconds she disappeared, swallowed by the crowd. I had to admit, there were times when I felt something real around her—a spark, a romantic connection—especially after it had passed.

———————

All morning, my thoughts kept returning to the flowers. I expected to receive two: the one I sent to myself and maybe, if I was lucky, one from Celia. After all, she'd gotten five free ones just like I did. But maybe she'd chosen to send them all to her girlfriends.

At Maxwell, homeroom was the mid-morning period when the teachers read announcements and took care of administrative paperwork while the students slept or ate contraband snacks from the vending machines. When I got there, I saw that my teacher, Mr. Mallet, had laid out flowers at the students' desks. Mr. Mallet was also the baseball coach. "I don't want to waste any time on this Valentine business," he barked. It only figured that a man of Mr. Mallet's hyper-masculine nature needed to distance himself from any activity involving flowers.

I looked for my desk at the back of the room, to see if there were two flowers waiting there—but there weren't.

There were four.

eleven

Mr. Mallet's reedy voice had been sharpened by two decades of yelling at ballplayers from the sidelines. He always read the daily announcements as if he were angry at them. But today, even Mallet's violent recitation wouldn't hold my attention. All I could see were the four flowers on my desk.

Sinking into my chair, I pulled the flowers toward me.

Hank, the kid who sat in the next seat, was staring. He was a meathead who towered over most people. Nearly every day, he wore a dark green windbreaker, ratty and worn, so in my head I'd nicknamed him the Incredible Hank. He wasn't bad looking, but I noticed he didn't have any flowers.

"Somebody's popular," he whispered. His breath smelled intensely of Doritos from the vending machine.

"I guess so." I looked around at the other desks. Nobody else had four. One or two maybe, but not four.

"Impressive," the Hank said. "Who is she?"

"Let's find out." I opened the first one.

Oooh, baby, when I see you in the halls,
I want to push you up against a
locker and cover you with sticky kisses.
Your bod is so hot—you could
fry an egg on that ass.

I smiled at Wesley's unmistakable sloppy handwriting. What a goofball.

I opened the second one.

Hey Jamie, you rock!
Love,
Yourself

Ho-hum. Guess I didn't need that one after all. On to the third:

Love is so very timid when 'tis new.
Byron

I closed my eyes, feeling almost sick. *Now this?* Why was a boy named Byron sending me a message? Had Crazy Paul told my secret to a kid named Byron?

I opened my eyes and studied the handwriting—loopy and careful. In fact, it looked like a girl's penmanship. (Was beautiful penmanship more girlish? Didn't boys care about writing neatly?) Maybe the message was from a girl after all. Maybe Celia. It seemed possible. *Please!* Then I opened the last one:

> *You're a deer! No wait—only a snake*
> *with antlers. Whatever wild species you*
> *may be, I suppose I can let you inside*
> *and feed you sometimes. Anyone for soup?*
> *Celia*

Okay, so this one was hers. Excellent. She sent me one, and it was funny. And yes, the penmanship was careful and girly. But who wrote the third one? Did another girl at Maxwell have a crush on me? And why would she call herself Byron?

"So?" the Hank whispered.

"They're all from a girl I like." I tried to sound bored. "Yippee."

"Congrats." He folded his enormous hands on his desktop, looking suddenly somber.

I lifted one of the flowers and handed it to him. "You can have one."

"Dude," he said, wincing. He showed me the wide pale palms of his hands. "I don't want a flower from a guy."

I shrugged and smiled. "No homo."

———

I took the flowers with me to the cafeteria, where I found Wes and Mimi sitting at our usual lunch table. We had established a system where only one of us went through the cafeteria line each day and got food for all three of us. Today it had been Wesley's turn, with predictably bizarre results: potato sticks, tater tots, and pickle spears. Wes was all about the sides.

"*Thank you for the flower*," they said in unison, and I bowed.

"You got four?" Mimi said. Her tone was distrustful.

"Well, one of them was from me," I said, a little embarrassed. "But thank *you*, Wesley, for the other one."

He grabbed the front of my shirt, all mock-toughness. "Don't tell anyone, see? Ruin my rep around here."

Mimi's gaze was riveted on my thin bouquet. "And the other two?"

"One is from Celia Gamez," I said, sitting down. I handed the flowers to her with some reluctance. "I don't know what to think about the other one." I began to eat, stuffing lukewarm tater tots into my mouth one after the other, like popcorn. I was always hungry after homeroom, but today my nerves had left me famished. I doubted that the odd meal Wesley had assembled was going to satisfy me.

"She likes you," Mimi said, after reading Celia's. "Weird, I've never seen the flirty side of her. Hell, I've never seen the friendly side of her. Are you psyched?"

"Stoked," I said. "Girls get psyched, boys get stoked."

She bristled. "What, I'm getting a sex lesson from *you* now?"

"This other one is wack," Wes said. "Why is a dude sending you a flower?"

I shook my head, feeling exposed. "I ... I can't explain it."

"Are you kidding me?" Mimi asked. "You jackasses, Byron was a famous poet. Lord Byron? It's some kind of quote. *Love is so very timid when 'tis new.'* I mean, please—who says *'tis* anymore? Wasn't that a clue?"

"I did wonder about that," Wes said unconvincingly.

Mimi added, "And relax, it's from a girl. Look at the handwriting. Some ridiculous, shy girl has a crush on you. Pathetic. But who?"

"I have no idea."

For a split second, I wondered if Mimi had sent it. Was it possible she was interested in me? As any kid on a playground knows, we harass the ones we like most. Plus, Mimi had expressed a more-than-usual interest in my love life. But I couldn't imagine her in romantic terms. She hardly ever cracked a smile; she was far too busy telling Wes and me what to do. Anyway, this theory was undermined by her next remark:

"You need to send Celia another one."

"That's what I was thinking," I said.

"It's like, put up or shut up," she added.

"Lay off, will you?" I said. "I'm going to go buy one right now." I hadn't eaten enough, but there wasn't much time left to go buy another flower. Getting up, I looked at Wesley. "Where is your flower, anyway?"

He flashed a goofy smile, his hand against his heart. "Saw someone on my way to lunch who just had to have it. Pretty girl needs to have a flower."

"I hope you had the brains to remove the tag first," Mimi said.

"Oops," he said.

Grabbing my books and flowers, I zigzagged through the cafeteria chaos, stepping around loose chairs and grounded food, to the front of the room. At a card table, Ivan and Anella sat with their cheeseburger baskets behind the cash box. Their sign said, *SEND A VALENTINE FLOWER TO YOUR—SPECIAL SOMEONE!—SECRET CRUSH!— FAVE FRIENDS!* A line of students waited to buy flowers. I stood at the end, trying to think of something clever to write on Celia's message. Did the tone of this next one need to be romantic? At the last minute, I decided that if one was good, two were better. One funny, one flirty.

"Two please," I said, when I got to the front of the line.

"Four dollars," Anella said, without looking up.

I handed her the money.

Ivan held up two tags, but when he saw it was me, he withdrew them playfully. "Hey, it's Jamie—you have come to help us!" A red carnation lay on the table beside his cheeseburger. Was it the flower I'd sent him?

"Give me those," I said, pulling the tags from him. I pushed them into my jeans pocket. I could fill them out later, when I had time to think.

"Sit with us," Ivan said.

"Please do!" Anella said. "Seriously, we require assistance." Until recently, she had basically ignored me, as if becoming friends with a freshman was a low priority for her. But now she waved me eagerly toward the seat next to her.

My impulse was to flee, but before I could go, Ivan

jumped up and pointed me toward his chair. "Sit," he com-manded.

I sat.

"Two dollars," Anella told a student. And to me: "Where's your girl?"

I hesitated. Did she mean Celia? "She has lunch later," I said, when it registered. "I wouldn't say she's my girl."

"She's single, then? Pay *her*," Ivan said to a customer.

I looked away. We hadn't exactly made things official yet. No public announcements or bulletins in the school paper. We hadn't even labeled it, whatever it was, ourselves. Was Ivan interested in Celia? Maybe, all along, that was the reason he'd been so nice to me. "Ask her yourself," I said in response.

"And you're single? How many?" Ivan asked a customer.

"I guess so."

"But quite popular," Anella added. "Two dollars, please."

"Me? Not so much."

"You're carrying *four flowers*," Anella said, ticking my neck. "I think we must start calling you ... Flowerboy."

This was the funny part. I *was* carrying four flowers— a fact that everybody seemed to notice. But I didn't have many real friends at Maxwell other than Wesley and Celia, and sometimes Mimi. I only *looked* popular, and only for this one day.

"Here, Flowerboy," Ivan said, moving behind me. He put his warm hands on my shoulders, squeezing. "If you sell for a minute, I can eat my cheeseburger."

For an ecstatic moment, I couldn't move. His spontaneous, casual gesture was no different from the thousands of gropes and punches that took place each day among male friends, but it sent a jolt through my chest that reverberated down to my feet.

I scooted next to Anella. "How many?" I asked a customer.

———————

I gave myself a pep talk as I crawled into bed that night. The important thing was that I admired Ivan as a person. He was smart, funny, good-looking—who wouldn't like him? And didn't guys always admire older guys? Even Coach Mallet must have admired his classmates when he was a teenager, guys like my father, the sports heroes. Everybody admired them. True, Mallet probably hadn't given too much thought to what my father looked like with his shirt off, the way I sometimes thought about Ivan. But I was working on that.

I was determined to dream about Celia.

Celia, who *liked* me. Celia, who sent me a Valentine flower.

What did Celia look like with her shirt off? I'd never even thought about that, but it was what I needed to focus on. Closing my eyes, I called up an image of Celia—smiling, confident Celia—then unceremoniously stripped off her shirt. In my mind, she looked amazing in her bra. I had to hand it to her, she was in terrific shape. Hands on her hips, she swiveled back and forth like a girl in a bra commercial on TV. Then I removed the bra—*poof, gone!*—leaving her boobs bobbling. Boobs, exposed to the open air like the ones I had seen for years in the pages of *Playboy* magazine, which Wesley pilfered on a regular basis from his father's workroom. Pleased with my powers of memory and imagination, I directed my fingers down to my shorts and waited for a reaction. *Oh,* I dreamed, *those boobs...*

Nothing.

Nothing.

Bobbling boobs did nothing for me.

But it was okay. I had the pills, and with time—when it really mattered—Celia's body would be all I thought about. Everything I wanted.

In the meantime, the weirdest part was? I really liked Celia.

And I fell asleep thinking of her.

———

I awoke in the middle of the night, my T-shirt soaked with sweat. Ivan's tongue was in my mouth again, heavy hands on my shoulders, his body on top of me like a blanket. I jumped out of bed, my heart racing. I wanted to scream through the roof or swear at the stars, but my grandparents were light sleepers. I had to stay quiet.

I turned on my desk lamp, then angrily opened the drawer that contained the pills. I had these damn drugs, so why wasn't I using them? I hadn't even mustered up the courage to take one yet. I closed the desk drawer, leaving the pills out, and resolved to take the first pill the very next time I was alone with Celia.

I scrambled for my backpack. I pulled the blank message tags from my binder and stared at them.

I sat on my bed and wrote the first one, my hand still shaking:

Celia,
Your body is so HOT—you could
fry EGGS on that ASS!
Jamie

If this wasn't direct enough, what would be?

I looked at the other tag, its blankness like a challenge to my brain. At the moment, I was in no mood to be clever or funny—for Celia or for anybody.

I realized I did have something urgent to say, just not to her. Again I printed with my left hand, so Ivan would never know who sent it. I wrote:

People like you make life really difficult for people like
me. I wish you were an asshole. Go away!

I knew two things for sure: (1) Ivan wouldn't know who it was from or what it meant; and (2) I didn't really give a shit.

twelve

Pre-dawn on the big day: I heard a knock on my bedroom
door, then a chirpy, strained, "Happy *Val-en-tine's* Day."

I opened my eyes and turned toward the voice, the bedroom door creaking. My eyes adjusted and I saw the dark
bony form of my grandmother's arm as she lobbed a bag
of M&M's toward my bed. Although her arm was the only
part of her anatomy she permitted to enter the room, the
bag landed expertly between my feet. *Thwack!* How did she
do that?

I cleared my throat. "Wow, thanks."

"From your mom," she called. "Don't eat them all at
once or you'll be sorry."

The door seemed to close by itself. I hadn't even seen
my grandmother's face.

I leaned forward and picked up the M&Ms with both

hands. It was a good-sized bag, but hard to tell the colors in the dark.

For years, my family had made a big deal out of Valentine's Day. There were handmade cards exchanged, bowls of chocolates set about for all to enjoy, even a pink-striped cake with dinner. But the year we moved in with my grandparents, the tradition had ended: no candy, no cards, no cake. The change was abrupt and unexplained. Maybe my parents were too busy that year, too cash poor, or maybe they thought I'd outgrown such gestures. The following year, I didn't make a card for them either. The holiday came and went like any other day, and so had all the Valentine's Days since then.

And now these M&Ms—arriving literally, it seemed, out of nowhere.

I might have felt cynical about it. I could clearly picture my busy mother dropping off this candy with my grandmother weeks before, easy and efficient, another item crossed off her to-do list. This Valentine's Day, however, I was not feeling cynical. After all, I had a to-do list of my own. I jumped out of bed, almost glad to be up early.

On my way out of the house, I stopped upstairs—in part to thank my parents for the candy, and more important, to discreetly grab some gift-wrap and ribbon. As it turned out, discretion was unnecessary since my parents were sound asleep. I found some paper and a pen, scribbled a note of thanks, added a sloppy heart, and left it on the dining room table where they would see it when they woke up. I helped myself to all the gift-wrap and ribbon I might need.

When I got to school, quite a few students lined the hallways, everyone doing the same thing as me—decorating lockers, tying up helium balloons, planning surprises. Nobody talking or horsing around. The work was serious and eerily quiet, a dutiful army of love zombies.

At Celia's locker, I began by covering the door with metallic-red paper. I taped all four corners, then twisted the pink ribbon in a border all around. I worked quickly, happily.

I'd realized that it was a mistake to keep our relationship so quiet. My dreams with Ivan were trying to tell me that. I *really was* dating Celia Gamez, and I was ready for the whole world to know. Once I told the world, maybe the world would convey the information back to me.

I got out the bag of M&Ms and glue. My plan was to glue the pink-and-red candies, one by one, into a big heart, with our names in the middle. *Inspired!* But the process was painstaking and tedious. It took more time than I expected to alternate between the two different colors of candy. Crouching, I had only completed the heart and Celia's name, when I heard my own name spoken behind me.

"Jamie?"

I recognized the voice, and my body instantly tensed. I turned to look.

Crazy Paul stood about five feet away, staring. He was wearing his black pirate hat with the red feather. The hat was more annoying than ever.

It had been only a few weeks since we talked, but it felt like a lifetime ago. Another world.

"Hey you," he said with a big, fake, shy smile. Pimply red chin.

I kept working, still in a crouch, but my heart raced full throttle. "Hey."

"Haven't seen you online for a while."

"Yeah, well, I'm taking a break from that," I said, and I hoped it sounded cold. I kept gluing the candy to the locker, one by one. Steady hands.

"Oh, I know the feeling. Sometimes you need a breather from all that *drama*, right?"

"Right."

I need a breather right now, as a matter of fact.

"And what are we up to here?" he asked—too familiar, too friendly, as if this conversation was part of an ongoing intimacy that we both enjoyed.

"What does it look like I'm up to?"

"A Valentine's surprise for . . ." He took a step closer. "Celia?"

"Good for you," I said. "You can read."

"Is that your girlfriend or something?"

"No, Paul," I said, standing and turning to look at him. "She's my personal trainer."

His eyes seemed to survey me, top to bottom. "What are you trying to do?"

"I'm not *trying* to do anything. I'm living my life."

True, the bag of pastel-colored M&M's and the glue in my hands slightly undercut the strength of my argument.

"Listen, Jamie, I'm not judging you. But I think you might be making a mistake. I want to help."

Yeah, I know what you want.

"I don't need your help," I said. "Honestly, I don't have time for this conversation." I needed to finish the locker. More importantly, I didn't want anyone to see me talking to this clown.

"Relax," he said softly. "Trust me. You *do* need my help. I'm older than you. I've already been through what... what I suspect you're going through."

"You don't know anything about me."

"Really?" He bent closer. "I mean, seriously? Do you want me to remind you of some of the things I know about you?"

I froze. The corridors were getting crowded, a few squeals of surprise and delight at the discovery of other decorated lockers. My time for this project was slipping away.

His voice softened again. "Jamie, if you go down that path, it won't end well. For her or for you. No matter how many different ways you try to justify it to yourself."

I resumed my work with the glue and the candy. "Thanks for your concern, but it's nothing for you to worry about."

Steady hands, steady hands...

"Good luck, then. Seriously, I wish you good luck." He began to move away.

"Wait, Paul—one question." I hated to ask, but I needed to know. "Did you send me a flower message?"

He looked at me, a coy smile on his lips. "Did you want me to?"

"Please just answer the question."

"Sorry to disappoint you. I did not send you a flower. I've got my own life, too."

I nodded, relieved. "Have a good one, then. See you."

He stood there a moment, as if waiting to say something else, then turned and scuttled off to his own life. Whatever that was.

The rest of the work was hasty and sloppy. I hadn't left enough space for my own name to fit properly in the candy heart. When completed, it looked like it said "CELIA + jawie." *Jawie?* Well, she'd get the idea. I finished within minutes of the first bell, picked up my trash, and then raced down the hall, still waiting for my breathing to return to normal. I wanted to get as far away from her locker as possible—as if I was embarrassed of the work. As if I'd committed a very minor crime.

———

Later, in homeroom, two new red carnations lay waiting for me on my desk. My seat neighbor, the Incredible Hank, stared at them longingly.

He looked up when I approached. "She really likes you, dude."

"Guess so," I said, slipping next to him. "Did you get one this time?"

"Nah," he said. "Most girls here are, you know, intimidated by my physique."

I nodded, acknowledging the tragedy of his massive size.

While Mr. Mallet snarled his way through the daily announcements, I opened the first of the two messages.

Celia had printed in neat, small letters that filled the tag:

Jamie, I've always been a steadfast cynic when it comes to this cheesy holiday, but this year I can't resist: Happy Valentine's Day! No irony intended. Be a good boy and keep this message in your pocket as a sign of my affection. Hart to hart, Celia

I slipped the message into my pocket, feeling proud, relieved, and a little strange.

I set the carnation aside and reached for the second one. Unsigned, another mystery. The note was written in the same loopy, careful handwriting as the earlier unsigned message:

Fishermen know that the sea is dangerous and the storms terrible, but they have never found these dangers sufficient reason for remaining ashore.
Vincent van Gogh

This time I recognized the name: Vincent van Gogh was a famous Dutch painter and *not* a boy at our school. That was a relief. Still, I was annoyed. If it wasn't Crazy Paul, who was messing with me by sending these flowers?

After homeroom, I went searching for Celia and found her in the library. I dropped into the seat next to her.

"My locker!" she whispered, kissing me on the cheek. "It's really—wow. Quite a work of art. Thank you."

She thanked me for the flower, but apparently I hadn't gotten the tone quite right in the message. "Fry eggs on my ass," she chuckled. "Perfect. I'm glad to know my ass might be good for something. Maybe someday I could go to disaster areas and, you know, prepare breakfasts at shelters." She noticed the two carnations in my hand. "Who'd you get the second flower from?"

"My friend Mimi," I lied.

"Just a friend, huh?"

"Absolutely and without qualification," I said. "Hey, I really liked what you wrote in your message to me."

"Really?"

"Yeah. I'll keep it in my pocket for a long time."

"That's sweet. And a relief! To tell you the truth, I was nervous about writing it."

"Why?"

She shrugged. "I didn't want you to think I was moving too fast. You know, in my head or anything."

"You're not. We're not."

"Wait ... not what?"

"Moving too fast in our heads."

"Right, good." She made a pantomime of wiping sweat from her brow, then leaned forward and whispered, "It's like we've planted this seed, and now we both have to wait and watch it grow. These things are sort of out of our control. Agreed?"

"Sure. We just let it happen."

"Effortless, automatic." She sighed. "You know, like in bad poetry, how a bud opens to become a perfect rose."

I nodded, feeling silly. "Or maybe it's like what they say about ... um, snowballs and avalanches."

She covered her mouth. "Yes, exactly! This thing could be like an out-of-control, speeding train."

"Oh, no."

Celia clutched my hand dramatically. "But there's good news. The train is on the fast track to a town called Love."

"*Aw*, yay! Or hey, maybe it's like Godzilla set loose in a sleepy Japanese city."

We were both sweating and shaking, trying to stifle our laughter. Any second, Mr. Covici would come and tell us to get to work.

"Maybe," Celia whispered, "it's like a wildfire that spreads and destroys everything in its path."

I paused, out of ideas. "Yeah, like... let's see, one of those old-time smallpox epidemics that killed all the babies in the village?"

"Yes, yes." She took my hands in hers, more soberly, and gave me the sweetest, most affectionate look. "Yes, Jawie," she said, "*that* is our new relationship in a nutshell."

This was what Crazy Paul could never understand: Celia and I clicked. We had something. I wasn't forcing a relationship with her because I was simply afraid of being gay. Celia and I *liked* one another. I didn't need the sarcastic good luck he had offered.

Besides, he wasn't aware of the legitimate good luck I had waiting for me in my desk drawer at home. Eleven doses of good luck.

———

My parents came down and joined us for a late supper. My favorite: spaghetti and "garlic bread" hot dog buns. My parents were in pretty good moods themselves. Like Celia, they had a new appreciation for Valentine's Day—in their case, due to all the package mail it generated. The challenge, from their perspective, had been to figure out where to store all the items that required refrigeration. Imported chocolates, stinky cheeses, expensive wines, grapes out of season, and New York cheesecakes. Both kitchens, upstairs and down, had been packed to capacity. A lot of people, I realized, look at Valentine's Day mostly as a way to justify eating like crap.

"Craziest week ever," my mother complained cheerfully. "Honestly, I think it's better than December."

My father looked at me, holding the Parmesan cheese over his pasta. "Did you get any valentines, buddy?"

"A few cards from friends," I said. "Thanks for the M&Ms."

"Well, I mean … thanks for your note," my dad said, a little awkwardly. "It meant a lot to your mom and me."

"Did you give anybody a valentine?" my mother asked me. Her tone was casual, but this was a test question. She wanted to see if I was violating the house rule regarding the age requirement for dating.

"Just to friends," I said. "To be nice."

"What about that girl you said you like?" my mother asked. "Celia, I think you said her name is?"

"Only to friends," I said.

My mother twirled spaghetti on a fork, and I wondered if she believed me.

My dad said, "We had a gal come in the other day with two packages. One for her husband, who's in California this week on business. The other for her 'old friend' Carl, to a work address in the suburbs. Guess who got the sexy underpants?"

My grandmother shook her head disapprovingly. "You're mailing underpants now?"

"Hell, we wrapped the packages." Dad laughed, throwing up his hands. "All the husband got was a stupid mug filled with Hershey's Kisses. Poor sap."

"We don't ask questions and we don't pass judgments," my mother said. "We just send out packages."

Packages. Packages. Packages.

"It's a big responsibility," said my grandfather. "You're in one of those professions that knows everybody's private business."

"Yeah, like a priest, huh?" my grandmother muttered. "Underpants."

My grandfather shrugged. "I was thinking more like bankers and dry cleaners. Dry cleaners know everything! We plumbers didn't get to know squat about anything, except—"

"Don't say it!" my grandmother interrupted.

"Except the people who can't control the size of their gigantic BMs."

"Not that again, please," my mother said.

Yes, this was my family, at supper, on what was supposed to be the most romantic evening of the year. Underpants, packages, and gigantic BMs. Somewhere in Heaven, St. Valentine probably borrowed Cupid's arrow and shot himself through the head.

After eating, I excused myself and went to my room. I refused to let my family spoil the spirit of the holiday.

I called Celia. "It's lucky you're nowhere near me," I told her. "I've had enough garlic bread to scare away an army of vampires."

"Hey, can we go to DePaul tomorrow after school and look for Amanda Lynn? Seeing this turquoise bracelet on my bureau every day makes me feel... you know, a little guilty."

"And you think we'll just run into her? Walking across the quad or something?"

"Yeah, I know. Long shot—but, you know, possible."

"Sure, we can go," I said. "As long as we're hanging out together."

"Cool. That'll be good, because I've got something important to ask you. But face to face."

"You're not breaking up with me already, are you?"

"You'll find out... tomorrow."

"Give me a hint."

"Nope."

"Please, one hint."

She hummed tunelessly, as if trying to decide what to say. "Okay, here's your hint. Tonight at dinner, my dad asked me something, related to you, and I've been thinking about it, and I'm just going to ask you. But to your face."

"Huh." Inside my stomach, the hot-dog buns turned in a circle and sat down again. "That's a little cryptic."

"Hints are supposed to be cryptic."

I couldn't think what to say. Her tone seemed oddly cautious. It was as if every time Celia let me know she cared about me, she nonetheless expected me to undergo a series of tests.

"Okay," I said, trying to sound breezy. "Well, I look forward to our adventure at DePaul then."

"See you in the sunshine, Valentine."

We hung up.

Her father had asked about me. Had he noticed, after all, that I'd taken the pills? *Celia, my darling, you should know something. Your friend Jamie is a thief, a criminal. And one other thing—he's gay as a goose.*

The unpleasant scenario replayed in my mind, again and again, as I finished my homework. Either (a) they'd discovered I'd taken the pills and I was screwed, or (b) they didn't know a thing and I didn't have a problem in the world.

Whichever the case, I decided to take my first pill in the morning.

What did I have to lose?

thirteen

I lay awake for hours, feeling giddy and anxious, then nearly overslept in the morning. Lifting my head, I saw the black clock radio glaring at me silently from the bureau. I rolled out of bed and scrambled around for something clean to wear—wishing, as always, that I had laid out my school clothes the night before. *Never prepared,* that was me. I would have made a terrible Boy Scout.

I scarfed down a granola bar in the kitchen and then took a glass of orange juice to my bedroom. I opened my desk drawer and retrieved the plastic baggie with the pills.

Was I really going to do this?

Yes!

I had waited too long already. I opened the baggie— *Don't eat them all at once, or you'll be sorry!*—and let a single pill fall into my palm.

This was the big moment. Good-bye to the old Jamie, hello to the new. Totally worth any risks or side effects.

Facing the mirror over my dresser, I placed the pill on my tongue. I swallowed it along with the juice and then studied myself in the mirror. Same tired eyes, same old me.

I grabbed my backpack and ran for the door.

On the bus, the minutes ticked by. I monitored all my passing thoughts, ready for new ones. I let my eyes roam over the girls my age, like a silly fool panning for gold.

The inside of my mouth tasted like pennies.

All morning long, I waited for the transformation, but it never arrived. I felt no different. I didn't daydream about cheerleaders or car-wash girls, farmer's daughters or any other stock fantasies. The thing is, I'd felt exactly the same way in the sixth grade, that endless yearlong wait to find something—*anything*—sexy about girls.

Instead, I only developed a slight headache, a focused pain, right between my eyes. Too much obsessing, I figured. I told myself to relax.

It would take some time for the medicine to kick in, I realized. Maybe several doses.

———

At lunch with Wesley and Mimi, our dynamic felt the same: Wes was still goofy, Mimi was still bitchy, and I was still the lone audience member for their asinine talk show.

"Where *are* you today?" Mimi asked me. "Somehow you are even less charming than usual."

I shrugged and smiled, opening my arms to them. "I'm

right here, enjoying the company of good friends." The truth was, I'd been dragging all day because of the headache. Occasionally, I still had a metallic taste in my mouth. Given all possible side effects, these weren't so bad.

Wesley asked, "Did you ever figure out who your secret admirer was?"

I shook my head and sent my fingers to forage for stray French fries among the empty baskets. "Mimi, you're still on the short list of suspects."

"Jesus, don't flatter yourself."

"Did you send *any* flowers?" I asked her.

She sneered. "Jamie, you and Miss Moneypants may choose to communicate any way you like, but I prefer to express myself less *commercially.* The old-fashioned way."

"Smoke signals?" Wesley guessed. "Pony express?"

She leveled him with her eyes. "Let me tell you something. If I'm interested in a boy, I simply let him know with a wink and a smile. That's all I need in my personal arsenal—one wink and one irresistible grin. Works every time."

"Funny," I said, considering this. "I don't see you winking very often."

"Or smiling," Wes added.

"Hell, I have to be careful," Mimi complained. "If I winked and smiled more often, I'd be *swamped.* And you two losers wouldn't be able to enjoy your lunches with me."

———

After school the day was warm again, with the sun melting all the snow. For the first time that year, the air smelled like spring. Celia and I walked a few blocks from school and found a bus going downtown. We held hands on the bus.

In the coming weeks, we would make a habit of roaming wherever we could, far from school. We wanted to see ourselves not as an ordinary Maxwell couple, but as something distinct, legitimate, even out in the real world. We took long, aimless walks when the sun was out. If the weather was bad, we used public transportation. We'd go to Warren Park or down to Lincoln Square. Soon we had a circuit of regular haunts: the comic book store, the used CD store, Village Thrift, even the big library on Lincoln Avenue to get homework done. We dropped in on Rita and drank a lot of free coffee. Rita began to call us *los banditos*. We'd walk in the door, and she'd smile and call out, "Oh no, here come *los banditos* again to steal all my milk and sugars. Help! Somebody stop them!" But you could tell she was glad when we came and sorry when we left. She seemed lonely.

"She needs some love in her life," Celia told me one day, after we left.

"Why doesn't she date?"

"Maybe she does. At her condo, I saw a brochure for a dating service. It was called something like *Más Amor, Por Favor!* For Latino singles. And good for her, right? After all, Abuelito won't live forever."

"Who is Abuelito? Your grandfather?"

"No, her cat."

We liked to sit on benches and bus stops, just to watch people. Celia liked to imagine whole lives based on quick observations. We invented a game called "Sex or No Sex?"

where we had to guess if a person had had sex that day. We based our decisions on clothing, accessories, and facial expression. This game soon evolved to "Regrets, Secrets, or Schemes?" where we randomly applied one of these three terms to a passing person and then justified our answer. Celia might say, "Regrets. That woman regrets the unkind words she used with her cleaning lady."

Or I might say, "Schemes. That guy schemes to poison the water cooler at his office."

Celia nodded. "Yes, totally creepy." It was essential that the other person supported the story. "And no sex," she added.

"Secrets," I said. "That woman secretly stole her roommate's credit card."

"Excellent, that's a secret *and* a scheme!" Celia said. "That guy, there—regrets. Bet he regrets buying that puffy white coat."

"Seriously, dude looks like a washing machine."

Secrets. This boy wants to love the girl, but he's gay.

Schemes. Thanks to a magic little pill, this boy can love the girl after all.

As for ourselves, no sex. We barely touched each other—a quick peck on the lips when it was time to go home. Sometimes a series of pecks. It never went further; we were never alone. The romance was in the roaming, the hand-held adventures, and the public picture we presented: two teenagers, one draped sloppily over the other, giggling. This worked for me, of course. I was meeting all the standard expectations and passing every test.

"Here's our stop," Celia said, when we were near DePaul. We stepped off the bus and walked west on Fullerton to the campus. We found the quad and nabbed a cement bench at a busy intersection. "I feel in it my bones," she said. "She's going to walk right by us today."

"And what are you going to say to her?"

"I'm going to say, 'Amanda, we have your wallet and bracelet. In return, we demand only two things.'"

"Which are?"

"Number one, lose the granny glasses. Number two, in the future, dear, please refrain from humping like a rabbit in my back garden."

Sitting there, we saw college students of every stripe. Students who were dressed like models. Students who were dressed like farmers. Students who were dressed like rappers and looked like models. Students who were dressed in tight little workout clothes, with their hair pulled up in ponytails on top of their heads so that they looked like the Whos down in Whoville. Students who dressed like accountants. Students who dressed like we did. None of them was Amanda Lynn.

There was a lull in foot traffic. Then another one of the accountants came down the path. He didn't look like a college student; he didn't look much older than us. I whispered to Celia, "Sex or no sex?" as if there was any question.

She smiled. Rather than answering, she jumped up and blocked his way on the path. "Excuse me, hello?"

"Hmm?"

"Yeah, hey—don't you sit by me in class?"

The guy blinked twice, as if shocked to be speaking to a beautiful girl. "Which class?" His voice was nasally, almost a whine.

"You know, first thing in the morning?"

"Statistics?"

Celia gave a big, flirty grin. "One hundred percent correct."

He let himself smile back at her. "That lecture hall is . . . you know, really big."

"Yeah, gargantuan. So do you think I could borrow your notes? I'm not getting to that class as often as I should. At this point, I am like seventy-five percent lost."

The poor guy looked fairly lost himself. Flustered, he tapped at his pockets with both hands as if searching. "I . . . I don't have those notes with me."

"You don't? Crap, that sucks."

"Maybe we could get together sometime and make copies."

"Well . . ."

"Or I could make the copies and bring them over to your dorm. Whenever it would be convenient."

"No biggie," she said. "Listen, I'll see you in class, okay?"

"Only if you make it," he teased shyly.

Her playful finger poked him in the chest. "Oh, I'll be there—looking for *you!*"

"Set your alarm!" he called, and went on his way.

Celia joined me again on the bench.

"You are cruel," I whispered.

"No sex," she said firmly.

We watched her new friend continue his way along the path. His encounter with Celia had left him with straighter posture and a confident new walk.

Knowing that Dr. Gamez's drug was in my body gave me a strange sort of confidence, too. "So anyway," I said, "what's so important that you wanted to say it to my face?"

"Can't I ask my boyfriend to hang out without a big reason?"

"Sure, but I thought something specific was on your mind. Otherwise, what was with the mysterious drama last night on the phone?"

Her eyes searched my face, as if giving herself a final moment to consider. She reached into her backpack, paused for dramatic effect, and then handed me a glossy brochure.

I opened it and stared. It was the travel guide I'd seen in her kitchen. Mexico's glorious dazzle. "You trying to make me jealous now?"

"No, dumb-ass," she said. "I want you to come with us for Spring Break."

"For real?" I opened the brochure to a random page: a stony ruin of a pyramid seen through ancient-looking trees. The thought of going—being in a foreign country for the first time—filled me with wild excitement and practical sadness. I handed the brochure back to her. "Thanks, but I can't go to Mexico."

"Think about it for two seconds, will you? It would be so romantic."

"It would be *awesome*," I said, "but my parents would never let me. It's too expensive."

"My dad will pay for everything."

"That's crazy."

"Jamie, he always lets me bring a friend. He'll cover the plane ticket, all the food. Look at this, the resort is huge!"

"Wait a minute. Your dad wants your *boyfriend* to go to Mexico with you?"

She scratched the side of her face. "He doesn't think you're my boyfriend, remember? He thinks we're just friends. In fact, he's the one who suggested that you come with us—last night at dinner."

He didn't miss the pills. So there was one relief, at least.

Was it possible I could actually go? I shook my head, letting the notion sink in. "It blows my mind that he'd let a boy go with you. He's pretty liberal, huh?"

She shrugged. "He's glad I have a new friend. I'm telling you, my father will do anything if he thinks it will make me happy."

"Man, I appreciate the offer. I'd love to spend Spring Break with you."

"Then come! Just think—one month from Saturday, you could be hopping a plane to the Yucatán."

I hesitated. One part of me said, *Jamie, you dope, when will you ever have the chance to go on a luxury vacation to Mexico, all expenses paid?* The other part said, *Run for your life. This is a bad idea.*

"Are you okay?" she asked.

I realized my fingers were massaging my temples, trying to rub away the tension I'd been feeling all day. Still, the confidence I now felt with Celia was worth any side effect, including low-grade pain. Confidence would only naturally lead to attraction, right?

"The thing is, Celia, my parents will never let me go to Mexico. With a girl? And with people they don't know?"

"Let's all get to know each other then."

"Trust me, my parents are predictable. They won't even discuss it."

"Don't worry," she said, reaching for me. "You always worry. I have a plan."

We gave up on finding Amanda Lynn. En route to Celia's house, we stopped on the Wilson Avenue bridge and looked out over the gray, slow-moving river. A red sun hovered on the horizon, and birds were going crazy in the bare trees. It was turning cold again. Celia and I pressed together, arms wrapped around each other's coats, and we kissed.

We really went to town.

So here it was, the fantasy Celia had described to me the very first day we hung out—her childhood dream, to kiss a boy on this romantic, arching bridge. She had waited years to make this fantasy come true. I knew how important the moment was for her.

I gave it everything I had. I really *tried.* But my body didn't cooperate.

I felt nothing.

Celia's affection wasn't enough. One pill wasn't enough. I was starting to realize that this process would require more practice, more patience, and a hell of a lot more pills.

fourteen

"Mexico?"

It was rare that a comment from me could stop my parents in their tracks. But for a long moment they stood there, frozen in the living room, still holding packing slips and job orders.

I tried to sound cheerful. "The school is paying for it. It's part of the club I'm in."

I showed them the phony permission slip Celia and I had created using her dad's computer. It looked official—fancy school letterhead that we designed ourselves. "You just have to sign this. It doesn't cost anything. Remember all the fundraising we did? We worked really hard, and now the club has tons of money."

"From the flowers?" My dad glanced at my mom, then surveyed the piles of boxes and packing clutter that surrounded him. "We're in the wrong business."

My mother looked skeptically at the permission slip. "I thought it was a *service* club."

"It is. We'll be working at a community clinic in Mexico. Dr. Gamez has arranged everything with some people he knows down there."

"Back in my day," my mother said, "being in a service club meant you got to decorate Easter windows at the nursing home on Harlem Avenue. We didn't jet off to foreign countries."

"The world's getting smaller," I said, shrugging. "Globalization."

"From selling *flowers*?" my father repeated.

"We'd need to think about this," my mother said.

"My grades are awesome," I said. "Don't I deserve a reward for hard work?"

"Honey," she said, "you seem tired. Won't this trip wear you out more?"

My father nodded. "Maybe you should stick around here during Spring Break. Catch up on rest."

This was the trouble with dreams. Once they settled into your thoughts, they held you prisoner. The funny thing was, a few weeks earlier, the notion of traveling to Mexico with Celia never would have occurred to me. In fact, the prospect of so much togetherness with Celia, all that pressure, might have sent me running in the other direction. But life changes fast. Now I had a pocket full of miracle pills and an invitation to travel. I wanted it all.

"Who knows?" I said casually. "Maybe this trip will

inspire me to study medicine. Lately I've been thinking about becoming a doctor." I had rehearsed this line with Celia.

Five minutes later, they both signed the permission slip.

Astonished and relieved, I went into the dining room to tackle some gift-wrapping. The number of boxes I found there surprised me. Baby gifts, wedding presents, birthdays, anniversaries, housewarmings—a little of everything waiting to be wrapped and shipped. Either business was booming or customer service was slipping. I looked more closely. Was this a backlog?

"Hey, some of these have dust on them," I said.

"It's been nuts around here!" my mother said.

"We've been waiting for you, kiddo!" my father called. "That's your specialty!"

"Yikes," I said softly. Whenever I took time to observe my parents at work, I understood why they had never gotten rich. They worked hard, sure, with energy to burn, but it was all too unfocused, too diffuse. They might spend a whole afternoon devising a clever marketing strategy while RUSH orders went unfulfilled. Meanwhile, Dr. Gamez had gotten rich by close observation and attention to detail. The contrast seemed instructive.

While my parents greeted customers, running between the door and the cash box, I faced the backlog and got down to some serious wrapping. I measured, cut, taped, and tied—one after the next, working without a break to get them all ready for pick-up. I wrapped until my fingers were sticky from Scotch tape. There were more than forty packages total, and in the end, I calculated that the work—at three dollars per gift—was worth one hundred twenty dollars for my parents' business. Not bad for an hour's work. It made me feel less guilty about lying to them about Mexico.

How much spending money would I need for a trip like this? According to Celia, we wouldn't ever stray too far from the resort. But I'd want cash to buy souvenirs or snacks. So when my parents were busy at the door with a customer, it didn't seem wrong to take another thirty dollars from the cash box. Thirty dollars wouldn't be missed. And after all, I was the one who had done all the work.

I began taking the pills with more confidence. One blue pill after breakfast, with a cold glass of milk or juice—a simple addition to the morning routine. For added security, I moved the baggie of pills from the desk drawer to a green plastic Army tank I kept on my bookshelf. I pointed the guns of the tank toward my bedroom door, in symbolic defense of my new life.

After the first three days, I didn't suffer from any serious side effects. Some sleeplessness, a metallic aftertaste. The headaches lingered, too, but this may have been my own general anxiety rather than a chemical side effect.

I didn't notice any major *benefits* either, except that I felt more confident around Celia. This may have been psychological.

For a week, I waited for the pills to take effect, to give me that hungry, boob-obsessed expression worn by all the boys in my school. I wanted to look at Celia the way Wes looked at every girl. I knew it wasn't going to happen fast. The pills, I imagined, would help to *build* attraction over time, the way sports supplements help athletes to build muscle. It would happen over the course of months, not overnight. In this matter, I could be patient.

———

Celia, of course, wasn't waiting for any drug to kick in. Our upcoming trip to Mexico had shifted our relationship into fast-forward mode. Now when we found time alone together, we went from conversation to kissing without delay. We made out on park benches, on dry patches of grass, and in secluded corners of the public library. We kissed each other at leisure and used our fingers to tickle ears and stroke cheeks. We let our hands roam freely and safely over clothing. She favored my back, my shoulders, and my butt. I started with these but I knew more was expected. Over time I moved to her breasts, soft under her shirt, guarded by her bra. My fingers sometimes traced the edge, thinking about lace and design.

Her hands never went to the front of my pants, which surprised me. I'd spent so much time worrying about my lack of an erection only to have it never come up, so to speak. Wasn't she curious?

I put my faith in the power of medicine.

The pills—or maybe it was this physical activity with Celia—did have one positive effect almost immediately: I stopped dreaming about Ivan. In fact, as soon as I started taking the pills, I stopped having any dreams at all. Upon waking, I couldn't remember one thing I had dreamed about. It was like all the lights went out in the movie theater of my sleep. Worked for me.

———

The First Knights were dwindling, as if in a losing battle. Keenan quit to play volleyball; the Mosinskey twins stopped coming to meetings as soon as we took the yearbook photo. Nonetheless, Mr. Covici saw to it that members of the club were on hand during every major and minor school event. The weekend of the school play, while some of us sold soda and popcorn, others kept the sinks clean and toilets flushed during intermission. The day of the blood drive, we were tasked with distributing orange juice and granola bars to dizzy blood donors. It was rarely the whole club, just two or three members selected by Covici for the event. On two occasions, Celia and I stuffed envelopes in the main office after school, giggling with private jokes, ambushing each other with tickles.

Celia always wanted to stretch out the afternoons. "What are you up to later?"

"Biology," I said. "Gametes and zygotes."

"Let's go hang out for a while. I'll teach you about biology." She stroked my thigh seductively.

"I can't." Truthfully, I didn't have enough pills to be a daily boyfriend. Almost a week had passed since I'd had one. "Plus," I said, "I don't want you getting sick of me before we even go to Mexico."

"I'm getting sick of not seeing you enough," she said. True, a statement like this had tons of whine potential, but on her tongue it seemed only flirty.

"Celia, I have to finish two chapters in the Bio textbook. And answer questions."

"By tomorrow?"

I nodded. With her, schoolwork was always a dependable excuse. Good grades were important to her, too.

"Tomorrow after school, then," she said.

"For sure."

"I wish we were in Mexico," she said wistfully.

"Me too," I said. "Just think, eleven more days." My eyes went a little blurry at the thought. *How was I going to get more pills before the trip?*

———

In homeroom, Mr. Mallet handed me a folded note. "Here's a message from your *library buddy*." His tone was so sinister he was practically hissing at me. I could only imagine the bad blood between Mallet and Covici. Their personalities were diametrical opposites, like the two sides of the Crusades.

"Thanks." I opened the note and saw Mr. Covici's neat handwriting:

> *Jamie, please come Saturday morning at*
> *8:00 to help with the School Board meeting.*
> *If this is a problem, just let me know.*
> *Mr. Covici*

I was a little surprised at the time commitment this club demanded. It was like being on a sports team, but without any of the physical or social benefits.

I stopped Celia in the hallway between classes. "Are you working the School Board meeting on Saturday?"

"Negative."

"I can't believe I have to be at school at eight o'clock."

"Better you than me," she said, swatting my ass.

———

Walking into the empty Commons on Saturday morning gave me an odd tremor of excitement. It felt like trespassing. The environment changed completely when students were absent. With the place empty, I couldn't help but notice the creepy Gothic details—arched windows and doorways, spooky dark hallways, and countless potential hiding places. I'd heard a rumor that the ghost of the mascot knight haunted the building. On school days, with the lights on and the hallways noisy, a ghost seemed like a silly school tradition. But now, as I walked down the long quiet corridor toward the conference room, my pulse quickened and I felt suddenly vulnerable. Weird, how sometimes you can *think* yourself into being afraid.

I heard footsteps. They were heavy and slow, coming from the other direction toward me.

Please, please, let it be Mr. Covici or one of the parents, and not a vengeful ghost knight, come for my young flesh!

"Hello?" I called.

"Jamie?" Ivan came into view, his hands stuffed in his jeans pockets. His green T-shirt hugged his broad shoulders. He seemed genuinely pleased to see me. "Good morning, comrade!"

Relieved that he wasn't a ghost, I still felt wary. "A little creepy here this early, huh?" I controlled my facial expression, limiting myself to a stingy, fleeting smile.

"Yeah," he laughed.

Until now, I had avoided being alone with Ivan. Maybe it was inevitable that he and I would be paired up eventually. I hoped I'd developed a resistance to him from Dr. Gamez's pills. Weeks had passed since Ivan had appeared in my dreams.

So why is my heart pounding now?

"Where's Covici?" I said.

Ivan shrugged. "Not coming. He called me to the library yesterday to give directions. He thinks we can handle it."

Just us, then.

Ivan repeated the instructions that Covici had given him. We were to get ice, food, and drinks from the cafeteria, take it all to the conference room, and set the table. During the meeting, we should be available to run errands for School Board members if asked.

"Let's go get everything set up now, so we can relax," Ivan said.

I had to admit, I loved Ivan's accent. When he said *go* and *so,* it sounded like "gow" and "sow." Also, his *th*'s were hard, like *d*'s.

Quit thinking about his mouth and hard tongue.

"Hold on," I said. "Back in two seconds."

In the bathroom, I felt around the wall in the dark, search-ing for the switch. When I found it, the fluorescent lights came on with a *clap*. I saw my face reflected in the mirror. I looked panic-stricken. I took a breath and reached into my pocket.

My last pill.

I'd been saving it for my next encounter with Celia. But if there ever was a time when I needed one, it was now. I swallowed it with quick handfuls of water from the sink. I wiped my mouth with my wrist and looked in the mirror.

Be cool. Now you're immune.

"Your accent is hardly noticeable," I told Ivan as we walked down the corridor. Sometimes I said the exact oppo-site of what I was thinking.

"I've been here for seven years," he said. "Almost half my life."

"Why did your family come here?"

"We were lucky. We had a cousin here. Over there, no money, no jobs."

"We don't have any money here," I said. "Maybe we should move to your old country."

I picked up the refreshments tray while Ivan got the ice. I envied his ease with the ice buckets, his broad back, the perfect symmetry of his shoulders. He was about my height, but infinitely more graceful. He had the body of an athlete, although to my knowledge he didn't play sports. No mat-ter how many pills I took, I would never have that body. I would still be me. Suddenly my tongue tasted like I'd been sucking on a rusty nail.

As the School Board members arrived, Ivan and I lingered

near the door like servants awaiting instructions. They took their muffins and juice, smiling as if they knew us. After they disappeared into a classroom, Ivan and I backed into the hallway and sat on the floor. Side by side, two feet apart. I could feel his body heat next to me. And his after-shave again—orange, cinnamon, and something else.

Thank God for the pill.

He whispered, "Now we wait."

"Yup."

"And you—have you always lived in Chicago?"

"Yup."

"In the same house?"

"No, different." I thought of the bedroom I'd had in our old place, before we moved in with my grandparents. A second-floor sunroom, three walls of windows. Different world, different boy.

I let some time pass, not sure which topics to raise. We were two years apart, with none of the same classes.

Say something!

"Do you shave every day?" I asked.

He rubbed his jaw with a rueful smile. "Yes, unfortunately."

I couldn't wait to start shaving. Shaving seemed like an essential part of a masculine life. "That's too bad," I agreed.

"Tell me about Celia," he said.

I leaned forward, smiling at my shoes, and wondered why he would ask. "She's incredible. So funny and smart. Don't you think?"

He nodded. "Is she your girlfriend or just a friend?"

"Girlfriend, for sure. But we're still getting to know each other. I've never had a girlfriend before. Is Anella your girlfriend?"

"No. I have known her so long. She's like my sister. You know, she is a very good girl."

When he called Anella a *girl,* it struck me as funny. She was so mature for her age, too sophisticated in her demeanor to ever seem girlish to me. At club meetings, she gave the impression of belonging in the real world rather than in high school.

"Do you have a different girlfriend?" I asked.

"No."

This seemed impossible. Such handsomeness, such sweetness.

He cleared his throat. "So, can I tell you something?"

"Sure."

"I don't have many friends at Maxwell. Besides Anella."

"Yeah?"

He nodded.

"Me neither," I said. "I guess it's not the friendliest place. It's too big."

"Maybe—" he began, and then stopped. He was shy. "Maybe we should hang out sometime. Away from school."

The hallway suddenly seemed very quiet. Could he hear the pounding of my heart? I bent to examine the sole of my tennis shoe, as if the dusty zigzag pattern contained hidden mysteries.

"Unless you're busy," he added.

"No. Yeah, that would be okay." Now the other shoe. "And do what?"

"I don't know. Do you like soccer?"

"Sure. I mean, I don't play it, or watch it on TV or anything."

He gave me a forgiving smile. Again, I was glad for the pill. But now the familiar side effect had returned, the line of pain across my forehead that would last all day. By nightfall, when I lay in bed, wide-awake and dreamless, my shoulders would ache as well.

"What do you like to do?" I asked.

He grinned. "To be outside, definitely. In the summer, I like to sail. Two years ago, my dad bought a used sailboat. He split the cost with Anella's dad and another family. Not a fancy boat, just twenty-four feet, two sails. We can't even sleep on it. But we take it out on Lake Michigan every summer day we can."

"Cool," I said.

My mind flashed back to the second mysterious flower, with Van Gogh's cryptic message: *Fishermen know that the sea is dangerous and the storms terrible, but they have never found these dangers sufficient reason for remaining ashore.*

Was it Ivan, after all, who'd sent the two secret messages? Did we both have crushes—on each other? No, this was impossible. So why did I feel the same surge of fear that I'd experienced earlier, when I was alone in the dark corridor?

"Maybe this summer," he said, "we can take you sailing."

"I ... I like movies," I said, trying to change the subject.

He smiled gamely. "Okay, me too. We could get a group together. See a movie."

I lowered my gaze to the floor. The thing was, I could not spend time with Ivan, even as a friend. I was already down an alternate path with Celia. I wasn't going to repeat past mistakes. I'd worked too hard. And now I was out of pills.

"I like *old* movies," I clarified.

"Yeah?"

"Scary ones, mostly."

"Excellent."

"I could lend you one sometime."

"Oh, thank you. That would be nice." His expression finally registered my meaning. Slowly he turned from me and faced forward.

Sorry, buddy, I need to play it safe. Nothing personal.

Awkward minutes of silence passed, and then the grown-ups began to emerge from their meeting, looking for pastry and juice. We jumped to our feet to attend to them. The break lasted fifteen minutes. We kept the platters filled. We collected the abandoned plates and cups and deposited them in the trash can. Ivan was all business, smiling at the Board members and not looking at me.

I felt bad for rejecting him. Not guilt. I felt a weird, unexpected... *loss*. It was like when I stopped emailing my Internet friends. *Click, delete, gone.* The suddenness of the sacrifice was harsh. But, I reminded myself, sometimes when the body had a diseased organ that threatens the rest, the damaged part has to go. Just like that—*gone*. Painful but necessary.

"Ready to start cleaning up?" I asked Ivan. I tried to make my voice cheerful.

He nodded, but kept his eyes on the pitchers of water. He seemed distant now, staring at the water but seeing something much farther away.

fifteen

I needed more pills. The ones I had taken were long gone, and now I faced a week in Mexico with Celia. While I knew exactly where to find more, getting my hands on them presented the challenge of metal doors and the lab staff, including friendly Dr. Gamez himself.

I called Celia. "What are you doing this afternoon?"

"Packing." She sighed contentedly. "Thinking about our adventure together."

"Me too. Can I come and see you? I'll help you pack."

"That's sweet. But I don't want you to see my swimsuit until we get there."

"I don't care about that," I said, which was completely the truth.

"Well, I do. Besides, in about an hour, I'm leaving to get my hair cut."

"I just want to spend some time with you before we go."

"Wow," she said. She wasn't used to this version of me. "If you come right away, we can have maybe thirty minutes together."

"Great!" I said, jumping up. "I'm leaving now."

I flew out of the house and ran to Western Avenue. The ten minutes I had to wait for a bus seemed like forever. When I got to Celia's neighborhood, I called her from my cell so she could meet me at the front door. I found her there grinning, with her arms folded. "Gee, someone's acting uncharacteristically romantic today."

"You bet." I leaned forward to give her a kiss.

"Not here," she said, pushing me away. "My dad might see."

I followed her inside and up the staircase to her bedroom. She closed the door and we kissed. All the adrenaline I'd built up racing to her house had made me sweaty. It felt nice to stop and hold her.

She'd lit a candle before I arrived, so the bedroom smelled like vanilla and coconut. I'd been in there only once before. It was a large corner room, painted soft green and pale yellow. In addition to the standard bed and dresser, she had substantial furniture—a grown-up desk, an overstuffed chair with an ottoman. On the walls, museum prints showcased the Getty Museum in California, the Tate Gallery in London, and the Prado in Madrid. These were mounted in real frames with glass, not just taped up like the movie posters in my bedroom. This was the room of someone who took her life seriously. When would Celia realize that she was *way* out of my league?

She pulled me down next to her on the bed, between the open suitcase and the pillows. "So, why are you really here?"

"To see you."

"Stop lying or I won't kiss you."

"Okay, the thing is—here's the deal." I took a couple breaths, my mind racing. "I'm nervous about flying."

Her head fell back with a laugh. "You've never flown before? That's so cute!"

"I wish I saw it that way."

"Flying is no big deal. You take your assigned seat, strap yourself in, turn on your music, and fall asleep. In no time flat, you're in another country and the vacation begins."

"Yeah, it's the *strapping yourself in* part that makes me nervous. As if there's a real possibility you could crash."

"The whole experience is boring, actually," she said. "You'll see." While listing the tedious aspects of air travel, she got up and returned to her clothes. I liked watching her pack, the way she created such neat, economical bundles. Compared to mine, her clothes were so tiny, stacks of pink and white squares, blue and yellow triangles. I fell into a kind of trance, far more interested in her wardrobe than was probably appropriate. I almost forgot the purpose of my visit.

"So relax, you'll be fine." She gave me a naughty grin and said huskily, "Honey, I guarantee, once you've done it the first time, you'll want to do it again and again."

To get the pills, I needed to be out of that bedroom and downstairs, closer to the lab. I stood. "I'm thirsty. Can I run downstairs and get us some drinks?"

"Sure, let's go."

I put my palms up like a snowplow. "You're swamped with packing. I'll be two minutes."

She shrugged. "Hurry back."

In ten seconds, I was down the hall and at the foot of the main staircase. The house always seemed empty. I never saw anybody except Celia, her father, and now and then a white-haired cleaning woman named Beatrice, who hummed while she worked and never greeted me. In fact, she never even seemed aware of us. "Don't take it personally," Celia whispered once. "Beatrice is on a mission."

Near the kitchen, I stopped at the big, white, metal door that I knew led to the laboratory. I peered through the small glass window in the door and didn't see anybody in the corridor beyond. I pulled the handle, guessing it would be locked. It didn't even budge.

Crap.

Next to the door, below eye level, there was a security keypad. I remembered what Celia had said, that the password for the house security system was her birthday. This one was probably the same. But all I knew was that her birthday was in November. Did I really have time to punch in all thirty combinations?

Idiot. Mr. Never Prepared. Do your damn homework!

I went into the kitchen and grabbed two Diet Cokes from the refrigerator. I had just closed the heavy, stainless steel door when I noticed a briefcase sitting on a barstool at the counter. It looked like Dr. Gamez's black briefcase—the same one I always saw with him—but I couldn't be sure. How many briefcases did most men have? My dad, as far as I knew, didn't even have one. But he didn't have a normal job, not like other dads. Dr. Gamez didn't have a normal job either. Maybe Dr. Gamez had a dozen briefcases, one for each different project he worked on.

Well, no harm in taking a quick look.

I stepped lightly across the room and set down the soda cans. I lifted the briefcase to the counter and snapped open the two locks, mindful of the noise. I froze.

Anybody hear that?

Beatrice's vacuum cleaner began groaning, nearly howling, in another room.

The briefcase lid lifted with a smooth glide and clicked into the open position. Black silk lining, leather loops holding expensive-looking pens, all very elegant. The main compartment held half a dozen manila folders and oversized envelopes. No brown drug bottles like the one Dr. Gamez had with him at the coffee shop, but there were several clear plastic bags, smaller than anything my grandmother ever used. I saw a variety of pills, none of them blue. I could only imagine taking the wrong drug and sprouting enormous breasts or unwanted body hair.

Hey there, ole hairy face! Nice jugs!

With a bongo drum playing in my chest, I bypassed the pills and looked at the folders. One of the labels said, *Rehomo—notes.*

I removed this folder and it flipped open randomly. The page showed a printed list of names and contact information, all doctors, all over the world: Manila, Milan, Mexico City. I flipped to another page. More doctors, more cities:

Sarajevo, Stockholm, Sydney, Taipei. Then pages and pages of handwritten notes—a nearly unintelligible scrawl. I tried to make out the meaning, but few words and phrases were decipherable: *"… essential…" "… cannot change the patient unless…" "… only alleviate…" "…potentially lethal…"*

Lethal.

My eyes stopped hard on the word.

I heard a noise. Someone was approaching. I dumped the folder back into the briefcase. When I tried to close the case, the hinge remained stuck in an open position. Frantically I attempted to unfasten the stupid thing.

"*Goodness sakes*, what is taking *sooooo* long?" Celia's playful voice rattled the silence as she shuffled down the hallway. The case was still wide open when she got to the kitchen. She skidded to a halt at the door.

"Hey there," I said. Then the hinge-lock gave way, and the lid closed automatically under my hand.

Her eyes went slowly from me to the briefcase, then back to me. "What are you doing?"

I felt myself blush. "Sorry, I don't know. I just saw this." It wasn't an explanation, just the truth. "It was sitting here."

Her face broadcast her confusion, and she folded her arms. "It belongs to my dad, obviously. What were you doing with it?"

I made myself smile. "I'm so embarrassed. I wanted to see what it looked like inside."

"Surprise, it's a briefcase."

"I know, but my dad has never had one." I lifted my

hands, searching for words. "And I wouldn't mind getting him a classy one. To show I believe in his new package business."

She remained silent, looking concerned.

"Yeah, this one is really sharp." I stroked the edge of the case appreciatively, to underscore my point. "Classy, you know?"

"Jamie, be honest." She came closer. She didn't look angry now, just serious. "Were you ... you know, looking for money?"

"Is that what you think?"

Her hand went to my shoulder. "Were you? You can tell me."

As she touched me, the fear released its own grip on my shoulders. "Celia, look at this." I opened my wallet and showed her the thirty dollars I'd taken from my parents' cash box. "I've got plenty of cash right here. And more at home."

Her expression softened, relieved. "Really?"

I nodded and put my wallet away.

Her own face reddened. "Now I'm embarrassed. I just figured ... we're leaving soon, and I thought maybe you were worried about not having enough money."

"You told me not to worry about that."

"I know, I'm sorry. I hope I haven't insulted you."

"Forget about it," I said, smiling. "Let's grab the sodas and go back upstairs."

Fifteen minutes later, Celia left for her hair appointment and I left without any pills. I wondered if I'd spent enough time with Celia already to make it through Spring Break without them. Maybe after eleven pills, my body had been conditioned to be comfortable around girls—to respond like any other boy. Maybe some gays had to take only one round of the pills to become straight.

Yeah, right. I was an idiot.

When I was on the bus, my cell phone rang. Wesley. We arranged to meet in Warren Park, a sprawling, flat park that was located between our houses. We had a favorite spot—an isolated bench far away from the tennis courts and picnic tables. We never could figure out why they'd put a bench so far away from the action, but in elementary school we'd spent many late afternoons there on our way home, plotting to take over the world with a loyal army of robotic squirrels.

He got there before me. "Look at this, they've got swings here now!"

"*Woo-hoo!* Let's swing!" I jumped onto the one next to him. It was a long rubber swing that wasn't designed for butts my size. It pinched my hips. But it was fun to be alone with Wes for once.

He said, "So you're leaving at the end of the week? South of the border? Promise me you'll extend my best wishes to my people."

"I'll try to bring back some sun for you."

"You are one fortunate fellow—off to a private resort with a beautiful girl. All expenses paid."

"I agree. And I owe it all to you and your encouragement."

"You bet your ass you do. I'll expect payback in the future."

"Only fair."

He slowed his pace. "Guess what? I took my last pill this morning."

"Really? Still going through with that plan?"

He nodded. "I feel good about it. Baseball tryouts begin the day we get back from break. At that point, my body should be completely drug free."

"I don't know, Wes. It makes me nervous. I remember what you were like back then."

"I was a bratty kid, that's all. I'm more mature now."

"I still think you should tell your parents first."

"Dude, relax. You're going to Mexico with your girlfriend and you're not telling your parents."

"That's completely different! I'm not putting anyone's health at risk."

He shrugged. "Me neither."

"My fear is that you'll get all Jekyll-and-Hyde on us. Let the record show, I like you the way you are now. Safely medicated."

"Listen, if going off them doesn't work, I'll start taking them again. Right? What's the risk?"

I nodded, kicking at the powdery dirt under the swings. He sounded so reasonable. I hoped what he said was true.

"Jamie, two minutes ago we agreed that you owed me, remember? So give me this. Give me your support."

"I'm trying to."

"Doesn't sound like it."

Later, walking home, I was struck by how unfair it was

that the universe had given Wesley an amazing drug he didn't even want while it denied me access to the one essential drug I really needed.

Stupid universe.

sixteen

So we went to Mexico.

We flew from Chicago to Houston and Houston to Mérida, a city on the Yucatán Peninsula. Two different airplanes. Despite Celia's claims, the experience was ten times more terrifying than I had predicted. When the wheels were stowed after take-off, it sounded like a small missile had struck us from below. Each time the captain changed the seat-belt sign, making that loud ring, I worried it was an emergency warning. My hand reached discreetly for Celia's.

"Sometimes," she whispered, "your palms are so clammy it's freaky."

"I am experiencing an unusual level of anxiety."

"No reason to," she promised.

No reason? We were 35,000 feet in the air, I was facing seven days alone with Celia, and I had zero doses of the

Rehomoline. On top of all that, my biggest concern was that Celia and I were going to share a room, and maybe even a bed. Dr. Gamez might have thought that she and I were just friends, but was he so trusting that he'd allow us to sleep in the same hotel room? As generous as Dr. Gamez seemed, I could not imagine that he'd pay for a separate room for a kid he barely knew. In my mind, I kept replaying the scene when Celia and I would climb into bed and lie next to each other in the dark, each waiting for the other to make a move. Two faces, staring at the ceiling with opposite expressions: one eager, one paralyzed with fear.

When the plane landed in Mexico, I gasped, thinking we'd hit the ground much too hard, and then clutched Celia's hand again as the plane struggled to slow down.

Do planes ever crash into airports? We're going to cra—

The plane stopped. We gathered our things and stepped into the terminal. The airport was small and hot and very crowded. There seemed to be just as many Americans as Mexicans. Because I was fifteen, I had to show my birth certificate along with a notarized letter from my parents that allowed me to cross the border with Dr. Gamez.

We took our bags outside. The evening air was humid and thick with flying bugs. Dr. Gamez said a car would be waiting for us. The one that met us was surprisingly shabby. Dr. Gamez shook hands with the driver, and then all three of us climbed into the back seat, Celia in the middle.

The car sped along a country road, and the headlights revealed, in thin clusters, a thousand tall skinny trees that we whizzed past in the dark. The terrain was woodsy and weedy, with few signs of human life—here a car abandoned at the side of the road, there a rusted-out piece of farm machinery. We drove farther and farther from the airport, into the dark landscape. Something about the route didn't seem right. Ten minutes turned into forty, forty-five, an hour.

This driver is taking us deep into the country to kill us.

Celia must have noticed my concern. She patted my knee. "It's always a long drive, just when you want to eat or climb into bed."

We came to a small town, not much more than the intersection of two roads, where a church stood. The church looked like it could hold fifty people max. Its rounded stucco exterior was painted beige and brown. The houses that surrounded it were one- or two-room structures built of cinder block. The roofs were made of tin or tile, and some out of grass. Several of the houses were painted brightly—light blue, yellow, red—and some were decorated with Christmas lights that outlined their windows or drew attention to a statue of the Virgin Mary.

"These houses," I whispered to Celia. "So tiny."

Dr. Gamez leaned toward us. "One room serves as the kitchen, living room, and bedroom. No beds, usually. They pull hammocks across the room for sleeping. One hammock for mother and dad, one for the kids."

For once, my grandparents' apartment in Chicago didn't seem so small.

We passed the town and drove for another mile, and then the car slowed and turned off the road. We cruised through a large gate with two tall stucco columns, then drove down a long gravel driveway flanked by palm trees. I thought I saw a house, but we passed it.

"That's not it?" I said to Celia.

She smiled. "That's a chapel. If you want to sleep there, we'll have to clear it with the *padre*."

The car pulled to a stop in a graveled circular clearing, and we got out. We were at the base of a terraced garden. I could hear the steady splashing of fountains.

The massive rustic house, looming above us, looked incongruously like something you'd see in a TV ad for spaghetti sauce. There was a central structure, plus two wings connected by elaborate arched colonnades. Everything was covered in stucco, which was painted dark red and mustard yellow, and dramatically lit with spotlights. I didn't see anybody except for a few members of the smiling resort staff, dressed in white jackets and black pants.

"The pool is in the back," Celia said, as if to reassure me. But it wasn't necessary.

"This is amazing," I said. "Already I want to live here."

"It's almost two hundred years old," Dr. Gamez explained as we climbed the steps toward the main entrance. "The man who built this would have owned much of the surrounding land. They grew *henequen*, or sisal, which they used to make rope. This is the Mexican equivalent of the plantations in the southern United States."

"Do they grow anything now?" I asked.

"Not here, not for many years," he said. "In fact, this whole estate, like many others, had fallen into terrible disrepair. Deep neglect. It was a ruin for many decades, until a wealthy American corporation came in and restored it. So often in these matters, progress is about transformation." He'd emphasized the last word—*transformation*—and I wondered if it meant the same to him as it did to me.

"They rent the resort for weddings and conferences," Celia added. "But we've got the whole place to ourselves this week."

I stood with her on the terrace while Dr. Gamez checked in at the front desk. Crickets filled the night air with a rhythmic beat. The resort property was thick with trees—palms and scrub—but lighted paths made their way through the branches. Despite my fatigue, I was eager to explore. For the first time in ages, I was sad that my parents weren't with me. They'd never seen anything like this.

Dr. Gamez returned with three keys, and relief flooded me. *Separate rooms!* I wanted to leap into the air with joy. He handed two to Celia. "The keys are rather a formality," he told me. "Your belongings will be safe whether you lock your door or not. As Celia said, we are the only guests here this week."

"The rooms are close together," Celia said, looking at the numbers.

"Are either of you hungry?" Dr. Gamez asked. "We can ask Fabian to send something to your rooms."

Celia glanced at me. Suddenly it was true: I was *starving*.

"He's hungry, I can tell," Celia said. "And so am I."

"Order something then," Dr. Gamez said. "I will leave you to enjoy it on your own. Celia, you will please remind Jamie about the importance of bottled water, yes?"

She said that she would.

He said, "Okay then. My plan is to rise early and get to work. I'll see you two in the morning." He kissed Celia on the forehead. "Sleep well."

"Thank you!" I called after him. "Thank you so much."

Celia spoke to Fabian, the porter. Her Spanish was perfect. Fabian was tall, with broad shoulders and tight black pants. Looking at him, I remembered why I needed to get my hands on some pills.

Celia told me, "I ordered two plates of fish tacos and two bottled waters. They'll go to your room."

"Great," I said, looking away from Fabian and down at my key. "I can't believe I have my own room. It's so generous."

"Are you disappointed?"

Knowing the correct answer, I opened my arms wide. "Devastated!"

"My dad's not an idiot. He wasn't going to let us sleep together." She took my hand, and I followed happily.

My room was large, with a high, beamed ceiling and a floor covered in painted tile. The humongous bed was made of dark wood and covered with a fluffy white comforter. Everything was made of wood or stucco. On the table next to the bed was a bottle with an orange ribbon, and I tried to read the label.

Celia watched me struggling with the translation. "See those gigantic mosquito-looking things, hovering on the wall near the lamp?"

I refrained from jumping. "Holy Moses."

"That spray will keep bugs away from your bed."

"Good to know." I set the bottle back on the table.

"Check out the bathroom," she said, leading the way.

The bathroom was nearly as big as the bedroom—cavernous and cool, with a stone floor. Fresh flower petals were scattered around the marble sink, filling the room with fragrance. The open shower stall was almost as big as my bedroom at home, and the showerhead was the size of a dinner plate.

"Sweet cheeses," I said, staring at the impressive plumbing.

"Yup, mine's probably the same way."

"This place is awesome," I said. "Celia, thank you so much for bringing me here."

"Now you may kiss me. To show your appreciation."

I laughed and pulled her to me, and we kissed. We kissed for a full minute and I was fine with it. I really liked her. But where it mattered, I felt nothing.

I need more pills!

A knock on the door interrupted us. It was Fabian with the fish tacos, and they smelled delicious. We sat outside in the courtyard, near a small bubbling fountain, and ate under the biggest canvas of stars I'd ever seen. Periodically, from beyond the high wall that surrounded the property, came the sounds of animals fighting: chickens, dogs, a yowling cat.

"So your dad's going to work while he's here?"

"Oh yeah. That's why he loves coming. No distractions, no employees to bug him. Nothing for him to do but think and work."

"Not much of a vacation," I said. "Do you know what he's working on?"

"We don't talk about it. It's a slow, boring process. It takes a long time for a drug to get tested and approved."

After eating, we wandered back to my room.

"Let's call it a night," Celia said. "I want to unpack and go to bed, so we can have a full day tomorrow."

"What's on the schedule?"

"Completely up to you," she said. "Swimming, exploring the property. We can visit a Mayan ruin if you want to. Or we can chill."

"Okay, I choose … all of the above."

"Agreed." Celia sat on my bed and patted the seat next to her. "Let's be sure to save time for some lovin'."

"Did you just say *lovin'*?" I laughed and jumped on her, and she squealed. I kissed her lips, her cheeks, her neck, my hands roaming up and down her arms, squeezing her shoulders. I buried my face in her hair, which smelled unusual—for once, more like Celia than like shampoo—and she pressed her face against my chest. I felt closer to her than ever. I'd never traveled with anyone outside my family before. I'd never been so far from home before. I'd never had a friend who'd been so generous, who'd made such a commitment to me. It felt fantastic to be part of a team that the world would approve of.

She pushed me away with a guilty smile.

"What?"

"Sweetie, don't take this personally," she said, "but you stink."

I jumped up from the bed, part embarrassed, part relieved.

"I told you I was nervous on the plane! And it was freaky *hot* in that taxi."

"Anyway," she said, "I'm dead tired. Would it hurt your feelings if I went to my room? I want to unpack my clothes before bed."

"Go on. Like you said, the earlier we go to bed, the earlier we can get up and explore."

"Don't forget, bottled water only—even for brushing your teeth."

"Got it."

"Kiss me again," she said, and I led her, lip to lip, to the door.

When she was gone, I unpacked and set my clothes into the wide, deep drawers of the bureau. I liked to imagine that this was my real bedroom, not the dark, cramped room back in Chicago. A ropy hammock lay curled on the floor, with one end attached to the wall. I pulled it across and hooked it to the opposite wall.

Maybe I'll sleep like the locals.

When I tried to get in it, it spun me around and dropped me to the floor. This happened twice.

The bed was a safer alternative. I doused the sheets with the fancy bug spray. Climbing into bed, I wondered if Dr. Gamez had brought any Rehomoline samples with him on the trip. This thought had preoccupied me earlier, on the plane, when I was trying to distract myself from the vision of crashing into the Texas desert. Like a mantra, I'd repeated: *Get more pills, get more pills.* More than a week had passed since I'd taken one. The side effects had worn off.

But would Dr. Gamez have brought any? Would he even be able to get drugs over the border? At first this seemed unlikely, probably even illegal, and I despaired. But then it occurred to me—maybe, as a health-care professional, Dr. Gamez had a special clearance that ordinary people didn't have. Maybe he had a letter from the FDA that permitted him to transfer pharmaceuticals to foreign countries for the purpose of testing.

Outside my door, strange insects chirped, repetitive and endless.

——————

In the morning, I stood in the enormous shower and felt overwhelmed by the downpour. I laughed. It was like someone pouring a garbage can full of water on me. I dressed in a T-shirt and shorts and stepped out of my room. The bright sun transformed the landscape: greener, more lush, and the flowers were more exotic, flashy.

I'm in Mexico!

I walked toward the main building, past rows of flowering azaleas and hibiscus, intense reds and oranges. Tiny lizards jumped out of my way, and I remembered being in Florida with my parents. I made a mental to-do list: *Write postcards. Find souvenirs. Get pills.*

Celia and I had planned to meet for breakfast at nine, but when I got to the veranda, I saw only Dr. Gamez, alone at one of the twenty or so tables. Next to his plate of food, the infamous black briefcase was open and file folders were set out for work. I had never seen him wear anything other than a formal dark suit; here, at an outdoor table in Mexico, was no exception.

He looked up from his papers. "Good morning, Jamie."

"Good morning."

"Sleep well?"

"Very well, thanks."

"Any headache? Shoulder ache?"

He sure asked a lot of questions. "No, why? Aren't you feeling well?"

He cut into his eggs. "Sometimes, you know, when we sleep in an unfamiliar bed, it can affect our body. Especially after a long flight, our head and shoulders may complain a bit the following day. That's simply why I asked."

A buffet table was set against the wall. I filled my plate with eggs, ham, and a glossy chocolate croissant. Then I faltered. I wasn't sure if I should join Dr. Gamez or sit by myself. Was it rude to sit at his table, or rude not to? I decided to take a seat at a table beside Dr. Gamez, facing the rear gardens of the resort. The central feature was the T-shaped swimming pool. Pale blue sparkling water. A series of cylindrical cement posts jutted up in a row, modern sculpture, like something you'd see in *Architectural Digest*.

"Nice pool," I said weakly.

"You'll need to wear sunscreen, of course. I have some in the room, if you need it. I don't worry about Celia, but your skin is fair. Did you bring your tennis racket?"

Sometimes, in the company of Celia and her dad, while I looked for things we shared in common, they seemed determined to discover the differences.

"No," I said. "I don't have a tennis racket."

"You may borrow mine then." In other words: *Of course, you will play tennis.*

A long silence passed when we both were chewing, our utensils scraping our plates. Just like at home with my grandparents.

"How's your research coming, Dr. Gamez?" I wondered if he would be as candid here as he was in Rita's café.

"Very well. In fact, we are now in the *testing* phase of the homosexual-therapy drug I told you about. Very exciting."

"Are you testing here in Mexico?" I tried not to sound too curious, but I hoped "testing" meant he would have some samples with him.

Dr. Gamez seemed ready to answer when his gaze moved past me. His expression changed as he called, "Good *morning,* Celia."

I turned. Celia looked half awake. She was still in boxers and a T-shirt. It amazed me that girls didn't have to shower when they woke up. If I didn't shower in the mornings, my wild matted hair made me look like Dr. Frankenstein's crazy lab assistant.

"What up, peeps?" Celia was always cheerful when food was in front of her. She went to the buffet and I jumped up to get more food. We began to fill our plates, and then Celia's eyes widened. "Stop!"

Moments before, I had dropped a seriously delicious-looking mound of melon onto my plate.

"Jamie, did you eat any fruit?"

"No."

"Repeat after me: No fresh fruit..."

"No fresh fruit?" *Oh right. Duh.*

"And no uncooked vegetables..."

"No uncooked vegetables."

"And no ice..."

"No ice."

"And no water, except bottled water."

"That one I know."

"Got it?"

I nodded, feeling stupid in front of them both.

The day was already hot, and Celia and I decided to spend the morning at the pool. We went back to our rooms to put on swimsuits and grab towels and sunglasses. We met on the path.

"Do you like my new swimsuit?" Celia asked, posing. The yellow bikini fit her body perfectly.

"Yow!" I had never seen her with so little clothes on. It made me feel self-conscious. I never had a problem with my body, but suddenly Celia looked a lot more like a grown-up than I did.

In the pool, the water was clean and cold, a pale blue-green. The color reminded me of the turquoise on Amanda Lynn's bracelet. If it was possible for a swimming pool to seem rich, this one did. The lining was made of blue mosaic tiles and sleek stainless steel. It seemed like the kind of pool James Bond would swim in.

Mmmm, 007.

Get the pills!

We swam and splashed around for about twenty minutes. Afterwards, we stretched out side by side on long wooden chairs as Celia removed items from her canvas tote—M&M's, gum packets, Tootsie Rolls, Starburst.

"You know what?" I said. "You have some explaining to do."

"For real?"

"Do you remember that time I brought treats to a First Knights meeting? You totally dissed my cookies. *Oh, did you bring anything healthy?*"

We both laughed, and she said, "Yeah, I did, didn't I?"

"But here we are in Mexico, and Miss Healthy Choice has got the whole Costco snack aisle in her damn bag. Celia, you're a secret snacker!"

"I admit, I occasionally indulge."

"Yeah, like every time we go anywhere. Ice cream, Skittles, mochas with whipped cream, microwave popcorn..."

She giggled, so I went on. "Pizza, all kinds, Dairy Queen, Big Macs..."

I loved to tease her. Not that she had any reason to watch her weight. And her skin was perfect, no zits or moles or random scars. I let my eyes explore a little, sadness creeping into my mood. The truth was, if I wasn't attracted to Celia—this perfect dream of a girl—I was a hopeless case.

How many truckloads of Dr. Gamez's magic drug would I need? Maybe too many.

A towering row of palm trees lined the edge of the resort. For the first time in ages, I thought of "the island" that my old friends online had joked about. Ironically, in this tropical paradise, the island seemed farther away than ever. Exactly how I wanted it.

I lay back in the chair, my head cradled on a fluffy white towel. I glanced toward the main building. I could see Dr. Gamez on the veranda, still bent over his work at the breakfast table. I wondered if his room was unlocked.

"Damn, I need sunscreen."

"Hurry back," Celia said, without moving. "Bring snacks!"

I strode across the lawn and down a flagstone path toward the rooms. The only people I saw were the grounds crew, watering and sweeping with funny brooms made from bundled twigs. They nodded shyly as I passed. My heart raced as I approached the row of guest rooms. One problem—I had no idea which room was Dr. Gamez's. All I knew was that my room and Celia's were right next to each other. Maybe Dr. Gamez had a room next to us. Or maybe he was on the other side of the courtyard. I tried the room next to Celia's and found it unlocked. I poked my head in. The room was empty, the bed stripped of linens. I pulled the door closed. Next I tried the room next to mine, and it too was unlocked. Also unoccupied.

"Señor?"

I turned and saw a smiling elderly woman holding a basket of clean, folded towels. She was maybe as tall as my chest.

"May I help you?" she added.

"Eh, no *gracias*," I stammered. "*Estoy ... un poco* confused." I walked straight to my room, closed the door behind me, and breathed deeply. I sat on the bed and waited two full minutes for the tiny laundry woman to move on before going out to try again.

Nothing to worry about, I reminded myself. Celia was safe at the pool, and Dr. Gamez was hard at work on the terrace. All I needed to do was find his room, walk in casually as if looking for sunscreen, and grab some pills.

I tried a dozen doors—all unlocked, a series of empty rooms. At last I reached the corner room. I opened it carelessly, thinking that it would be empty like the rest. It was not. The bed was made up, and Dr. Gamez's enormous leather suitcase sat open on the sofa. The curtains were closed and the light was off.

I stepped inside and closed the door behind me.

Now my heart threatened to jump through my chest. I looked at my watch. Only five minutes had passed since I left Celia at the pool.

Just find the pills and go.

I turned on the bedside lamp and considered my options. In addition to the suitcase, Dr. Gamez had two other bags— a small leather bag and a square metal case. I went to the leather bag first, unzipped it, and found shoes. Two pairs, expensive looking. Next I glanced at the metal case, but saw a lock on it. This seemed like the most logical place to keep medicine, but I wasn't about to break a lock. Maybe I'd get lucky elsewhere. I moved to the suitcase. Dr. Gamez hadn't unpacked yet, which surprised me. He seemed so fastidious, like he'd have all his identical suits neatly ironed and on hangers, ready to wear. He wasn't the type to tolerate wrinkles. I crouched on my knees to reach under his clothes, feeling around without disturbing his things. I thought I might find one of the plastic pill bottles. My left hand stopped on something hard, and I felt hopeful. But the object was cold metal and heavy. I pulled it out and nearly dropped it. A gun.

Holy crap.

I pushed it back under the clothes and stepped away from the suitcase, as if it might shoot me all by itself.

Holy crap. Holy crap.

Maybe Dr. Gamez felt he needed a gun for protection. Celia had mentioned that in Mexico, parts of the countryside were notorious for bandits. Bandits who preyed on rich American tourists. Perhaps Dr. Gamez took the gun whenever he left the resort or went on excursions. This seemed reasonable, but it still freaked me out. My parents would never allow a gun in our house. When I was young, even toy guns were off limits.

Maybe the FDA required that drug researchers keep weapons when they travel in foreign countries—to prevent the drugs from falling into the hands of warlords or drug kingpins. Because imagine, if one of *those* guys got his hands on this stuff, he'd—

Quit making a movie out of this!

My breathing quickened, approaching a full-scale panic attack. I decided that if anybody came into the room right now, I would pretend to faint. Fall to the ground with my eyes closed and play dead. When I came to, I would claim to have no idea how I got here.

Where am I? Somebody, please, call my parents in Chicago.

I glanced at the bureau. I ran to it, switched on a second lamp, and opened the top drawer. A Bible in Spanish. A guide to the Yucatán. A plain envelope, which, I happened to notice, was full of American twenties. Over a thousand dollars cash, at least.

Dr. Gamez had always been generous with me. I wouldn't consider stealing money from him. I put the envelope back in the drawer.

Then I saw the pills. Tucked in the back of the drawer was a reclosable plastic bag, bigger than the size for sandwiches, filled with blue pills. I couldn't believe my luck. It was like the universe was giving me an instant reward for not taking any of the cash.

I lifted the bag and studied it, hundreds of pills all pressing against the plastic. They seemed to be competing to show off their elegant little *R*s.

Hello, my friends! Glad to see you again!

It felt like a beanbag in my hand, the kind you throw for points in kindergarten. I opened the top and poured about thirty pills into my palm. *How many can I take without Dr. Gamez noticing?* Twenty? Thirty? Thirty pills weren't so many. It seemed like a safe number. I sealed the bag and then returned it to its hiding place, closing the drawer without a sound.

I didn't have a pocket in my swim trunks for the pills. Frantic, I turned in a circle, trying to decide where to stow them. Finally I stepped into the bathroom to grab a washcloth. I folded it around the pills like an envelope.

When I came out of the bathroom, Dr. Gamez was standing in the doorway.

"Oh," he said, calm but clearly surprised to see me. "Hello."

There was a long silence when my mouth couldn't form words. For a split second, I considered the fainting act, but if I did it, the pills would fall from my hand.

He took a step forward, and I flinched. The time had arrived when I would finally be exposed for what I was—a gay teen, a petty thief. An ungrateful friend.

He did not smile. "Have you come for the sunscreen or my tennis racket?"

"Sunscreen," I said, my voice a whisper.

He moved past me, pausing at his suitcase. Would he reach for the gun? I nearly pissed myself. But then he shook his elegant finger at the suitcase. "No, not in there." He went into the bathroom.

He'd left the door to the courtyard wide open and I could hear the gardeners' banter. I might have fled if my knees hadn't felt so weak.

He returned with the sunscreen: Neutrogena Sensitive Skin SPF 50. He smiled, almost bashful. "Perhaps you think I'm overly cautious…"

I took it with my free hand. "It's fine, thank you." I turned to go, almost free. But when I reached the door, he called my name.

"Jamie."

"Yes?"

"The next time you need something, I hope you will simply ask." His voice was kind.

"I will," I said.

I raced down the cobblestone path toward the pool.

"That took long enough," Celia said, squinting into the sun. She was sweating almost as much as me.

"I had to get sunscreen from your dad," I said.

"He had some? There's a shocker." She sat up and reached out a hand. "Let me rub some on your back."

"Excellent," I said. "But hold on—I gotta pee."

Discreetly I took the folded washcloth to the changing rooms next to the pool. There was a bathroom there, and I closed the door. I opened the washcloth and stared down at the pills, more relaxed. I smiled. *My pills!* I hadn't seen them in more than a week. Sure, I'd had a comfortable spell without headaches or sore shoulders, but I was willing to welcome those back gladly if it meant I could be straight. I was ready for Celia and me to move forward in our relationship. I put one pill in my mouth, then bent down over the sink and drank water from my hand.

Maybe three sips of water, that was all.

I wasn't thinking.

seventeen

It was ugly. In the six hours that followed, my stomach emptied its contents. Like Linda Blair in *The Exorcist*, my body was possessed. I couldn't believe I had so much crap inside me. Whenever I thought, *That's . . . gotta be . . . all there is*, my body respectfully disagreed and I raced back to the fancy bathroom. Afterwards, sweating and desperate for rest, I climbed into bed. Within minutes I was back at the toilet.

Worst of all, I wasted a pill. Dumb-ass risked everything by going into Dr. Gamez's room for the pills and then sent the first one right down the toilet.

Celia was attentive but seemed suspicious. "Are you sure you didn't eat some of that fruit salad?"

"I may have," I lied. "I just don't know."

She sat on my bed and stroked my forearm. "Are you

lying to me because you're embarrassed to be such a stupid gringo?"

"I bet you say that to all the boys you bring here," I said, batting my eyelashes at her pathetically.

At regular intervals, Dr. Gamez came to check on me. He stood stiffly next to my bed, hands clasped behind his back, asking about symptoms. He was formal with me, professional, and demanded every detail, every ache or pain. At times he seemed annoyed; I wondered if he regretted bringing along such a careless guest, one who would squander the opportunity to be in paradise. All I knew was that I felt lucky to be under a doctor's watchful eye.

For the next three days, we didn't leave the resort. I was afraid to be too far from a bathroom. On one hand, I had certainly learned my lesson about the local water. But I didn't feel so steady on my feet yet. I was not up to exploring the town or scaling ancient ruins. Dr. Gamez made me email my parents every day, using his laptop, to let them know I was okay.

Secretly, I took a pill each morning—with bottled water. The metallic aftertaste returned, along with the headaches, the afternoon stiffness in the shoulders, and the restless, dreamless sleep. But all these side effects, I knew, would be worth it.

Instead of touring, Celia and I lay by the pool, playing Gin Rummy and Solitaire or reading magazines we'd bought at the airport. We took short walks around the estate. We dutifully sat through a Spanish Mass in the adobe chapel. Afterward I took a postcard from a wooden box in the vestibule. The postcard showed the hand-painted altar, so I sent it to my grandparents:

Mexico is beautiful and fascinating. Some nights I sleep in a hammock. I got sick, but I'm feeling better. Most of all, we are happy to be helping the impoverished local people at the clinic.

By the fourth morning, I felt almost normal again. My appetite had returned, and Dr. Gamez told me it was safe to do whatever we wanted. After breakfast, Celia and I rode in the resort van back to Mérida. It was old and crumbling, with narrow streets. Even the tiny cars were vintage, unspoiled by snowfall and salt. We took pictures of each other in the town square, a plaza surrounded by rows of palm trees, ornate Colonial buildings, and a big stone cathedral. We wandered and shopped. Celia bought some colorful bracelets and a cloth coin purse. I bought a brass key-chain shaped like a donkey; I thought maybe I could hang it on our Christmas tree at home. After two hours, we were bored.

That afternoon, back at the resort, we changed into our swimsuits and headed toward the pool.

"Before we swim, I want to show you something," Celia said. She led me down a series of stone steps into a woodsy landscape. A well-defined path led to a clearing under a canopy of trees. There was a small round pool of greenish water, maybe twenty feet wide.

"Cool," I said. "Is it a natural spring?"

"No idea. It may be rainwater. It's called a *cenote*."

"Very pretty. Let's go back to the pool."

"Let's relax here first." She pulled off her T-shirt, so she was standing there in her shorts and bikini top. "It's kind of romantic, don't you think? Come on."

"Really?" I leaned toward the water, peering. "Don't you think there are a million bugs in there? Scorpions? Snakes?"

"Don't be such a girl. You're the boy, remember?" Her shorts dropped to her feet, and now she was standing in her yellow bikini.

I suddenly felt vulnerable. "If this were a *Friday the 13th* movie..." I began.

"It's not," she said, irritation creeping into her voice.

"Right."

"The *cenotes* are meant for relaxing. We sit in them every time we come."

I swatted a fly away from my face. "We don't even have towels."

"Come on," she said, gingerly stepping into the water, exploring the bottom with her feet. "Don't be a pussy."

I had no choice. I doffed my shirt and followed her. "I don't want to put my face in."

"Me neither. So we won't put our faces in."

The murky water was tepid, almost lukewarm. I didn't see the attraction. Compared to the pool, this looked like a sewer pit. Celia crouched at one end of the *cenote*, only her head sticking out of the water, and I crouched opposite her. I waved my arms on either side of me to ward off critters.

She was grinning wildly. "What do you think?"

"I don't know. It still feels...sketchy." I slapped my neck—another fly, or maybe the same one.

She came toward me. "Let me get your mind off the bugs."

I recoiled. "So, um, Celia, when is your birthday, anyway?"

She made a funny face. "Is now the ideal moment to update your calendar?"

"Something like that."

"November 30. Same as Mark Twain and Winston Churchill. Yours is in October, right?"

"October 24. Same as Kate Winslet and Nicky Hilton."

"Cool. Must be the birthday of sexy, smart, creative people."

"Yeah—and party-loving hotel heiresses."

She nodded, not smiling, in a sultry way. She lifted her hands to my face to kiss me.

When we kissed, I reached behind my back to steady myself on the slimy rocks. I realized she was giving my hands permission to wander, but I didn't want to touch her under water. It seemed too intimate, too open-ended. Her own hands moved easily from my face to my shoulders, then to my chest. She played with my nipples, which made us both laugh.

As her hands traveled south, I realized what would be expected of my body. There needed to be a transformation…down there. I prayed that the pills would kick in for once and give me a miracle:

Under trees, among bugs, and still feeling iffy,
To Jamie's surprise, he got a huge stiffy.

Inevitably her hand brushed against my shorts, and I jumped.

"*Celia*," I sputtered. "Wait, I—I saw something."

She blinked at me. "Close your eyes then."

"I swear, I saw something in the water *right there*." I pointed over her shoulder, at nothing, but her angry eyes didn't stray from my face. "It was like a spider lizard," I said. "Or a lizard spider!"

"Jesus Christ, what is *wrong* with you?" she said. "You're in a private swimming hole with a half-naked girl, and you're freaking out about a lizard?"

"I'm sorry." I shrugged. "I'm a wimp when it comes to the great outdoors. I'm a city kid who never—"

Now she rose out of the water, arms folded and dripping. "You know what? I'm starting to get really pissed off. I bring you all the way down here so we can spend some romantic time alone together. First you get sick and you need to rest all the time. Now you don't even want to touch me?"

I shook my head helplessly. "Please just give me some more time. I've never had a girlfriend before. Don't hate me for being inexperienced."

"Jamie, I don't care that you're not experienced. But I'd expect you to be a little more *enthusiastic*."

"I'm nervous. And really—kissing in this scummy little swamp?"

"No, it's not just here." She closed her eyes, lifted her hand, and rubbed her forehead hard. It was the same place my head ached. Then she looked straight at me. "Whenever we're together, being intimate, you seem reluctant. Almost... indifferent."

"Give me a break, Celia. I've been sick."

"Not just this week. *Always*." She flailed for a second, literally stomping her feet in frustration.

"I don't know. Maybe I'm not the right guy for you."

"Yeah, well, that's becoming obvious."

We walked back to the pool in silence. She dove into the water and I lay on a chair, feeling pathetic and desperate.

Dramatic storm clouds had filled the sky. Loud birds gathered in the palm trees, shrieking at each other angrily. Within minutes, for the first time since we'd been in Mexico, it began to rain. The first big drops crackled as they hit the paving stones around the pool.

"That does it," Celia said, getting out of the water. "Time for a nap. Alone. *Adiós.*"

We retreated to our bedrooms.

Supper was another elegant buffet prepared especially for us—platters of grilled fish and vegetables, warm corn tortillas, a pot of beans, and plenty of colorful fresh fruit that went untouched.

Celia was chilly with me, as she always was in front of her father. It was all part of the Great Friendship Charade that we performed for Dr. Gamez's benefit. Terse and polite, we answered his questions about our visit to Mérida. We talked about tropical rain, about how much harder it rained here than at home. Celia never looked in my direction.

Dr. Gamez said cheerfully, "Tomorrow the weather will be fine, and we will go see some fantastic ruins."

But already, sir, we are viewing the fantastic ruin of a grand relationship—one that was rocky to begin with.

"I have a tiny headache," Celia announced. "I'm going to bed early."

The waiter gave us three umbrellas, and we separated.

In my room, I lay on the bed, listening to the thunder. I missed Chicago. I missed being in my own bed. I actually missed my grandmother's bland cooking. I thought about Wesley, going off his Ritalin, and I felt worried. I wrote him a postcard:

Hola buddy—
Mexico is cool, but I'm keeping you on
my radar screen. Wish you were aquí.

Sprawled on the bed and listening to the rain, I'd never felt so miserable, so lonely. I'd finally been exposed as a fraud. Not a real boyfriend, hardly a real boy. My brain kept replaying all the mistakes of the previous weeks and months: the lies, the excuses, the thieving from my parents and Dr. Gamez. I'd been pushing my friends away, even potential friends like Ivan, and for what? What had made me think this trip would be a good idea? Obviously I wasn't ready for a real relationship with anybody.

I heard a knock at the door and sat up.

Celia entered, wet head and shoulders first, almost shy. "I hope I'm not intruding."

"I'm glad you're here," I said, and I was.

"My head's a little better."

"That's good."

"I'm annoyed at you, but—I don't like being alone out here."

"Me neither," I said.

"Anyway, I brought a peace offering." She reached into her bag and pulled out a deck of cards.

"More Gin Rummy?"

"And one other thing." She had a dark bottle. Its label was edged in gold. I wasn't sure if it was wine or champagne. She handed it to me.

"Where did you get this?"

"I asked Fabian, and he brought it to me."

"Wow, they're nice here."

"Okay, so listen. I realize that neither of us drinks. Honestly, I don't care two shits about drinking."

"So why'd you get it?"

She shrugged, still not smiling. "I thought if we had a few sips, who knows? Maybe we could both be more relaxed around each other."

"Worth a try."

She reached into her bag again and pulled out a corkscrew. "Fabian needs it back tomorrow." The corkscrew was silver and complicated. It looked like the skeleton of an exotic marine animal. Neither of us could figure out how it worked. In the end, we just twisted the screw part into the cork and pulled. A team effort, one pulling on the bottle, the other on the corkscrew. Eventually we got it open. I grabbed two short square glasses from the bathroom and Celia poured.

It was red wine, and it tasted like wet chalk. Celia made

a face. We both drank the first glass quickly, then poured another. We sipped the second, and it still tasted awful.

We began a game of Gin Rummy. Within a few minutes the blood in my veins felt warm, my head a little heavy. Celia won the first hand and we clinked our glasses together. She said, "Want to play best two out of three?"

My heart wasn't in it. I put down my cards. I spun around so that we both were sitting against the wooden headboard. I reached out and took her hand. She was wearing the bracelets she had bought in town, and we examined them together without speaking. Another minute passed. I thought randomly of Covici's hand-painted plea for silence: *Silence is a mansion where dwell my greatest notions.* Outside the room, the rain kept splattering on the cobblestone path; the crickets were quiet for once. Celia let her head drop against my shoulder, and I smelled the chlorine in her loose, shiny hair.

"Celia?"

"Hmm?"

"Are you ever going to tell me about your mom?"

She looked down at my hand, stroking hers. "I wondered if you were ever going to ask."

"I wasn't sure you wanted to talk about it."

"I'm not going to burst into tears, if that's what you're thinking. The reality of it sunk in a long time ago. What do you want to know?"

"I know she died in a car accident. That's all."

"That's pretty much it. An ordinary school day. The principal's voice came over the loudspeaker in my Social Studies class, and she called me to the office. My dad was waiting there. He took me out to his car. And he told me... I mean, she was a terrible driver. Always. It was a one-car accident—what they call a 'no fault' accident—and I remember thinking, *She died in a car and we're in a car right now. And it's nobody's fault. Weird.* It was two years ago last November. Almost two and a half years now."

"Does it seem like a long time ago?"

"The day of the accident seems recent. It's so vivid. But when I think about how different things are now, it seems like forever ago. Another life."

"Different how?"

"Just being alone in the house with my dad. Being each other's only company at dinner. Making small talk in the car. It's a strange pressure I never expected." She sipped at her wine, so I did too. She gave a regretful smile. "In retrospect, I guess I should have spent more time getting to know him when I was growing up. We're bonding now, though."

"And you have your siblings."

"We're spread out—nine years between my sister and me. And she's on the West Coast. My mom was, like, the glue. My sister and I connected mostly through her. Now whenever my sister calls or visits, she seems more interested in talking to my dad. Grown-up stuff. Investments."

"But she works in Hollywood. See, to me, that's fascinating."

"She's in the business side, not the creative side. She raises the money to make movies. I bet there are plenty of times when she doesn't even watch the finished movie."

"That's weird."

"Honestly, she's not a happy person."

"What about your brother?"

"He's fantastic. Hilarious, more like my mom. The thing is, Mom died only a couple of weeks after he moved to Rome. He came home for the funeral, and he must have had so much to tell us, but all we talked about was our mom. It was all we could *think* about. We were planning a service. And now when I see him or email him, and he talks about his interesting life, I remember how we didn't talk about any of it during that first trip back. It was the first time I realized that there's, like, a filter. And there probably always was, always *is*, a filter between people, no matter how close you are. I never knew that before. Oh, man—am I rambling? Stop me."

"No, this is what I wanted. To know you better."

"Okay. Let me think." She seemed to focus on the orange-colored lampshade across the room. Funny what a person looked at when there weren't a lot of choices. I kept staring at her. In the dim light, she looked prettier than ever.

"The whole thing was surreal. At the time, everything seemed like a movie. We had to dress a certain way for the funeral. We had to act a certain way at the dinner table. I'm not sure if it was respect or expectation or what. But I felt like I was playing a role. And I also kept thinking about how quickly the car accident had become a permanent part of my life. It became a *fact*, an unchangeable part of her life story. And mine. We spend so many years trying to imagine what it would be like if our mom or dad died, and then when it happens, it's like, okay, *this* is what it's like. And not only that, but *this is*, once and for all, how that part of my life will go."

"That's interesting."

"It was surprising to me how much thinking I did about it, in addition to just processing it emotionally and being sad."

I nodded.

"And, God, there was one other thing."

"What?"

"It's embarrassing." She sat up. "Let's play more cards."

"Just tell me."

"Okay, um," she said, settling back. "After my mom died, I was, you know, obviously upset. I was so upset, in fact, that my hair literally began to fall out. It came out in *clumps* every time I brushed my hair. Bizarre, right? And I went to my dad in a panic, and he took me to a doctor and to a psychiatrist, but nobody knew how to help me. It just..." Her voice cracked. "It just kept happening. Even the hair on my legs stopped growing. It was so...weird."

"You must have been really stressed."

"Tell me about it. Within a few weeks of my mother dying, I lost about half my hair! And it still kept happening until I was nearly freaking *bald*. Eventually I had to wear a shitty wig for about nine months, until my body calmed down and my hair began to grow again."

Now she was crying. I pulled her toward me. "It must have been awful. I'm really sorry you had to go through that."

"I can't believe I told you. It's the last thing I ever wanted you to know about me—that I was a complete weirdo bald freak!"

"I'm glad you told me. Hearing that story makes me love you even more."

She looked at me. "You *love* me?"

"Yeah—I mean, *of course.*"

She was still crying a little when we kissed again. I tasted the salt on her face.

I do love her.

We didn't need the rest of the awful wine. The rain outside fell and fell, and the room was humid and cool.

She reached under my shirt and ran her fingernails across my back, which felt terrific. I closed my eyes, but Celia fell asleep first. It seemed like such a grown-up experience—a luxury, having her sleep in my arms. I loved smelling her hair, feeling the touch of the whole length of her, warm and soft, pressing against me.

An ancient memory surfaced, out of nowhere, of crawling into my parents' bed when I was very young, taking a spot between them, enjoying their body heat and the comforting sound of their breathing. Falling asleep, snug between their beating hearts.

My head was spinning from the wine, but I smiled. I thought: *This is what intimacy feels like.*

I had forgotten.

eighteen

After Mexico, Chicago felt gray and wet and heavy.
We landed at O'Hare airport, where a shiny black
car picked us up. It was late afternoon; traffic inched along
with too many stops. Nobody said anything. We were tired
from the flight. I actually looked forward to being home,
returned to the quieter life I was used to. Plus, after days
of pills and headaches, sleeplessness and sore shoulders, I
needed a break. My vision was getting blurry.

It was officially spring, but it hadn't warmed up for good.
The trees didn't have leaves yet, and ugly muddy patches lined
the sidewalks. It was strange to be back after being so far away.

When the car pulled up in front of our apartment, I discreetly squeezed Celia's hand before getting out. I would see
her in the morning at school, but I would miss her tonight.
This thought cheered me.

I said, "Dr. Gamez, that was the most amazing week of my life."

And I repay your generosity by stealing from you and lying to your daughter.

He shook my hand, formal as always even after spending a week together. "Great having you with us, Jamie. Please thank your parents for trusting me with your care."

I took my duffel bag inside and found everyone waiting in my grandparents' kitchen.

"Welcome home!"

The kitchen was decorated with balloons. The table was set, with a red tablecloth we normally reserved for Christmas.

"Let's eat!" my mother said. In an email she had promised a special dinner to celebrate my return, but I was slightly horrified now when my eyes focused on the table—Old El Paso tacos with their unnatural yellow shells. The ground beef was unseasoned, in consideration of my grandparents. Cheddar cheese from Wisconsin. A bottle of hot sauce. And a big pot of Minute Rice on the side. We sat down to eat.

"You know what's interesting?" I said at one point, "Mexican food isn't really like this. I didn't see one hard taco shell the whole time we were there."

My dad looked surprised. "What did you eat?"

"Lots of those corn crackers, I bet," my grandfather interjected. He called tortilla chips "corn crackers." He didn't know better. He called granola bars "cookies." When it came to keeping up with food lingo, my grandparents gave up in about 1978.

"Some tortilla chips." I nodded. "And rice, beans. Lots of fish and chicken."

"You got sun, but you look tired," my grandmother said. "Like you could use a good meal. I should have made pot roast."

"This is perfect. Just what I wanted." I couldn't help but rub my eyes. "How's business?" I asked my parents.

My parents looked at each other but didn't say anything. "Tell us about the clinic," my mother said.

My father nodded eagerly. "Did you save anybody's life?"

"No, Dad." The best strategy was to downplay the volunteer aspect of the trip. "It was a community clinic—a free clinic. Mostly it was just talking to people, running errands for Dr. Gamez and the other doctors. I mopped floors and washed dishes."

My grandmother perked up. "Hell, I could do that. Maybe I should take a fancy trip to *Mex-i-co*."

The comment hung in the air, and I noticed some tension. "So what's been going on here?"

Nobody said anything.

"How's business?" I asked my dad again.

"Slow, actually. It's been a little slow."

"How slow?"

"Well—" my dad said, shrugging at his plate.

"Anyway," my mother interrupted, "I bet the trip did wonders for your Spanish."

I nodded, but in fact, I hadn't spoken more than a few sentences of Spanish the whole time. I wanted to say something truthful about the experience. "The thing is, where we were on the Yucatán, the people are very poor." I described the cinder-block houses, with their altars and Christmas lights, and the general poverty I saw in the villages. "It's not like anything we see here."

"Not like anything *you* see here," my dad said.

"Makes you appreciate what you have, I hope," my grandfather said. "At your age, it's important to learn the concept of… *appreciation*." He said the word like it was a scientific process.

"Gratitude," my mother corrected.

"You look like the dead," my grandmother said to me. "Did chickens keep you up at night?"

"I feel fine," I lied. I could barely focus, and my shoulders felt bruised.

Once I felt that I had described the trip to everybody's satisfaction, as well as underscored my *gratitude* for my own circumstances, I excused myself. I went to my room and closed the door. I was never more excited to see my familiar little bed.

My forehead throbbed, but I had one essential chore to do before sleep. I went to my duffel bag on the bed and opened the zipper. My travel clothes smelled rank. I threw them into a pile near the door—everything except for one clean sock, curled in a tight white ball. I held it in my lap for a second before unfolding it and shaking the pills onto my black bedspread. There were two dozen left, a constellation of bright blue stars against a night sky.

Before leaving Mexico, I almost flushed them down the toilet. It didn't seem possible to make it across the border without the customs police discovering them. But then I remembered that Dr. Gamez had brought them to Mexico without incident. Maybe, since these drugs weren't on the market, they weren't illegal yet. From the perspective of customs, they didn't even exist. Besides—worst-case scenario—if the customs police found them, I would have looked to Dr. Gamez to explain it all away. I would have had some explaining to do myself, of course, but I was willing to take the risk.

Risk. The price of admission to Planet Hetero.

I guided the pills, two and three at a time, into the plastic Army tank and returned it to the bookshelf. Back where it belonged, newly stocked with ammo.

I was still staring at it when my left arm flinched, a kind of spasm. My knuckles hit the dresser.

Whoa.

I took a step backwards. You know your body is beyond tired when you lose control of a limb.

Then it happened again—my forearm jumped, just for a split second.

I needed to sleep. Without even removing my clothes, I collapsed into bed and trapped my crazy arm under the pillow to hold it still.

I closed my eyes and thought about Celia. I missed her already.

Does she still like me?

I had let her down in Mexico, no question, but she seemed to believe my excuses. We had experienced so much together in a week. At this point, there was nobody in my life I felt closer to. Celia had talked so candidly about her mother's death, and her grief and her hair, that I knew she wasn't pushing me away. I knew that if I could hold her interest a little bit longer, the pills would kick in and I would be an excellent boyfriend.

I wanted to buy her a present. Something significant, to convey my thanks for the trip. She'd always been so generous with me. A piece of jewelry would do the trick, but it would require more money than I'd ever had. How could I ask my parents for money to buy jewelry for a girlfriend I wasn't allowed to have?

A sound came from the window. Two quick, deliberate knocks. I got out of bed, shuffled across the room, and lifted the shade.

Good old Wesley!

I turned the lock and lifted open the sash, hoping the noise wouldn't be heard from the living room. "Hey," I whispered. "Good to see you!"

"Dude, I have to say, you're almost *tan*. If I didn't see it with my own eyes, I'd never believe it. C'mon."

"Hold on a second." I put on my sneakers and grabbed a sweatshirt.

Ten minutes. I am going to be back in bed in ten minutes.

I pulled the window closed behind me, leaving only a crack for my return. We darted across the back grass and out the alley gate. A dark green Toyota Corolla was parked behind our garage, hazard lights blinking. The hubcaps were laced with rust.

"Whose car is this?"

Wesley grinned. "My cousin's."

I peered into the car. "Mimi's family? Is she here?"

"Nah, different cousin. Let's go."

I opened the passenger-side door. "Wait a minute. Who's driving?"

"I am." He got into the driver's seat—a full year away from taking Driver's Ed, much less having a license.

"*You* are? Since when?" I slid into the seat next to him and before I could protest, he had the key in the ignition and we were on our way.

I fastened my seat belt with unusual *gratitude*.

Wes pulled out of the alley, made a couple of fast turns, and then we were heading down Sheridan Road, as normal as anybody. We drove past the currency exchange, Payless Shoes, the liquor stores. Boring storefronts I'd passed for years took on an edgy new glamour with Wes behind the wheel.

I had to shout over the radio. "When did you learn to drive?"

"Over break! You're not the only one to have a few adventures this week."

When Sheridan Road turned to Broadway, I thought about my vow to be back in bed in ten minutes. "How far are we going?"

"Up to you. I was thinking the lake. Foster Avenue beach!"

"Can we turn the radio down a little?" My head felt like it might explode.

He reached for the dial but didn't seem to lower the volume.

I saved my questions for the red lights; it didn't seem

wise to distract Wesley when the car was moving. "So your cousin lets you drive his car? That's cool."

"He didn't exactly sign a permission slip."

"But he gave you the keys?"

Wesley's shrug was kind of a dance move. "It's an extra set." He reached over and slapped the back of my head. Playful, but it stung. "Relax!" he shouted.

Then my left arm flinched again. Shot up big time, like ballplayer shaking off a cramp.

"Whoa! Down boy." Maybe Wes thought I was trying to punch his shoulder.

"Heh heh," I said. This spasm thing was freaking me out.

Something was different about Wesley, too. He was so charged, like his energy level had been switched to turbo.

After cruising down Broadway for a couple of miles, we turned east on Foster and drove to the empty parking lot near the beach. The lot was so full of potholes that Wesley had to cut back and forth like a slalom skier. He finally cut the motor and I jumped out, relieved to be out of the car and on my own feet. The water was black and choppy and loud.

"So what's been going on?"

"Look at your watch," he said. "What's the time say?"

"Nine o'clock."

"Exactly. I knocked on your bedroom window at *precisely* eight forty-five. Fifteen minutes from that moment to now."

"And?"

He smiled and grabbed me by the shoulders. "Look

around! We've got the car keys, we can *move*. This is what it's all about—being a teenager."

"What? Stealing cars and sneaking out without your parents knowing?"

"Freedom, dude!" He jumped up and down. "Freedom!"

"You're going to lose your freedom pretty quick if you act like a lunatic."

I followed him to the rocky shoreline. We scrambled over the first section so we could get closer to the water. The wind was blowing and I could feel the spray when the waves crashed. Wes was picking up little rocks and throwing them into the lake. He had a quick, determined pace, picking up and throwing in rapid succession as if he had a job to do.

"So," I said, "this is what life's like off the pills, huh?"

"Absolutely."

"Baseball tryouts begin tomorrow, am I right?"

"After school, my friend," he said. "I'm ready for all the lunges and wall-sits the coaches want to give me."

I nodded. If he acted this crazy at tryouts, he would never make it past the first cut.

"Freedom!" he shouted again, as if reading my thoughts. "I'm all about freedom these days."

"Quit jumping in my face." I didn't mean to be crabby. I just wanted to be in bed. "You sure you feel okay?"

"*Okay?* Like I'm *alive*, dude," Wesley said. "Like the gates have been opened and my brain can run free."

"That sounds a little intense."

He looked at me sideways, momentarily somber. "Just—

just forget about it." He threw rocks for another minute without speaking. "So how was Mexico?"

"Wes, it was unbelievable. Celia's father rented this amazing resort, the whole thing. This romantic old Mexican estate that's totally renovated, first class. We had it all to ourselves. And the swimming pool was so cool, like something you'd see in a James Bond movie."

"Her dad sounds all right."

"He really is."

"Letting you and your girl hang like that."

"Well, you know, we didn't rub it in his face. He didn't see us making out or anything. We all had separate rooms."

"You had your own hotel room?"

"Yeah. Dr. Gamez is, like, super generous."

"But you and Celia slept together, right?"

This was, technically, true. I figured I was entitled to a little bragging. "Yeah, we shared a bed when we could."

"How was that?"

"What do you mean, *how was that?* It was awesome."

"What's she like between the sheets?"

"Wes, I don't want to talk about that. I really like her."

"C'mon, I'm your best bud."

"Let it go."

"Tell me about some of her favorite tricks."

I winced. "Shut up."

"Just give me a taste."

"Forget it, will you? Let's go." I turned and started back toward the parking lot.

"All right, I'll drop it. Relax, dude."

I kept walking toward the car.

"Jamie, I'm sorry," he said, grabbing at my arm. "Wait a minute."

"What's with you tonight? You're being a complete dick."

"I said I'm *sorry.* I just wanted to hear about your trip. This is getting serious with you and Celia, right?"

"Obviously, yeah."

"So let me in sometimes."

We leaned against the car, both trying to cool down. My left arm made the spaz-ballplayer move again, and I tried to conceal it with a full-body stretch. This was more than fatigue. Maybe the pills had some freaky side effects I hadn't seen yet. This could be a problem. Headaches weren't noticeable, but spasms were hard to hide.

Wesley grinned. "So, Mr. Jumping Bean, this girl is important to you."

"She really is."

"I'd like to get to know her then."

"She said she wants to know you guys, too," I lied.

"Excellent. Truly excellent. We'll talk to Mimi tomorrow and set something up. Mimi's been wanting us to go bowling."

"Bowling?" I said. "Mimi bowls?"

"She says she does."

I wondered how a limb spasm, combined with blurry vision, would affect me in a bowling alley. "Fine by me."

"Okay then, let's organize it. Make it happen."

We got in the car and drove home, radio blaring, and my heart pounding all the way. He dropped me in the alley behind the apartment. I shut the car door with as little noise as possible. I opened the back gate and saw that the lights were off upstairs. Everyone was asleep. I crawled back in through my bedroom window.

Wes was right, after all. We could handle a little freedom now and then.

As tired as I was, the trip to the beach had left me feeling wired, exhilarated. I tiptoed to the kitchen for a glass of milk.

In the moonlight, my eyes caught the sparkle of my grandmother's wedding ring. It was on the windowsill near the sink, along with the other jewelry she typically removed for washing dishes.

I thought again of a piece of jewelry I could buy for Celia—a simple bracelet, maybe, or earrings. I sighed. With the money I had left from the trip, I could barely afford to buy her a *candy* necklace.

My grandparents, I knew, always kept some emergency cash in the cupboard under the sink, hidden in a box of steel-wool soap pads. I opened the cupboard door and crouched on my knees. The S.O.S. box never held too much money, usually only enough to pay for newspapers or an occasional pizza.

I turned the box upside-down and shook out its contents. A wad of crumpled cash fell into my hand. I unfolded the scraggly bills, which felt thin as tissue, their texture almost oily from age. Listening for the sound of my grandparents' bedroom door, I counted quickly. I was surprised. Ninety-one dollars total. If I took it all, they might ask questions. I took seventy and left the rest.

My grandparents would never think I took it. They would blame their own faulty memory before they suspected me.

The funny thing was, for once I didn't feel guilty. I was only a boy who wanted to buy a nice present for a girl. And the one thing I had known since childhood was that the whole world smiled upon simple, romantic gestures between boys and girls.

nineteen

Until the limb spasms began, I'd never thought the drug might kill me.

"What has gotten into you?" my grandmother said at the breakfast table.

"What do you mean?"

"You think we can't feel you kicking your damn leg?"

I bent down, pretending to rub my calf, and locked my foot behind a table leg. "I've got a cramp. Trying to shake it out."

"You're acting like a defective."

"Don't say defective," my grandfather said, looking up from the newspaper. "Say handicapped."

"I'm not handicapped." I sat on my hand before it could flinch again. I hadn't slept well, and I felt grumpy. Were the pills I'd gotten in Mexico the original formula or something new? I could conceal headaches, sore muscles, even blurry vision. But I couldn't easily explain a spastic arm or jumpy feet. The drug seemed to be affecting my brain, as promised—a result that had sounded ideal in concept but was scary in practice. The dangers of self-medicating were becoming more and more evident.

I pushed away the fear. Already the pills had gotten me through a trip to Mexico. My relationship with Celia was more intimate than ever. I was eager to continue treatment.

When my grandmother got up for more coffee, my grandfather leaned close. "You know, Jamie, your folks are in a bit of a pickle. Financially speaking."

"I don't have any money," I said defensively.

No money from under the sink, that's for sure.

"Think about getting a job this summer," he said.

"I'm not sixteen until October."

"Cutting grass then, or painting fences. Walking dogs for yuppies. Use your imagination."

My grandmother turned from the sink. "How's a defective like him going to make any money?"

"Don't say defective," my grandfather said. "He can walk a dog, can't he?"

So now it was *my* responsibility to fix my parents' financial situation? The suggestion drove me crazy. The fact that my flaky parents weren't money savvy annoyed me to the extreme. As much as I loved them, it was hard not to compare them to an authentic success like Dr. Gamez.

"I'll think about it." I got up and reached for my backpack. "By the way, are *you* hiring?" I asked my grandfather.

His eyes went back to the newspaper. "Sorry, we don't have a dog."

At the First Knights meeting on Tuesday morning, Celia and I sat side by side, sleepily comparing forearms. Her skin was still a smooth golden brown from the trip. Mine, peeling and irritated, looked like a moonscape.

Across the table, Ivan spent most of the meeting avoiding eye contact with me. He hadn't greeted us or asked about Mexico. Clearly I had gotten my message across—*we can never be friends*—but I hadn't intended to hurt his feelings.

Mr. Covici's somber gaze moved around the table, resting on each of us. "Okay, club members, we have a unique problem." Finally he broke into a big grin. "We need to spend all this flower money!"

We gave a half-assed cheer.

"How much do we have?" Ivan asked.

Covici looked over the club ledger. "Three thousand dollars, give or take."

As expected, Perfect Gwen's hand shot up first. "Maybe, since we do so much clerical work and hang up so many posters around the school, we could spend the money on office supplies. New staplers and staples, tape and stuff."

Nobody said anything.

"Dream bigger, Gwen," Mr. Covici said gently.

Ivan smiled. "What about new laptops for all of us in the club?"

"Not quite that big," Covici said.

Gwen was chock-full of ideas at seven o'clock in the morning. "How about some new American flags for the school? With so many soldiers back from the Middle East, I think it's important to honor them. We could put up big beautiful flags all over the place."

Another suggestion met with silence.

"A noble intention," Covici answered. "But flags seem more like the realm of the History Club, or even the Sewing Club. You guys are the Knights—"

She nodded. "Right, and knights were like soldiers!"

"Flags are one idea," Covici said. "Are there any others?"

I stayed quiet. Given recent events, I was likely to steal the damn money. Plus, the creativity tank in my brain was on *empty*. I was too tired to think. Tired from the trip, tired from not sleeping enough, tired of schlepping to school at daybreak for this stupid club. Next year, I resolved, I would join a different club—a club that met *after* school. A club whose members sat around after school and watched old movies. That sounded perfect.

My hand went up as soon as I thought of it. "What about using the money to buy a new movie screen for the auditorium?"

"That's a little random," Gwen said with a huff.

"There's a film club here at Maxwell," I said. "They've got camcorders and supposedly they make funny short films. But there's no big screen to show them on."

Celia leaned forward. "That's awesome. *And* we could

show regular movies as fundraisers, even for other clubs. It would make fundraising, like, really easy."

When no one else said anything, I turned uncertainly to Ivan for support.

He shrugged. "It could work," he said. "We could show movies on the first night of every month. First Nights, sponsored by the First Knights."

Covici looked pleased, but perfect Gwen wasn't going to back down. "Isn't it *illegal* to charge admission to rented movies? It says so, right at the beginning of every DVD."

"Well," Covici said, "maybe we wouldn't charge for the movie. We'd charge for the refreshments, and for the opportunity to socialize before and after the movie. Plus, we would suggest a donation to support any club or cause we wanted."

Ivan was nodding. Apparently his dislike for Gwen was more potent than any bitterness he felt toward me. "And the movie," he said, "would be a free gift to express thanks for supporting the fundraiser."

"Exactly," Covici said.

"It sounds like a lot of work," Gwen muttered.

Now Anella came to my defense. "Not compared to the flower sale. All those tags, *ach!* Selling them, putting the *leetle* tags with the flowers and distributing them to homerooms? Compared to that, movie nights would be easy."

"All in favor of a new movie screen," Covici said, "raise your hand."

All hands went up, except for Gwen's.

"I like it too," Covici said. "A movie screen serves a need, fills a gap. Well done, Jamie."

I felt myself grinning. I looked at Ivan and mouthed, *Thank you.*

He returned a quick, shy smile, then turned back to his book bag.

Celia and I got up and moved closer to the library doors, waiting for the first bell.

"Bowling, huh," she said, talking to herself. I'd told her about Wes' invitation before the meeting. "This weekend will be interesting, to say the least."

"It'll be fun," I said. "Trust me."

The truth was, I felt nervous about bowling under the drug's jittery influence. I pantomimed throwing a bowling ball. My throwing arm had a slight tremor, but maybe it wasn't noticeable. I tried it again, concentrating on a smooth underhanded arc.

Ivan was standing near us. "Let me guess. Is it ... tossing breadcrumbs to pigeons?"

I smiled, embarrassed. "We're supposed to go bowling this Friday. But I may have pulled a muscle in my arm. Or something."

"Ah, bowling." When Ivan pantomimed the bowling act, the gesture was graceful, one arm in front of him, leg raised behind him, perfectly balanced.

"Come with us, Ivan," Celia said. "Please? The more, the merrier."

"I have never bowled before," he said, his voice full of hesitation. "But I will mention it to Anella. I know for a fact she would like to spend time with you." He gave me a lingering, sideways look. There had been a time, not long before, when I would have spent hours recalling and analyzing any look from Ivan. *What did the look mean? What secret message was he trying to convey?*

But that was the past. I realized I didn't think about Ivan very often anymore. And when he did cross my mind I didn't feel much of anything, except slightly guilty for rejecting his offer to hang out. I didn't dream about him. I didn't look for him at his locker. My crush on him was over—vanished, like a minor cut that had healed, leaving no trace. For the first time, it struck me:

The drug really is working.

Sudden joy washed over my body, a downpour of joy. Everything Dr. Gamez had said was true. The treatment was working. And not since I first grabbed a handful of the pills at Rita's café did I feel such unrestrained hope about my future as a heterosexual.

As a result, the notion of spending time with Ivan didn't threaten me at all. "Sure, Ivan," I said easily. "Come bowling with us."

He smiled, as if taken by surprise. "Really? Okay … thanks."

"Whoa, look." Celia pointed behind us and we turned. "What is that man doing now?"

Mr. Covici had the ladder out again and was leaning against the farthest wall, the remote corner where the students went to fart. He climbed the rungs slowly with another can of paint.

"Another message *from the wall*," Ivan said gravely, as

the first bell rang. "Who knew the library walls had so much to tell us?"

We all headed to our first-period classes.

Before lunch, I stopped by the library to print out an essay for English. Right away, I saw Covici's latest handiwork. Above the bookcase, green letters rose and fell in a wavy line: *OPPORTUNITIES ARRIVE LIKE TRAINS AND THEY DEPART LIKE TRAINS.*

———

On Friday, the plan was for my parents to drive, stopping by Wesley's house to pick up him and Mimi. Celia told me she would meet us at the bowling alley, where we would find Ivan and Anella, too.

I always hated for friends to ride in our van, a humiliating relic from my dad's print shop. It wasn't like a regular minivan—it was a hideous gray delivery van. The walls and ceiling were all exposed metal and there weren't any windows in the back. It looked like a van for transporting hostages.

As predicted, Wesley had not made the baseball team. He hadn't gotten past Day Two of tryouts. He was thrown out for talking back to an assistant coach. Although Wes did not seem devastated by disappointment, he didn't want to talk about it.

Instead, he and Mimi sat in the back seat of our van and argued about school. Wes was under the impression that *The Scarlet Letter* and *The Crucible* were the same story—one in novel form and the other a play.

"I've seen them both on TV," he insisted. "They're the *same thing*."

My mom settled the argument. "Different stories," she said. "Same costumes."

Mimi stared out the window. "Sometimes," she said, with genuine sadness in her voice, "I wonder how it's even possible I'm related to him."

"Mimi," I said, "I'm counting on you for some coaching tonight."

"All right," she conceded. "As long as you know I like to win. My main advice is not to compare yourself to me. Or, in your case, to anybody else."

Mimi and I had developed a routine. I complimented her and she fought back. It was an unusual kind of friendship, but it seemed to work for us.

All day I had wondered how the evening would go, these people from different parts of my life getting together for the first time. I liked to keep the separate parts of my life separate, the way I kept my things organized in rubber bins at home. Old toys in one bin, CDs in another, movies in a third. Tonight I felt like all my stuff was spilling together onto the floor in an unholy mess.

On the plus side, Celia already knew Ivan and Anella from club meetings. Mimi and Celia knew each other from middle school. And Wes could make friends with anybody. Everybody had somebody to latch onto, but for the first time in my life, I was the glue.

We met the others inside the front door and wandered toward the counter. The bowling alley was loud and bright.

Fluorescent and neon lights curled across the ceiling, blinking to the sound of the music. The worn dark carpet had an abstract pattern of what looked like humongous pink and orange slices of toast repeating in endless swirls and circles.

"My treat," I told Celia.

"I can pay," she said, but she didn't protest further. I could tell she was pleased. She looked even better than usual, dressed in tight black jeans and a lime-green T-shirt. I felt proud to be with her. "Okay," she said, "while you guys pay, I'll use the time to find the perfect bowling ball."

"You do that, dear," Mimi said, not very sweetly.

Wes and Mimi accompanied me to the counter.

"Let me pay for you guys, too," I said.

I wanted Mimi to smile, but all she said was, "Oh, is her money rubbing off on you?"

"Mimi, give her a chance," I said. "Maybe she's changed."

She shrugged. "Maybe she's perfect for you."

"At least she's friendly, unlike some people."

Wes wasn't going to get involved. He was sort of hunched over. I thought he was taking off his shoes, but when he straightened up, he was holding a cigarette.

"What, you're smoking now?"

He showed me his lighter: SPANKS FOR NOT SMOKING! "You want one?"

"Put that out, Wes. You're not supposed to smoke in here."

He laughed and swatted at my ass.

"Seriously," I said, "you are defective."

Off in their own little world, Ivan and Anella seemed

delighted by the entire experience. They eagerly traded their tennis shoes for brown-and-red leather rentals. They played with the hand-dryers and took prolonged interest in selecting the right bowling balls. With childlike enthusiasm, they surveyed the dozens of options—heavy blacks, lighter reds, iridescent greens, metallic purples—like it was the ice-cream counter at Baskin-Robbins.

Mimi was the best bowler among us. It was like she *bossed* the ball from her hand straight to the pins; there was no arguing with her strength and aim. Now I understood why she had wanted to set up a bowling night. She was generous with advice for Ivan and the girls, but to Wes and me, she barked out commands as usual: "Wes, go get us some soda. Jamie, you do the scoring."

Obediently, I took my place in the captain's seat. I knew how to score. The problem was, I couldn't really see the pins.

"Hey, Anella," I said. "Come here and score with me."

"What an invitation!" Anella said, fanning her face theatrically, and everybody laughed. "Don't be jealous," she said to Celia.

"Oh, I'm not." Celia draped her arm around me and sat on my knee.

I showed Anella how to do the scoring. When it was my turn to bowl, I stood at the line, squinting. The white pins shimmered at the end of the lane like ghosts. At least I knew which general direction to throw the ball. Praying the limb spasms wouldn't interfere, I took a breath, stepped forward, and threw. My arm felt okay, straight. Three seconds later, I heard a crack of impact.

A miracle!

But at the end of the lane, the pins still shimmered, unchanged. As I turned toward my friends, my left arm flew out like a wild noodle. "How'd I do?" I said, before anyone could comment on my arm.

"You have a few more to take down," Ivan said helpfully. "You got one."

I pumped my fist. "Watch and learn."

"He needs glasses," Celia said to someone. "I've been telling him that for weeks. When we were in Mexico, he couldn't read street signs."

"I told you. My Spanish sucks."

"You don't need to speak Spanish to know *Avenida San Diego* from *Avenida San Miguel.*"

"No *hablo Español.*" I put my fingers in my ears. "*No entiendo nada.*"

My green metallic ball appeared and I took it to the bowling line. I tried to concentrate, to focus. I drew back, laid it down, and waited... *Gutter!*

"Awww," Mimi said loudly. "Next!"

I took my seat. In the lane next to ours, some college guys were bowling and partying, drinking pitchers of beer. Fraternity brothers, maybe. They were tall and broad-shouldered, dressed in jeans and tight pullovers that showed off their bodies. I suppressed a smile. Not long ago I would have watched these guys, scrutinized them up and down. I would have imagined them with their shirts off, powerless against my own curiosity. But the fact was, I didn't care about them now. They only caught my attention because—this time—they wouldn't hold my attention.

The drug works. The treatment is working!

The bowling alley was packed. Even with blurry vision, I could see that. We were lucky to have gotten a lane. The management was blasting songs from the 1980s: Beastie Boys, Guns N' Roses, Journey. The loud music, along with the crashing of balls against pins, made my ears ring. I sipped my Coke and waited for my turn to bowl.

That's when I noticed. Two lanes away, someone was staring. In the middle of this complete chaos, a solitary figure stood absolutely still, his gaze locked on me. I thought of the Hitchcock film *Strangers on a Train*, the famous scene at the tennis tournament when the hero, Guy, looks up in the stands, at all the hundreds of faces turning back and forth, following the tennis ball. Only one face is frozen, staring right at Guy—the psychotic killer Bruno.

In this case, it was just as bad. Paul Tremons.

I almost dropped my Coke.

His companions were laughing and clowning around, but Crazy Paul kept staring. As if he'd been waiting for me to notice him. Like a lunatic, he smiled and raised a hand in greeting.

I turned back to my friends.

Go away. Go away. Don't come over here.

Anella brought me back to the game. "You're up next, Jamie."

My chest thumped in full panic mode. It didn't seem fair. I had done everything I could—avoided him, stopped going online. I had the pills. But I was never going to escape those old mistakes as long as this one freak still knew my secret.

Celia jabbed me in the rib. "What's wrong? Shoes too tight?"

"Nope." I stood and put my drink into the cup holder. "Just concentrating on my game." I reached for the green ball and moved to the bowling line, conscious that Crazy Paul was probably still watching me.

Steady hands, steady hands.

I took two steps forward and threw the ball. It careened to the right gutter as if pulled by an invisible string. My wrist was out of wack.

From the sidelines, Wesley offered characteristic support: "Dude, you suck at this."

"Keep your wrist straight!" Mimi snapped. "Your shoulders are crooked."

"Honestly, I don't care," I said. "But thanks." When the ball emerged from the chute, I grabbed it and returned to the line.

Still watching me, freakazoid?

I steadied my shoulders and concentrated on my aim.

Damn limp wrist.

I took a breath and threw. My wrist turned. Another gutter.

"Awww," Mimi called. "Next!"

"I have to pee," I announced, as if it was an excuse for my pathetic performance. I needed to get away before Paul approached all my friends.

I navigated through the crowd, around people who were taller and clearly happier than me at that moment. The weaving made me dizzy. To my relief, the bathroom was nearly empty, just one tall guy talking angrily on his cell phone: "Do you believe that shit? Or do you believe the words of the man who loves you?"

There were four urinals, all in a row. No partitions. I stood at the one in the corner, breathing deeply, and hoped no one would come in when I was peeing. I wished the cell-phone user would leave. I really needed to pee.

In any case, I was glad to have the chance to think for a second. I had to believe Crazy Paul would not mess with my friends. Would he be stupid enough to let on that we knew each other?

Indignant Cell-Phone Guy said, "You take some time tonight to think about who matters to you. I don't need this drama." He ended the call. I could hear him at the sink, the sound of a spray—two quick squirts. When he left the bathroom, I was alone.

There had to be an unspoken code. You don't "out" a person without his permission.

Especially if he's made such an effort to be straight!

"Jamie?"

I turned my head.

And yes, here was Crazy Paul, three feet away. Full focus. I had forgotten about the oily forehead, the close-set, pale gray eyes.

I zipped and flushed. "Oh, hi. I wondered if that was you back there."

Seriously? You followed me into a bathroom?

He smiled. "I waved, but you didn't seem to recognize me."

"I'm not wearing glasses tonight." That was the truth, at least.

"You wear glasses? Funny, I've never seen you in them."

"That's because I don't wear them." It was like talking to a five-year-old nuisance. "But, you know, I could be getting some soon."

"Okay," he said, studying my face. "Yeah, I can see you in glasses. You've got the kind of face that would look good in glasses. Not everybody looks good in glasses."

Every time he said the word *glasses,* I thought my head would explode. Since when was Crazy Paul the expert on what looked good on my face?

Why am I even talking to you?

I stepped around him to use the sink.

He folded his arms, getting comfortable. "Hey, I'm so jealous. Those guys in the lane next to you are hot! No wonder your game's a little bit off tonight."

"Um, I hadn't really noticed."

He laughed. "Yeah, right."

Don't act like we're the same.

He wasn't backing down. "How's life? Besides the eyesight and the bowling, I mean."

"Everything's great, thanks."

"So, I've got to ask—is one of those girls your girlfriend?"

None of your damn business.

I nodded, washing my hands. "Something like that."

Go away, Crazy.

"Things getting serious with you two?"

"Yup."

"That's ... grand," he said, his voice dripping with sarcasm. "Hey, in case you hadn't heard, we started a gay-straight alliance at Maxwell back in January. We've got nine members. Not bad for a new club. It's fun—in fact, that's who I'm here with tonight."

"Cool." I glanced at the door and wondered how long it would take for Wesley to come looking for me.

He moved a little, as if blocking the exit. "You should come to a meeting sometime."

"Okay," I said quickly. "Thanks for the invite."

He grabbed my shoulder and whispered, "You know, you don't have to be gay to be a member. Half the group is straight."

It turns out, I don't have to be gay at all.

Silence.

I stepped around him. "Speaking of which, I've got to get back to *my* group. See you around."

I bolted out of the bathroom, wondering if he would follow me. Maybe he really needed to take a leak. Doubtful.

I jogged back to our lane just in time to take my turn. Two more gutters. My concentration was shot.

I dropped into the seat next to Celia. I leaned against her and lightly rubbed her knee. "One thing I know for sure," I said. "I'm not impressing my girl tonight."

"Hey, who is that boy?" she whispered.

She saw him. She knows.

My heart jumped twice. "Who do you mean?"

"The one who followed you to the bathroom. I recognize him. He goes to Maxwell."

What kind of perv follows people into the bathroom?

"Him? Yeah, he recognized me, too, but I can't remember his name."

Celia's attention returned to the bowling. "Almighty crap, what is it now?"

Wesley had passed the foul line by at least ten feet. He was crouched on all fours, his skinny butt wiggling high in the air. He scurried toward us, backwards like a crab, trailed by cigarette smoke. Whatever else he was doing, he hadn't knocked down any pins.

"He is a nut," Celia whispered matter-of-factly.

"Only sometimes," I said.

"Well, he may get us thrown out of here."

I sat on my hands, hoping she was right.

twenty

My supply was limited, so I took the drug only on days when I knew I'd be spending one-on-one time with Celia. The limb spasms let up a bit, but my vision remained weak. And I needed weekends to catch up on sleep. Lucky for me, it didn't strike anybody as strange for a teenager to spend Saturday mornings in bed with all the shades pulled down.

I heard a knock. The door opened a crack and my father poked his head in. "Got a minute?"

I sat up fast, rubbing my eyes. The alarm clock glowered 11:00.

I always felt uneasy when my father came into my bedroom. Such visits were rare. His gaze seemed to roam the neat-as-a-pin décor with suspicion, as if the tidiness might be covering up some sinister enterprise.

He leaned against the doorframe. "Get up, sleepyhead. Let's go for a walk."

"Yeah, like, to where?"

He shrugged, smiling. "Anywhere."

"Just you and me?"

"Sure."

My trouble radar sounded an alarm in my head. As I swung my legs to the floor and reached for my tennis shoes, I wondered if he would ask me outright if I'd taken money from my grandparents. If accused, I would deny it. The day after the bowling trip, I'd used the leftover money to buy Celia a simple silver bracelet with an engraved pendant that read, "Don't hide your hart from me." I wrapped it using a sheet of the most elegant paper my parents had. When I presented the box to Celia, she nearly cried. I'd never seen her happier. She couldn't stop hugging me. For the first time since Mexico, it felt like we were really back on track.

On the sidewalk, I had to hustle to keep up with my father. My legs were finally the same length as his, but his pace was quicker. Was he nervous too? At the same time, I remembered the pleasure of being out in public with him. Now and then, his hand pressed against my back as we maneuvered around lampposts and street signs. Neighbors in every direction were occupied with outdoor chores—breaking up fallen branches, sweeping driveways, acting like it took only a token of human effort to make spring arrive sooner.

Enjoying the walk, I almost forgot about the inevitable Inquisition.

Dad cleared his throat. "I wanted to talk to you, buddy, and I don't want you to be defensive."

I wasn't going to make it easy for him. "Defensive?" I asked. "About what?"

"Your mom and I are worried about you. You seem tired all the time. It's pretty clear you haven't been sleeping well. We can see it in your face. In your personality."

"Who knows? Maybe I'm going through a growth spurt or something."

"No, not a growth spurt. We think something else might be going on. And we wonder"—he paused on the sidewalk, but kept his voice even—"if maybe you've been experimenting with drugs. Weed, or pills, or..."

My mind entertained a paranoid thought: Was my mother *at that moment* going through my dresser drawers and bedroom bins looking for drugs? If she picked up the tank, she'd find my stash of Rehomoline. I'd be screwed.

I sighed, as if bored. "Dad, you know me better than that."

"Well, you're in high school now. And we don't know the scene there..."

I forced a little laugh. "Yeah, well, I don't know *the scene* either. I'm sure there are plenty of kids using drugs at Maxwell. I just don't ever see it."

"You can be honest with me about this. You know you can."

I started to walk again. "Dad, please. I want to go to college. I'm not doing *drugs.*"

We walked to Peterson Avenue and turned west. We

were almost to Wolfy's, a hot-dog place we'd been going to for years.

"Let's grab some lunch," he said predictably. He was trying to lighten the mood to show he wasn't angry with me. He was too nice to engage in an actual argument with anybody.

At Wolfy's, we ordered the usual: chili dogs and root beer. The girl who brought the food to our table was pretty. Her sleek dark hair was pinned in shoestring loops behind her head. Her uniform was tight. The moment she walked away, Dad grinned at me. "Nice looking," he whispered.

"Dad, she's a teenager."

"I meant, don't *you* think she's nice looking?"

"Meh."

We began to eat.

"Say, what happened to that girl you liked a few months ago?"

I chewed, forming an answer. It was tempting to tell him about Celia—just let the whole romantic story spill out. He would be pleased. But then if he shared the information with my mother, she was likely to put a quick stop to our after-school outings. I couldn't take that chance.

"Nothing much. She's cool."

"You know, when I was your age, I had a lot of girl-friends. That was the best part of high school for me. Girls were the *only* good thing I had going besides baseball. I don't think that's unusual."

I nodded.

"I guess what I mean is, your mom has her rule about

dating, but it's okay with me if you want to go out with someone. I wouldn't tell."

"Thanks, Dad."

He leaned forward and tapped the table next to my food. "And buddy, I was thinking, maybe that's the reason you seem so tired—keeping some girl happy. Not a bad reason for a guy to lose sleep, eh?"

"Jeez, I'm *telling* you, it's a growth spurt. No girls, no drugs. Okay?"

He wiped his mouth with a napkin. "Yeah. Okay, sure."

I looked back towards the counter. "The only drug I really go for is caffeine. You think they have iced coffee here?"

"Iced coffee? Are you bullshitting me?"

"Dad, it's my new favorite thing!" I had to give him something.

Revealing this tiny fact only made me more aware of all the things I couldn't tell him. How could I convey to my father that my life now was richer than his was, my world bigger and more interesting? It wasn't just the trip to Mexico. For the first time in my life, I was discovering the city of Chicago beyond our boring little neighborhood. It bewildered me that my parents didn't seek out the kinds of activities that Celia and I did, like window shopping on Michigan Avenue, prowling used bookstores in Wicker Park, or even seeing foreign movies at the Music Box on Southport Avenue, where the painted stucco walls rose around us like a Moroccan castle and the ornate ceiling twinkled with stars. At Rita's café, I had developed a taste for warm scones with whipped cream and jam, and French bread toasted with goat cheese and herbs. I now craved all sorts of hot teas: Darjeeling, Ginseng, San Francisco Spice, Gunpowder Chinese. With Celia by my side, I had unlimited access to a world of culture, privilege, and adventure.

As much as I loved my dad, I suspected that my days of chili dogs and root beer were numbered.

———————

It got to the point where Celia and I helped ourselves at the Bound & Ground. We invented a special coffee drink, involving steamed milk, cinnamon, and half a Hershey bar. I kept a supply of chocolate in my backpack, and Celia mixed the drinks. If I had taken a pill and felt a headache coming on, the magic coffee drink was the only thing that made me feel better.

We were still careful with Rita, though. We didn't let her see us kissing, or even touching. In her eyes, we were best friends, just *los banditos*, and that was it.

One afternoon, Rita seemed giddy, all aflutter as she worked the register. When she got a break she came and sat with us, her gold bracelets knocking against the table. "Hey there, *banditos*," she said. "Listen, I'm glad you're here because I have great big exciting news. I'm moving—to Albuquerque!"

For a long moment, nobody said anything.

Rita's face never changed. Her expression remained one of crazy joy. "I've met someone and I'm going. We've been emailing for six months, and we've seen each other three times. He's a perfect gentleman. His name is Rudy, and he's a roofer. Isn't that funny?"

Celia looked shell-shocked as she stared at her drink. "You're *moving?*"

"Now I know," Rita said, "that I've kept it a secret, and it seems like a big step. But sometimes you have to take risks for love."

"Amen," I said out loud, without meaning to.

"Exactly, honey," Rita told me. "You can't stick to the sidelines or always try to play it safe. Someday you kids will understand."

Celia reached for Rita's forearm. "I don't want you to go."

Rita chided her. "Don't you want your Tía Rita to have some love in her life? Hey, look at me. I'm not such an old lady, Celia."

"I know," she said. Now she was almost crying.

I asked, "What about the café?"

She shrugged, a little defensive. "Selling it, closing it. Don't know yet."

How ironic, I thought painfully, that she would abandon a successful business like the Bound & Ground while my parents would cling forever to the sinking ship of their doomed enterprise.

Rita seemed at peace with her plans. "This was fun while it lasted," she said, looking around. "But you know what? This place is cute, and I've put a lot of time into it. I'm proud of it. But at the end of the day, an adorable little café can't love me the way a man can."

"I'll miss you so much," Celia said.

"It'll be hard for all of us at first," Rita said gently. "But, Celia, you're at the age when you can jump on an airplane and come see me anytime. Come for a nice long visit in the summer, and we'll shoot snakes in the desert."

Celia sniffled. "That'll be fun, I guess."

"You'll come too, Jamie, okay?"

I nodded to be polite, even though the notion of snake shooting seemed cruel and scary. I'd never held a gun in my hands, except for Dr. Gamez's handgun in Mexico.

"Now listen, Celia, I haven't told your dad yet. He won't be pleased."

"He'll miss you."

She waved away the notion. "Get serious. Your dad won't give a tough taco that I'm going. But he'll be annoyed that I'm closing the café, after all the time and money he's invested. I can deal with him, though."

When Rita got up to attend to customers, I patted Celia's hand. I wanted to put my arm around her, but feared Rita might see. We sat in silence for several minutes, letting the news soak in.

Finally, Celia wiped away her tears with a paper napkin. "Oh, what the hell," she said. "Speaking of taking risks for love, I've been meaning to talk to you about something."

"You've met a roofer named Rudy, too?"

Finally, I got my wish; she smiled. "Be serious."

I made the universal gesture for buttoning the lip.

"Thank you. Okay, James, I wanted to say, this thing we've got going? It totally rocks."

"Yeah, it does."

"Now listen a second. I love being with you. I love the quiet, thoughtful way you have. I like how well you listen. You're so cute, and you're a great kisser, and smart, and you're fun to cuddle with. You have been *a perfect gentleman*, as Rita would say."

I blinked, making sure to smile. "At this point, it sounds like you're going to dump me . . . for a snake shooter."

She ignored me. "So I wanted to say, you know, that it's fine with me that we're taking things slow—physically. Like you, I want my first time to be with someone I trust. Someone I care about."

Now it was clear. This was a rehearsed speech, with an agenda. Suddenly I felt anxious. I waited a moment before speaking. "We agree on that."

"The thing is, I do trust you and care about you. Completely."

"I feel the same way."

"And when I think about why you haven't been very aggressive with me, in the physical sense, I wonder if maybe it's because you're scared of what might happen."

This seemed like a prompt. "That's putting it mildly."

She nodded. "Right. Sex is a big deal. A huge deal, with real consequences. It's the biggest deal."

"Right."

"Well, I wanted you to know—I mean, the thing is . . ." She gulped, as if she was more nervous than me. "I don't want you to judge me or anything after I tell you this."

"Trust me, Celia. Just say it."

"Okay, here goes." She took a breath, leaned close, and whispered, "I'm on the Pill."

I wanted to say, *Is that all? That was one of the first things I ever knew about you!* But I feared what was coming next, so I kept my mouth shut.

She gazed out the window rather than looking at me. "Yeah, so it's something my dad wanted me to do as soon as I hit puberty. Obviously he would prefer that I don't have sex when I'm so young. But he also doesn't want a pregnancy to disrupt any plans I have for college or a career."

"Celia, I don't think differently about you because you're on the Pill."

"The thing is, it's a *safety measure*. It makes the idea of sex a little less scary, right?"

I nodded. "Less scary, yes."

She stared, as if waiting for a different response. More enthusiasm perhaps.

A smidgen of enthusiasm?

She gestured with her hands as she spoke, as if they were helping her to search for words. "So, if you've been holding back, or taking things slow or whatever, because you're scared of me getting pregnant—you don't need to be."

I nodded again like an idiot, my brain scrambling for something to say. "Does the Pill prevent one hundred percent of pregnancies?"

"No, but—"

"Does it prevent STDs?"

"Jamie!" She pretended to look angry and insulted, then burst out laughing. "You know I don't have a friggin' STD.

We both come to this with zero experience. Unless you've been lying to me. Which you better *not* have been."

I grabbed her hand playfully, but she drew it away. "Relax," I said. "I was kidding."

"Okay, so, in fact—when you think about it—we're never going to have a safer experience than the first one."

"True."

Across the room, the espresso machine hissed and gurgled.

"So, what do you think?"

I sat back in my chair, trying to contain the panic that was rising in my gut. I knew the pills made me less attracted to boys, but I wasn't sure if they would get me through sex with a girl—yet.

I remembered to smile. "Okay, great! Thank you. That gives me something to think about."

She raised an eyebrow, annoyed. "You'll think about it? That's what you have to say?"

"Well," I said, then stopped. "Look, I don't know what you want me to say."

"Whatever." She pushed away from the table and reached for her bag. "Listen, I've got to get back to school. I've got Latin Dance in twenty minutes, and I'm going to be late as it is."

She was still frosty to me when we got to the sidewalk. *Another iceberg to navigate.*

"Celia, in the first place, where exactly do you expect us to *have* sex? On the bus? In your backyard, like Amanda Lynn?"

She rooted through her backpack as if she didn't want to look at me. "What's wrong with your house? You're always telling me your family leaves you alone."

"How am I supposed to explain having a beautiful girl over? I'm not allowed to date, and neither are you."

"There's always an excuse with you. *My* house, then."

"Celia, I don't understand why your dad is so trusting. He lets me come and go, hanging out in your room like I'm any ordinary friend. Your dad's a freaking genius. Why is he so naïve?"

"Oh, about that." Her smile was sarcastic. "Here's the other thing I've been meaning to tell you. And don't freak out or anything."

"Tell me."

She turned away again, facing the street. A garbage truck rattled by, its brakes screeching as it slowed at the corner.

"My dad thinks you're gay."

I stepped backwards. "Whoa. Why does he think that?"

"Because—I told him so."

He thinks I'm gay.

He knows.

"It's funny when you think about it," she said, her voice softening finally.

It was so Not Funny when I thought about it. At that moment, the old phrase *the blood drained from his face* applied perfectly to me.

"Relax, will you? Jamie, my father would *never* let you come to the house if he thought you were my boyfriend. Or even if he thought you were any random straight boy.

Please. I had to tell him something. We were just lucky he believed me."

"Yeah, but—"

"Don't you think it's worth that tiny, silly, stupid lie so we can spend time alone together?"

"Maybe."

"So what's the problem? In my dad's view, you're welcome at our house any old time. We can have sleepovers! Problem solved. No more excuses."

I shook my head, speechless. I remembered the private conversation I'd had, all those weeks ago, on a rainy winter day with Dr. Gamez inside the café.

"Wait, when did you tell him I was gay? Just recently?"

"No, a long time ago."

"When? Tell me the day."

She shrugged, as if growing impatient. "I don't know. When we first started hanging out together."

"Before Mexico?"

"*Of course*, before Mexico. Jamie, keep up. My dad would not have let you come with us otherwise. Okay, I remember. I told him after the first time you came over—when we designed those stupid flower tags. I didn't want to get in trouble for having a boy over." She smiled, a little bitterly. "At the time, I had no idea how useful it would be for us."

Now it all made sense. Dr. Gamez could not have known I'd be at Rita's café that rainy day, but when I walked in, he saw his chance and took it.

Opportunities arrive like trains and they depart like trains.

Celia looked at her watch. "I gotta run."

"Me too."

"Bye."

No kiss.

After she ran off, I stood in front of the café, trying to process this new information. I reconstructed the story from the beginning. As soon as we'd met, Celia had lied to her father to allow us to spend time together. Dr. Gamez, thinking I was gay, told me about his "secret" new drug, and then immediately gave me the opportunity to steal the pills. He invited me to Mexico to monitor the effect of the drug, and even let me take more pills when I wanted them. All along, he'd been using me as his guinea pig. He knew the truth all along.

The only person who didn't know was Celia.

twenty-one

This time I was prepared.

With Celia safely at dance class and the six digits of her birthday in my head, I had no trouble getting past the security checkpoints and into the house. My anger made me confident. I knew what I was doing. Inside, the place was quiet. Late-afternoon sunlight poured through the front windows, landing on the carpet in intervals like warm spotlights. I stepped lightly down the hallway toward the kitchen and stopped in front of the white security door that led to the lab. I punched in the birthday code and reached for the metal handle. It released, turning with a cold *click*. Easy as opening the refrigerator at home.

The lab corridor was long and brightly lit, a series of five office doors. My sureness wavered a little as the door shut behind me. Dr. Gamez's lab assistants would be gone for the day, but I listened for sounds of activity anyway. Nothing but distant, slow piano notes. Classical music.

I crept along the linoleum floor, taking slow steps. Fleetingly I remembered that scene in *The Silence of the Lambs* when FBI agent Clarice Starling approaches the evil Hannibal Lecter's jail cell for the first time. She faces a row of scary-looking cells, and the audience knows by instinct that Lecter's cell is the very last one; likewise, I knew that Dr. Gamez's office would be the farthest away.

The air was sterile-smelling and familiar, like the old tin of Band-Aids in my grandparents' medicine cabinet. At each office door, I paused, taking a quick peek. Four indistinguishable offices, each with a cluttered, messy desk. Corkboards lined the walls, decorated with charts, photographs, cartoons ripped from magazines. I didn't see anybody. Across the hall, a door led to the big lab—elegant rows of black Formica counters, chrome fixtures, glass beakers.

I paused just before the last office. The classical music was louder than ever. I wanted to catch Dr. Gamez by surprise. I tilted my head forward, expecting to find him bent over papers or working at his computer.

Instead, he was looking right at me. He stood behind his desk, facing the door, his fingertips resting on the desk surface in front of him. His stare and his smile rattled my nerves. "Good afternoon, Jamie!" he said cheerfully.

"How did you know I was here?"

"Why wouldn't I know it?"

He gestured toward a security monitor in the corner of the room. It looked like the little TV in my bedroom. Its black-and-white screen showed the entire lab corridor, one end to the other.

"Dr. Gamez, you haven't been honest with me."

"What do you mean?"

"The pills. You've known all along."

"Of course, yes, I know about the pills. I invented them."

"You haven't been playing fair."

He smiled, unflustered. He turned for a moment to lean down and silence the classical music. "I might say the same thing about you. You stole many pills from me."

"You practically handed them to me! You set them down in front of me and walked away. After Celia had *told* you I was gay."

He shrugged, grinning, as if embarrassed to be caught. "The funny thing is, Jamie, I could not know for certain if Celia was telling the truth. Teenagers lie all the time, as you well know."

"If you weren't sure, why did you show me the pills?"

He crossed his arms. "It was a safe gamble. If you had no interest, you would have left the pills alone. I knew that you had taken them the moment I left the café and got into my car. It was a simple matter of counting. I gambled and won. Celia may have thought she was lying to me, but she was telling the truth."

"Is that why you invited me to Mexico? To study me?"

"You may see it that way. There were a lot of reasons. Celia wanted your company, obviously. The fact is, you were safer under my watch. I needed to monitor the effects of the medication on your body."

I didn't buy it. "You were using me. You still are."

"Some might say you were using me. Naturally, I was eager to see if the drug would work. In retrospect, Mexico was a waste of our time, due to your carelessness with the local water."

"Does Celia know about you experimenting on me?"

For the first time, I saw a flash of something dark in his eyes. His tone was firm, but his voice remained even. "Now listen. Celia is innocent. She knows nothing about any of this, and we need to keep it that way."

"Maybe I'll tell her."

"No, that's not a good idea. Or do you want your *girlfriend* to know that you are a homosexual?"

"Girlfriend? What makes you think—"

"Jamie, let it go. I have known since the beginning that you and Celia are seeing one another. I know my daughter. I could see how she felt about you from the start. She may be naïve, but I'm not."

I didn't know what to say.

He smiled. "Given the time you have spent together, I certainly do not want Celia's feelings to be hurt at this point."

"Whatever. We don't tell her then."

"Jamie, please don't be angry. I wanted to help you, and I still do. You have already put forth such an *effort*. It seems to me that you are very close to being cured."

"It doesn't matter. I don't want to take them anymore."

I spoke in a rush of anger, but the words lingered in the air as a sort of question to myself. Did I really want to stop taking the drug?

"We both committed to this process the day you stole those pills from me at the café."

"I'm done with it," I said stubbornly.

His stare was powerful, full of disappointment. "I have to say, Jamie, I'm surprised at how ungrateful you seem. And foolish."

"To be honest, Dr. Gamez, I don't care what you think of me. I've got about fifteen pills left, and unless you want them back, I plan to flush them down the toilet."

He stood up. "Not recommended. The development of this medicine is of vital interest to my company. It's too late to stop what we're doing here. I'm sorry, but if you choose not to continue with the experiment, I will need to have you arrested for theft—grand larceny—and it will take every dollar of your parents' and grandparents' money to keep you out of prison. They'll be bankrupt."

Probably too late for that.

"Face it," he continued. "Your family cannot afford an attorney. And even if they could, he or she would be no match for my legal team, the best that money can buy. I take this work very seriously, Jamie, and I can afford to protect my interests."

I didn't know how to respond. I couldn't argue with the facts.

He added, more gently, "This whole argument seems so unnecessary, since I am helping you get what you want."

"You have no idea what I want," I mumbled, but it was true. If the drug worked, I still wanted to be straight. To be normal. I wanted to be obsessed with girls the way Wesley was. I wanted to be like every other boy at Maxwell. And I wanted the option of someday having a wife and children of my own. Maybe, if I kept taking the pills, all this would happen.

Dr. Gamez pulled his chair under him, sitting at the desk as if he intended to return to work. "Here's what you want," he said calmly, not looking at me. "You want to curb the attraction you feel for the boys in your class. You want to stop hating yourself for never fitting in, always having to hide your secret desires. You want to stop feeling like an outsider in your own family."

There was a long silence.

I nodded, ashamed. He was exactly right.

"Do we agree then?"

"Yes," I said, my voice barely more than a whisper.

He sighed. "Thank goodness. Honestly, I have had quite enough of this *negative attitude* for one day." He pulled open a desk drawer next to him and busied himself with the files inside.

"I need to go," I said.

"Wait, before you leave, I want you to answer a few questions. Sit down. Over here, next to my desk. Hurry up."

My instinct was to flee, but I did as he instructed. I didn't want him to "out" me to my whole family. Even more, I still wanted the pills to work.

From the desk drawer, he pulled out a folder. It was thick with papers, what looked like his notes. Next he grabbed a legal-size yellow pad, the kind Celia sometimes brought to school, and flipped the pages until he came to a clear sheet. "All right then. How often have you been taking the drug?"

"Only when I think I need it. Before seeing Celia."

He frowned. "Is that all?"

"Or when I see a boy at school."

"One particular boy?"

I nodded.

He wrote something in his notes. "I thought so. And since taking the drug, what has the response been? Do you think about this boy as much as you did previously?"

No, I mouthed.

"What was that?"

"I said no."

I don't dream at all anymore.

"Excellent. Any side effects?"

"Yes," I said quickly. "Lots of them. It started off with my spit tasting like pennies, and I got headaches. And now my vision gets blurry. My friends think I need glasses."

"Perfectly common. Anything else?"

"Sore neck and shoulders. It's hard to sleep sometimes."

"Normal."

In Dr. Gamez's view, everything I'd experienced was *normal* or *common.*

"And if I take the pills for several days in a row, my arms get all spastic."

He was writing it all down. "Spasms in the upper extremities," he said. "One arm, both?"

"Mostly my left arm. Sometimes even my leg. People notice, and it's hard to explain."

"Yes, very inconvenient. How many pills do you take each time?"

"One."

He looked up from the notepad. "Only one? I need you to start taking two. Every day, without skipping days. Take them both in the morning, starting tomorrow. Understand?"

I nodded.

He stood and went to a stainless steel refrigerator. He removed a large plastic container of the pills and set them on his desk. He asked, "Have you been refrigerating your pills?"

"I didn't know I was supposed to. Besides, I couldn't. Someone would find them."

"Where do you keep them?"

"In my room. In a plastic bag."

He mumbled some words of displeasure. I guess it was a good thing I didn't mention the plastic Army tank. He opened the container and poured about twenty pills onto a sheet of plain white paper. My friendly blue pills looked a bit less friendly under these circumstances. He took a baggie from a desk drawer. "Take these for the coming week. Keep them in a cool dark place."

"Won't taking two pills every day make the side effects worse?"

"Jamie, you must trust me. I'm a doctor. Based on what you said, I'm giving you a slight variation of the original formula. As soon as you get home, you may flush the others down the toilet. Just as you wished."

I nodded, feeling skeptical. At the same time, I wanted

to believe he was right and I wouldn't suffer more side effects. I put the pills in the bag, two and three at a time.

He watched me. "You need to start coming every week at this time. That way, I can examine you and you can get more of the drug."

"How am I supposed to explain coming over here like this?"

He took several deep breaths, thinking it over. "Very simple," he said at last. "You need service hours for school, yes? We could use assistance here in the lab. Sanitation services. I expect you can be handy with a bucket and a mop and not make a mess of things."

He spoke with such obvious condescension. Had he only *pretended* to like me all along? My neck felt hot with sweat.

"Unless you have any other questions," he said, seeming very pleased, "we're finished here for now. We need to get you home."

He led me out of the laboratory and through a door in the garage, then up some damp concrete steps to the back garden. He didn't want us running into Celia or the housekeeper any more than I did.

The sky was dark. I could hear the river in the distance, fast and high after the spring rains. The circular terrace was bordered with the first signs of daffodils and tulips, and the curving hedge was turning green. The garden was more beautiful than the first time I was there, but also muddier. We walked through the spongy grass to the side of the house and stopped at a high iron gate, secured with a padlock and chain.

Dr. Gamez got out his keys. He spoke in a low voice. "I am very glad we came to a shared agreement, Jamie. We both have much to gain by working together."

I nodded, staring over his shoulder. I just wanted to get away.

He inserted the key into the padlock and opened it. "See you next week."

"Right," I said.

I ran to Western Avenue as if I were being chased. The bus came immediately. Riding north on Western, I fell into a sort of daze as we passed all the familiar sights: Maxwell Tech, used-car lots, gas stations, and the dark cemetery with its high cement wall. The fluorescent lights inside the bus were so bright that I mostly saw my own ghost-green reflection in the window glass. My eyes looked hollow and there was a deep crease between my eyebrows. I looked like I'd been crying, even though I hadn't been.

On one hand, I didn't need to worry about getting the pills anymore. I had a dependable source now—*the only* dependable source, in fact. And I was relieved that Dr. Gamez now knew about the side effects. For the first time in weeks, I felt less worried about my health.

But how was it possible that someone I had trusted and admired as much as Dr. Gamez could turn out to be so selfish? All those months of his generosity and warmth—was it only a strategy? An investment of superficial kindness in the interest of a gigantic financial payoff?

Worst of all, now two people knew my secret: Crazy Paul and Dr. Gamez.

All I'd learned so far was that when people discovered my secret, it gave them power over me, and I hated that.

twenty-two

took the pills as instructed—two pills each day, first thing in the morning.

On Wednesday afternoons, when Celia had dance class, I took the bus to check in with Dr. Gamez. Each visit, he checked my vitals. He asked too many questions about my private thoughts and daydreams. He taped tiny monitors to my chest and wrists, then showed me pictures of models torn from *Seventeen, Teen Vogue, GQ,* and *Men's Health.* Hundreds of pictures. Sometimes I'd get distracted, thinking about how much cash he must have dropped on magazine subscriptions.

His note taking was *rigorous* and *thorough*—"the hallmarks," he said, "of good work in a laboratory."

Quiet music always played on his sleek little stereo. He preferred Bach: slow piano notes, rising and falling, with occasional flourishes. The effect was either calming or creepy, depending on my mood.

His office was filled with interesting things. World maps, fancy silver scales, a doll-sized plaster statue of the Blessed Virgin. I was curious about a white metal contraption that looked like a cross between a desktop computer and the fancy chrome espresso machine at Rita's café.

"What is that thing?"

He followed my gaze. "That *thing* is an electron microscope."

I studied it more closely, thinking of the cheap desktop microscopes we had at school. In comparison, this thing was badass. I wondered if it could show me eyelash bugs.

"Hands off," Dr. Gamez said, without looking up from his notebook. "That piece of equipment is worth more than the ramshackle apartment building you live in."

I withdrew my hand.

A row of plastic pill bottles on his desk reminded me of the window ledge in my grandparents' bathroom.

I picked up one of the bottles. "What are these for?"

He looked at my hand. "Those have been on the market for years. They alleviate the very common phobia of public speaking."

I put them down, picked up another. "And these?"

He barely lifted his eyes. "Used by veterinarians … to eliminate aggression in dogs."

An antique table next to his desk was arrayed with more things to look at: the security monitor, a waxy gray skull, and two glass jars of what looked like white marshmallows in liquid. I pointed. "What's that stuff?"

"Those are lithium hydroxide pellets from Argentina. Lithium is commonly used as an anti-depressant." He sighed as if annoyed. "Now, Jamie, that is enough. I am not your teacher, and I need to concentrate."

I had to admit, it was a relief to be under a doctor's care. The process of becoming straight didn't seem half as dangerous. But I always dreaded his final words as I left the office, some variation of, "Please be sure to clean the bathroom before you go." Or, "The floors in the lab require mopping, Jamie. Please go over them again—this time *thoroughly*." He seemed to take perverse pleasure in this aspect of our relationship, signing off on my service-hours form like a sadistic parole officer.

Celia didn't like this development any better than I did. "I feel like you're my father's *maid* suddenly," she said. "Can't you cut lawns or something?"

"It's not about money," I said. "I need the service hours." But this reasoning didn't make her any happier.

Sometimes I still had bouts of blurry vision. Dr. Gamez suspected this was ordinary eyestrain—"perfectly *common*"— and he suggested I see a regular optometrist about glasses.

On some mornings, I felt the familiar ache in my shoulders. Dr. Gamez assured me it had nothing to do with the drug. "Normal tension," he said. "Your family's financial situation may very well be the source of that."

This might have been true. My parents' package business, as I had long dreaded and expected, was a flop.

"It's a seasonal business," my father explained, waving away my concerns before school one morning. It was late April. I sat on their dining room floor, eating a cold Pop-Tart. Next to me, rolls of Christmas gift-wrap were still stacked against the wall.

"We were busy during the holidays, we'll be busy again," he said. "Wait until May and June. Mother's Day, Father's Day, graduations, weddings. We'll be *buried*."

My mother looked up from a computer spreadsheet. "Honest to God, I don't know where all the money went. I thought I was getting pretty good at accounting."

"In the meantime," Dad said, "Ronnie's got me up the wazoo with landscaping projects."

I cringed, imagining my father and me competing for jobs in the summer.

My brain reviewed the few times I'd taken money from the cash box. It couldn't have made that much of a difference.

I sneezed. On top of everything else, I'd caught a cold. I sneezed three more times while I finished the Pop-Tart. It was the generic kind, but it tasted better than anything I could find in my grandparents' kitchen.

"Stay home," my mother suggested. "Spend the day in bed."

"I can't miss today. Too much going on." I didn't like being around them when things were so tense financially, even if I was partially to blame.

———

Things were changing between Celia and me. She'd been angry ever since our conversation about birth control. I thought I had been appropriately casual about her big revelation, but now I realized I'd been too cool. Had she really expected me to leap into bed with her just because she was on the Pill? Would most straight boys have jumped at the chance? Whatever happened to waiting until junior year to have sex?

Celia stopped meeting me in the Commons before school. At her locker, her smiles seemed forced. In the library and the cafeteria, she spent more time sitting with her girlfriends, whispering stories with a long-suffering expression. She was letting me know I'd blown it big time.

In homeroom, Mr. Mallet raced through the daily announcements. His tone was a combination of anger and boredom, as if he were only reading us our Miranda Rights so he could arrest us. I couldn't believe I'd ever thought those silly, tight coach's shorts were sexy.

I grabbed a tissue from his desk and blew my nose. My snot was dark red, almost brown.

You have the right to be surprised by bloody snot.
You have the right to be grossed out.
You have the right to be concerned.

This wasn't a normal nosebleed. I excused myself and went straight to the bathroom, holding the tissue against my nose.

In the bathroom, I encountered a familiar face standing at the sink.

"Jamie, hi," Ivan said.

"What are you doing here?" I asked stupidly.

What else do you do in the bathroom, perv?

Because of the drug, I didn't get the same spark from Ivan that I once did, but somehow I still managed to act insane around him.

He held up a notebook. "I can't study in homeroom. I've got a Chem quiz in five minutes, and this was the best place I could think to go. Is something wrong?"

"I'm sick." I stared at myself in the mirror. My face looked paler than ever, my eyes were bloodshot. I tried to see up into my nostrils. "I have a bloody nose, but I think I'm really sick."

"Celia will take care of you."

"Maybe. We're going through a rough patch."

"Yeah?"

I nodded. "These days, she'll be happier to let me suffer."

"Too bad." He gave me a small, sympathetic smile, but then glanced down at his notebook. Whenever we were alone, Ivan continued to keep his distance, as if I'd taught him a hard lesson he wouldn't forget.

I went to the stall for some toilet paper so I could blow my nose again. More bloody brown gunk.

Oh my grossness.

This was freaking me out—scarier than blurry vision or spastic joints. I felt light-headed.

"You know, Jamie," Ivan said slowly, "I want to talk to you about something."

I sort of froze above the toilet. "Yeah? Hold on a sec."

I wiped my face with tissue and stepped out of the stall. "What's up?"

"It probably doesn't matter anymore, old news. But since we're alone, maybe there's no harm."

"No harm in what?"

He smiled again, a little guiltily this time. "I don't want to get in trouble for saying this."

"Trust me, I won't tell anybody." What kind of secret did Ivan have to share with me?

Opportunities arrive like trains...

"It's about the flowers."

Did he mean the unsigned flowers I had sent him? That was ancient history. I leaned against the sink, steadying myself with my hands. "Which flowers?"

"From the Valentine's fundraiser. The unsigned ones."

My heart nearly burst through my T-shirt. I was totally busted. Maybe he'd known all along. "Okay, about those—" I started to say, but he interrupted.

"Those came from Anella."

...And they depart like trains.

I stared at him. I wanted to say, *No, dummy, they came from me!* But then I realized he meant the other flowers, the ones I had received. "Anella sent those?"

"She likes you very much."

It had never crossed my mind that Anella had sent the mystery flowers. I always assumed it was Mimi, or maybe some random classmate. Anella hadn't even made a blip on my radar screen. Just like I never made a blip on Ivan's.

"Jamie, I'm only telling you this now because if you and

Celia stop dating, our friend Anella would be interested to hear it."

"Thanks. Like I said, I think we're only going through a rough patch."

He nodded.

It struck me that there were probably people like Anella all over the school—all over the world—wasting too much time with people they didn't have the slightest chance with. This knowledge made me feel worse than ever.

The bell rang, and Ivan tapped his notebook. "Time to go kick some butt in Chemistry."

"Wait—Ivan. Please don't tell Anella that Celia and I are having problems. I don't want to get her hopes up, you know?"

He nodded as if he understood, and walked out.

Ivan, too, had no idea what he'd once meant to me. Now, thanks to Dr. Gamez and his pills, he'd never know. Maybe that was for the best. I felt bad that Ivan was lonely, but given the circumstances, I wasn't the right guy to be his friend anyway. He was better off without me.

I blew my nose again. Scary Gunk City.

I returned to homeroom to grab my books. Celia used to wait for me there, but she'd stopped coming. Just as well, I thought.

She doesn't care. It's really over.

It would have been difficult to imagine a day that sucked more than this one did. I needed to go home. I went to the main office to call my parents. As I entered the reception area, I heard a loud whisper: "Hey!"

Wesley was sitting in one of the wooden chairs outside the dean's office. His flannel shirt was torn and he had a black eye. He looked awful.

"Holy crap. What happened to you?"

He grinned and lifted a finger. "A case of mistaken identity, as it turns out. Which got a little out of hand."

"I guess so." I sat uneasily in the chair next to him. This was a notorious spot at Maxwell. It was where students waiting for parents could often be seen vomiting. The area always smelled like floor polish and vinegar. "Are you okay?" I asked Wes.

He shook his head and raised his eyebrows, staring into space as if he knew very little about the situation himself. "They're calling my parents. I think they're going to suspend me."

"Damn, really?"

"Hey, take this." He handed me his yellow *Spanks For Not Smoking!* lighter.

I stuffed it into my pocket. "You're giving up the smoke?"

"That's a *loan*. I don't want my parents finding it. I'm in enough trouble."

"Wes, listen to me. Tell them about the Ritalin."

"Nah."

"You've got to. This is enough. First the baseball, and now this? Ever since you stopped taking it, you've been acting like a nut."

His lip twisted defensively. "Only sometimes."

"No, all the time."

"How do you know how I act *all the time*? We never see you, now that you're with Celia."

I hesitated, acknowledging the truth of this. "Being off the pills isn't good for you, Wes. Mimi and I have talked about it."

He leaned toward me, eyes blazing. I realized he was furious. He was as pissed-off at me as he was at the rest of the world. "You and Mimi? Have talked about it?"

I nodded, even though he'd caught me in a lie. But a tiny lie, in comparison to all the others.

"I doubt that." He sneered. "Give me a break. Mimi doesn't even like you."

This stung for a second. Since the very first day I'd met her, I had tried to be nice around her, despite how mean she was to me.

"Is that true?"

He tapped the bottom edge of his bruised eye with his fingers. "Dude, she thinks you're a loser. She says you try too hard."

I didn't respond.

"Haven't you noticed she's always picking on you?"

"I ... I thought maybe she had a crush on me."

"Then you are one clueless clown."

I had to agree with that. I felt like a complete idiot. First I'd mistaken Anella's distance for indifference, and now Mimi's meanness for flirtation. It struck me that I had developed a dangerous habit of seeing things the way I wanted them to be, rather than as they were.

Weirdest of all, Mimi wasn't *my* favorite person, either.

She'd teased me ever since our first lunch together, and now it turned out she honestly meant every bitchy remark she made. What a colossal waste of time. It was like I'd been constantly gift-wrapping myself for a person who never, ever wanted what was inside the box. Why had I *ever* tried to get her to be my friend?

"What are you doing here, anyway?" Wesley asked. He looked away, down the hallway toward the exit doors. "Don't tell me you're in trouble too."

I stood and picked up my books. "I am, Wes. Big trouble."

He swung back around to face me. "What kind?"

I bit my lip. After all that Wesley and I had been through together, I still couldn't tell him my secret. I wasn't ready.

I whispered, "The thing is, I can't talk about it right now. But as soon as I can, I'll tell you everything."

"You better."

"I will."

"In the meantime, what are you going to do about it?"

"Excellent question," I said, rising to my feet unsteadily. My stomach felt queasy. I needed to get out of there fast, before I joined the wretched ranks of those who had puked their guts onto that cursed ground.

twenty-three

The next twenty-four hours passed in a blur of dizziness and head congestion. I hid out in bed, barely able to breathe. I was afraid to blow my nose in case more of the scary brown glop came out. This wasn't normal or common, despite what Dr. Gamez might claim.

My dad offered me cold medicine.

"Take one, kiddo," he insisted. "You'll feel better in twenty minutes."

"I'm fine," I lied. "I just need rest."

"Quit whining, then," he said, pulling my bedroom door closed behind him.

The truth was, I was afraid to take any other pills. I didn't know how cold medicine might interact with the Rehomoline. And since I didn't know Dr. Gamez's personal phone number, I had to wait until I could sneak over to their house and talk to him in person.

One thing was clear: I needed to get off the pills. It didn't matter what Dr. Gamez said. I didn't want to keep taking them, waiting for them to start working for real. True, I didn't feel attracted to Ivan anymore, or to any other boy. But I also didn't feel attracted to Celia or to any other girl. Not the way I should have. How long was a person supposed to wait for a drug to start working? I missed the excitement, the obsession of attraction. I used to think about sex all the time. Now I felt numb—maybe the way Wesley felt on his Ritalin. For the first time, I could understand why he'd wanted to stop taking it.

I lay in bed, staring miserably at the ceiling. In the past, I would have jumped at the chance for a lazy day with nothing to do. I would have listened to music, re-read favorite books, watched a movie. But even these old pleasures had lost their appeal.

My cell phone rang. I looked at the number.

Celia.

I answered uncertainly. "Hi."

"Why aren't you at school?"

"So . . . you're talking to me now?"

"Answer the question."

"I'm sick."

A pause. "Sick again. There's a shocker."

I sniffled, as if supplying evidence. "Thanks for the sympathy. I have a cold."

"And I have about two seconds before the bell rings. Here's the deal. I just found out that my aunt is going to New Mexico this weekend, visiting Rudy."

"Good for her."

"She asked me to stop by her condo to check on Abuelito."

I didn't know what to say. "Cool."

"So," she said slowly, as if giving me time to catch up, "I was thinking that maybe you could go over with me, and we could...be alone for a while." Her tone was unusual, half flirty and half impatient. "It's the opportunity we've been waiting for, right?"

"Celia," I said reluctantly, "you know I'm allergic to cats."

"So you'll take a pill or something."

Please, no—for the love of God, no more pills!

"Maybe we should wait and see how I feel this weekend."

She didn't say anything.

"Celia, let's talk about this in person. Not over the phone."

"I need to go."

"Celia," I said, but she had already hung up.

Immediately, I knew. The next time we saw each other face to face, we would break up. Either she would say it, or I would.

Let her say it.

The thing is, I loved everything about her—her confidence, her humor, her brain, even her beauty. She was the most interesting, exciting girl I'd ever known, and the most fun. I just didn't want to have sex with her. The pills were taking too long, and Celia was going crazy in the meantime.

It wasn't fair. I knew she would hate me. Most of all, I would miss her as a friend.

I felt nauseous, sicker than ever.

I got out of bed and went to the kitchen. My grandmother was sitting at the kitchen table, going through a stack of utility bills.

I put my head down on the table and groaned.

She laughed. "Melodramatic, as usual. Why don't you go back to sleep?"

I mumbled, "I can't sleep."

Hello? I haven't slept in four months.

"Get back in bed. Miracles can happen."

I lifted my head. "You know what? I don't believe in miracles anymore."

"That's too bad."

"Do you?"

She ripped a check from her checkbook. She stuffed the check into an envelope, grinning a little as she licked the flap. "Yeah, I do," she said.

"Why?"

"I see them happening. Look right here, it's a miracle we can pay our bills every month."

"But miracles like in the New Testament? Or in your book of Bible poems? I don't buy it. I think they made that stuff up to convince people that Jesus was God's son."

She breathed heavily, as if annoyed. "Let me put it this way. Do I think that at the wedding at Cana, Jesus really changed water into wine? Well, that seems like magic, and I don't believe in magic."

"So you admit, they made that stuff up."

"Not exactly. I think that Jesus had such a loving presence that the people didn't *need* wine at that wedding party. They had just as much fun with water, because of Jesus' company. The water became like wine, because they were all so happy."

I wasn't convinced. "What about the loaves and the fishes? Jesus was so loving while he was preaching that people didn't get hungry? I doubt it."

"Who knows? Maybe Jesus' preaching was so effective that people were inspired to share what they had. Maybe people went to their homes and got more food to share, in the spirit of the sermon. And in that way, a tiny bit of food became a whole lot more."

"Maybe."

"Jamie, think of miracles as changes in *perception*. All those stories about Jesus healing blindness—it's such a powerful metaphor. What were these people blind to? Their selfishness? Their ego or fear? Jesus showed people a way to be happier in their lives. And yes, I do think that kind of miracle happens. More often than you might expect."

"So you're saying, for example, that Mom and Dad's business failing is only a matter of their perception?"

She seemed to choose her words carefully. "I'm saying that if they changed their perception, maybe they would understand what they are *supposed* to be doing to make money."

"And my not being able to sleep is just a matter of changing my perception?"

"Who can say? Maybe you're not *supposed* to be sleeping. Maybe you're supposed to be doing something else. You don't appear very tired to me right now. You seem unhappy and crabby, as you have for several months. And it wouldn't be the first time in the history of the human race that a teenager felt that way, so I'm not exactly in a panic about it."

"Thanks a lot."

I got up from the table and went back to my bedroom, closing the door behind me. I sat on the bed, taking big breaths to fuel my frustration. Nobody ever understood how I felt. It didn't seem fair for her to sit there and talk about miracles happening through changes in perception when her goddamn medicine cabinet held enough pharmaceuticals to heal the whole goddamn neighborhood. Obviously she wasn't relying on a miraculous change-of-perception to keep *her* healthy.

I filled another two tissues with black gunk. Then I changed into jeans and a sweatshirt and snuck out through the bedroom window.

———

Running past the Bound & Ground, I noticed it was dark inside, all the lights off—odd for a weekday afternoon. Then I saw the red "For Sale" sign posted in the window. Rita sure didn't waste any time. She was taking her chance on love, all right.

I pushed through the iron gate of the Gamez property and jogged up to the front door. I entered the security code and walked in. I no longer felt like a trespasser. After spending so much time there, I felt like I finally belonged. But the school day was over, and I knew that I risked seeing Celia. I went straight down to the lab.

Dr. Gamez looked up from his desk when I knocked. "Good afternoon, Jamie," he said. "You are not expected today."

"This isn't working. I'm sick."

"Yes, I can hear you have a cold." He stood up and came around the desk to me. He placed his hand on my forehead, then behind my neck. "No fever. Just a cold, I suppose."

"May I?" Boldly I took the handkerchief from his suit jacket pocket. I blew my nose—a satisfying, wet honk—and handed it back to him. "Here's the latest problem."

When he looked into the handkerchief, his face made an expression that would have given me some pleasure if it weren't so alarming.

"I see."

"And I still have the blurry vision and the aching muscles. And I still can't sleep. And I don't think any of this is *ordinary* or *normal*. The drug is causing it."

"A logical conclusion." He returned to his side of the desk and sat down. He opened a drawer and pulled out a folder of notes. "A new drug goes through many generations before it's ready for the general public. We change the dosage, alter the formula, improve the *taste*, even. It's common for early stages of medicine to have minor side effects."

Those words again: *common, minor*. "I don't think of these side effects as minor. What is that *freaking gunk* coming out of my nose?"

He was writing notes. "Unclear. Harmless, I assume. It looks like a combination of coagulated blood, mucous membrane, perhaps cerebral fluid."

"*Brain* fluid?"

"Please, calm yourself. Jamie, you understood all along that the drug would affect your brain. That's what it is targeted to alter. Not your knees or your toes, for goodness sake."

"But when will it make me … attracted to girls?"

"What do you mean?"

I sank into the chair across from his desk, nearly in tears. "Dr. Gamez, so far, the pills have only made me less attracted to boys. When will they make me more attracted to girls?"

He looked up from his writing as if surprised by the question. "Never."

"Never?"

"That's not the purpose of this drug. Listen to me now. Months ago, when we first discussed this, I told you exactly what the drug was designed to do. I compared it to a pet-allergy pill, remember? This drug is intended to diminish an unwanted response to a very specific stimulus."

I nodded, recalling the conversation.

"And it appears, from your experience, that the medicine is successful in that effort. Your libido seems to be virtually numbed."

"But…" I choked, "I thought … I thought they would make me attracted to girls, too."

He folded his arms. "Then you were mistaken."

"So I won't ever be attracted to girls?"

He smiled reassuringly. "A different pill, maybe, in the

future. That is the wonderful promise of medicine. If there is a large enough demand for it, then a pharmaceutical product naturally will be developed. You must not give up hope for that."

I wiped my face with my sleeve, embarrassed to be crying in front of Dr. Gamez. "You misled me about the drug. You made it seem like a miracle or something."

"In the eyes of many people around the world," he nodded, "it will be a miracle."

"But you encouraged me to date Celia. Wouldn't you say that was a little misleading?"

"Be reasonable. Would I have let you spend so much time alone with my daughter, both here and at a romantic resort in Mexico, if I honestly thought you would try to *screw* her?"

His crassness stunned me into silence.

"I need you to be quiet for a moment, Jamie, so I can think of something to give you to decrease the loss of cerebral fluid."

"Not necessary." I pushed the chair away from the desk. "I'm done with the drug."

He sighed impatiently. "We won't have that conversation again. You need to continue to take it until we have arrived at a satisfactory formulation of the medicine."

"No."

"Really?" He took a breath, and for the first time he raised his voice. "Then I have no choice but to have you arrested for theft and thrown into juvenile detention. Your family will go broke trying to secure your release. I will see to that."

I leaned forward, wanting to hit him or strangle him. "Do

you want your daughter to learn what you've been doing? That you've known all along that her boyfriend isn't really attracted to her? Don't you think that will make Celia a little bit angry? Seriously, I'm not taking another single pill."

He glared at me. "When I first met you, you may recall that I complimented you on your powers of observation and your sensitivity, not your intelligence. Are you willing to risk the side effects that will come if you abruptly stop taking the medicine?"

"What side effects?"

"Ones that would make the minor discomforts you've endured so far seem like a day in the park."

"I don't believe you."

"Are you foolish enough to take that risk?"

I leaned back in the chair, nearly shaking with anger. He was right. I had no idea what withdrawal from the pills might be like. I was already freaked about the weird fluid leaking from my brain.

I felt defeated, paralyzed. "What happens next?"

"We need to figure out what is wrong with the current formula. We might not have even noticed a problem if it were not for your cold, so we must be grateful for that. We need to work quickly."

"What's the hurry?"

He stood from his chair and reached for a thick medical reference book from a shelf. "In the coming weeks, we will begin testing at sites in Asia, Africa, and South America. My assistants have been traveling for the past month, finding subjects willing to participate in the study."

I recalled the list of names I'd seen, so many weeks ago, in his briefcase. "Will you give *them* the complete information? Or just half, like you gave to me?"

He pretended not to hear me as he consulted the book's index. "Once the foreign tests have been conducted, we will begin conventional testing in this country and apply to the Food and Drug Administration for approval." He thumbed through several pages, scanning for the information he needed. "Ah, good enough. I may have something in my lab for you to take for a few days, until we can correct the drug formula. Sit still for a moment while I get it." He lowered the book and smiled at me, almost warmly, but I knew it was his control over me that pleased him most. "I assure you, by tomorrow your young snot will return to normal."

He left me sitting in the chair, looking around the room in a daze. At the books and maps, the statue of the Blessed Virgin, the fancy microscope. My eyes finally settled on the big glass jars of marshmallow pellets. Staring at the jars, my vision blurred, the white pellets all running together in a gooey mass. I felt powerless and despondent under the weight of something strange—something so much bigger than me. How long had I been feeling that way?

It's embarrassing now to admit, but it wasn't until that moment that I realized: *This doctor is a villain. This drug is evil.*

Dr. Gamez was like a wack-job evil doctor from a bad sci-fi movie. He had a sinister plan, and I was only one small part of it. If he was successful, how many people would be taking Rehomoline all over the world? Religious extremists could use the formula to repress the desires of gay people. In countries where homosexuality was still a crime, gay men could be forced to take the pills by law, against their will. I could envision a whole category of people whose hearts had been numbed. An army of robots.

What good could come from a pill that removed a person's capacity for desire? I couldn't believe I had willingly taken the pills for months, thinking they would make me straight—a whole different person. Instead, all they did was strip away the essence of what *made* me a person.

I was definitely not ready to come out. I was still too afraid to face those hard conversations. But I knew one thing for sure: I wanted to be a human being, not a robot. I wanted to fall in love, like everyone else. I wanted to share my future life with someone who loved me, too.

I needed to get out of that office.

My instinct was to get up and run, but I wasn't sure Dr. Gamez would let me. Would he physically stop me from going? He had so much to protect. Even if I could get away, would he accuse me of stealing the pills from him? I couldn't put my family in worse financial jeopardy than we were already in.

To protect myself, I needed solid proof that Dr. Gamez had engineered the experiment from the beginning. Otherwise, in a courtroom, it would be his word against mine. Celia knew nothing. My friends knew nothing. My family knew nothing. I hadn't recorded our conversations or kept a journal. Dr. Gamez was a respected, successful doctor. A jury would have no reason to believe my word over his. I didn't stand a chance.

Unless I have the notes.

The complete account of the experiment—*rigorous* and *thorough,* in Dr. Gamez's own handwriting—was right there on the desk. Everything I needed to prove my case. But he would never let me take them. Not willingly.

Down the hall, a cupboard door opened and closed. A metal stool squeaked against a linoleum floor. Dr. Gamez would be back any second.

I had never thrown a punch in my life. I didn't even know how. Besides, my body was too weak to fight him.

I rose out of my chair and looked around. There had to be something I could use to stun him—just temporarily. I approached the expensive white microscope. Too heavy to lift. The Blessed Virgin statue might be painful on impact, but would it be enough? The security monitor was about the right size. I picked it up, yanked its wires out of the wall, and carried it to a hiding place behind the door. The monitor was the heaviest thing I'd ever lifted above my head. I stood there, waiting, terrified.

I am not a violent person!

Dr. Gamez entered the room and the monitor dropped effortlessly, guided by gravity. The monitor landed with a painful crash, and a second later the doctor followed, buckling at his knees. The bottle of pills he'd brought with him skittered across the carpet like a little brown mouse.

My arms shaking, I bent to examine Dr. Gamez. No blood that I could see. He was out cold, but still (*thank God*) breathing. I dragged him by his ankles out of the office and into the hallway. I rested a second, and then dragged him to the lab. He had to be out of the way for what I needed to do next.

My *simple goal*, as Dr. Gamez would have put it, was to destroy everything in that office. Anything remotely connected to the stupid, worthless, evil project.

I had the foresight to set aside a few items for my defense. First I took the file folder with Dr. Gamez's notes in it. Several manila folders lay in the same pile, all labeled "Rehomoline," so I grabbed them. I set this pile near the door. Everything else, as far as I was concerned, could be trashed.

I opened several of the file drawers and pulled a dozen folders to make a heap on his desk, and then made another pile on the antique table. It felt strangely satisfying to see his office in complete disarray.

I reached into my pocket and found Wesley's yellow lighter. I lit a few paper corners and stepped back. Then I did the same to the papers on the antique table.

Good-bye, notes. Good-bye, research. Good-bye, exotic marshmallows from Argentina.

I went to the taller metal file cabinets in the back, looking for the drawer marked *R*. I opened it, pulled out all the files that my arms could carry, and added them to the two burning piles. I was only trying to be as *thorough* as Dr. Gamez had taught me to be.

Good-bye, Rehomoline.

You are not needed in this world.

In less than a minute, the fires gained strength, smoke

reaching up to the ceiling. Even from the door of the office, the heat was intense. The fire alarm would go off any second, which would activate the water sprinklers on the ceiling. The structural damage to the facility would be minimal, but I hoped the paper loss would be significant. My eyes began to sting from all the smoke. I grabbed the important files and closed the door to his office behind me.

I faltered.

Celia was coming down the corridor. She saw the smoke and screamed, "Oh my God!"

"There's a fire, Celia. We gotta get out of here."

She lowered her eyes, grimacing, as if it caused her physical pain to see me. "What are you doing here? Where's my dad?"

"He's in the lab. Please, let's just go!" I reached for her hand, but she pushed me away and slid by.

"Celia, come with me."

"Daddy!" She turned and disappeared into the lab.

I continued down the corridor and threw open the back door. I scrambled up the wet concrete staircase, letting the door slam behind me. A siren began to wail deep inside the house, and I wasn't sure if it was the smoke detectors or the security alarm.

I raced across the brick patio to the grass. Already the big moon was visible in the dark sky. Beneath my feet the ground was soft and springy, a winter's worth of moisture finally loosening. I raced to the side of the house and stopped. High fences protected both sides of the Gamez estate. I didn't have the key to the padlock on the gate. I was trapped.

The only option was the river.

I ran back across the lawn and down the rocky embankment, but hesitated at the water's edge. I didn't know how to transport the files without getting them wet. There was a steep drop, nearly ten feet to the water. I might have taken the plunge if I hadn't heard Dr. Gamez's voice.

"Stop where you are, Jamie. Turn around."

I glanced back. Part of me was relieved—I hadn't killed him.

He was standing on the brick terrace, near the iron table and chairs where Celia and I had spent our first afternoon together, drawing pictures. He was about thirty feet away from me. In the moonlight, I could see the flash of metal in his hand.

A gun—maybe the same pistol I'd seen in Mexico—with the barrel pointed straight at me.

"These games have gone on long enough," he called. "And now you try to destroy my research?"

"You are destroying my *life*!" I shouted.

Celia had followed him. She was crying. "What is going on?"

"Come back inside, Jamie," Dr. Gamez said calmly. "We have all had enough of your selfish melodrama lately."

This accusation seemed a bit ironic, coming from someone holding a gun.

I didn't believe he would shoot me, not in front of Celia. Not outside, where people could hear. The river was only two hundred feet wide at this point. Neighbors on the other side would go to their windows if they heard a gunshot.

Celia approached her father, her hands outstretched. "Daddy, what is happening?"

"Celia, I've got to talk to you," I said.

"Close your mouths. Both of you." He waved her away. "Jamie, I need those folders."

I couldn't go back inside with them. If we were inside, there was no telling what he might do. No one knew where I was, or where I was supposed to be. But it was hard to argue with the barrel of that gun.

"Celia, I'm *sorry!*" I called, wondering what I could say next.

It was the last thing I ever said to her.

That was when the infamous "explosion" took place. Truth is, it wasn't much of an explosion. A few basement windows burst—incredible, magenta-colored flares, followed by clouds of smoke. The force of it knocked Dr. Gamez and Celia off their feet, and they reached for each other in the wet grass. They were probably as surprised as I was.

Who knew lithium was so freaking explosive? I was still two years away from taking Chemistry.

The smoke detectors in Dr. Gamez's office must have summoned an emergency team, because we heard the roar of the fire trucks as they arrived on the opposite side of the house.

In retrospect, this was where I made my biggest mistake. I should've run straight to the side gate near the house, called to the police and firefighters, and passed all the folders through the iron bars. I should've found a police officer and said, "This is crime evidence—protect it!"

Instead, I just wanted to get away. From Dr. Gamez, from Celia, from the entire situation.

After the explosion, when the others turned back to the house, I dropped all the files at the river's edge and jumped into the water. The river was stunningly cold and muddy, filled with sharp rocks and duck shit and probably rats. A horror movie of a river. But the trees overhead blocked the moonlight, so my path was dark. I kept my head low in the water, trying to hide as I swam. I swam until I reached the other side, without looking back. I scrambled up the bank, freezing and wet and relieved to be safe. Dr. Gamez never fired his gun.

Whether the notes were lost in the river, or he destroyed them, I don't really know. Maybe he and Celia scoured the riverbank to salvage the files and keep them. According to public record, nobody ever saw those papers again.

twenty-four

Apparently I presented an unforgettable face on the Western Avenue bus that night.

That was the testimony of numerous witnesses who spoke at the trial. My clothes were soaked, my face and neck covered in mud and slime from the embankment. I must have stunk up the whole bus. One old guy who was interviewed on the TV news remarked that I looked like *The Creature from the Black Lagoon.* I appreciated that.

I got home, still wet and shivering, and marched straight upstairs to find my parents. My dad turned off *Wheel of Fortune* and my mother nearly dropped her Sudoku puzzle.

"What happened to you?" she asked. "You're … you're covered in mud."

"*It came from beneath the lake,*" my father intoned.

"Give me one minute." I went into the bathroom and

closed the door. I turned on the shower and plunged my entire head and torso—fully clothed—under the water. I was generous with the soap and shampoo. It was time to come clean.

I grabbed an armload of thin towels and returned to the living room, shoes squishing and clothes dripping. I dropped a towel on the edge of the coffee table, right between my parents, and took a seat.

"Okay, guys, so here's the thing…"

And then I told them.

Was this an unforgivably *melodramatic* way to come out to my parents? Guilty as charged. Not recommended to anybody. But at least I told them.

For years, I had not felt close to my parents. It was like we were separated by this mysterious distance, made only worse by living in different apartments. But suddenly here I was, spilling my big secret. I'd already been through hell. What was the worst that could happen now? I could handle it if my parents got angry, if they put up more emotional walls between us. Even if they kicked me out.

I'd survive. I'd probably end up on the infamous island my old Internet friends joked about. Maybe we'd be reunited there. I could see it so clearly—all of us standing around, talking about the families and friends we left behind, comparing battle scars but looking fabulous in our tiny little Speedos. It would be a strange and unfamiliar world, but it would certainly be better than the solitary confinement I'd been living in.

I told my parents, and I braced myself for the worst.

And then a funny thing happened. The longer I talked,

the more my parents leaned forward, not back, in their seats. At one point, my father reached out and put a reassuring hand on my wet knee. My mother got up from the sofa and joined me on the coffee table. "Honey, we love you," she said, her arm around my shoulders. "Listen to me—we *love* you."

I felt my body collapse under the weight of her arm. Their response stunned me. In a way, it felt like I had finally swum over to that long-imagined, long-dreaded island and found my own parents standing there. Like they'd been standing there for years, waiting for me.

We've always known this about you.

Maybe, all along, I'd been the distant one. Maybe the only thing *normal* and *common* about my experience was the confusion I'd felt for so many years—and the overwhelming fear that prevented me from saying something sooner. The fear that Dr. Gamez had recognized and exploited.

"I'm so glad you told us," my father said, his voice a whisper. "Trust me, you have nothing to worry about anymore."

———

Well, little did he know. The police arrived before I could finish the whole story. They said they needed me to go over to the station to answer some questions. My parents rode with me in the squad car, all of us covered in a wool blanket to keep me warm.

"What I still need to know," my mother said, "is why you smell like a burned-up garbage truck."

"Oh yeah," I said. "I hadn't gotten to that part yet There

was a minor incident involving an explosion along the north branch of the Chicago River."

We spent about six hours at Precinct 24, answering questions. More accurately, *avoiding* answering questions. My parents called a lawyer friend, who strongly advised me not to say a word. At midnight, my parents demanded that I be allowed to go home and sleep. The police didn't have enough evidence to hold me. Due to my age and lack of a criminal record, they let me go, but told me I couldn't leave the country for any reason until after the matter had been adjudicated.

Within days, my school yearbook picture was on the front page of newspapers and Web sites across the country. *BOY BOMBER IN FAMILY PHARM*, according to the *Chicago Tribune*. The *Sun-Times* was even worse: *DID SPURNED BOYFRIEND BURN LUXURY LAB?* These first stories were all the handiwork of Dr. Gamez's PR team, who he hired even before the trial began.

Reporters camped out along the sidewalk in front of the house. My grandparents were mortified by all the attention. We didn't even tell them about the gay part until that aspect of the story made the papers.

I missed the last three weeks of school, including exams, but it wasn't at the top of my mind given the bigger problems at hand.

———

Dr. Gamez hadn't been joking when he said he would prosecute to the full extent of the law. Due to a lack of evidence, all the criminal charges were dropped, but in the civil court, it came down to this:

The prosecution argued that over the course of five months, I stole expensive, untested drugs both from Dr. Gamez's lab and from Dr. Gamez's personal property. Moreover, I had intentionally destroyed a state-of-the-art laboratory and caused significant damage to the basement level of the mansion, with losses totaling more than five million dollars.

With the help of a family friend who provided *pro bono* legal representation, we counter-sued. Our suit claimed that Dr. Gamez had performed an ongoing and illegal drug experiment on a minor without parental consent. First, we argued, Dr. Gamez had lured me with experimental pharmaceuticals that were not approved by the FDA. Our lawyer stressed the word *drug* a lot during his remarks. Moreover, Dr. Gamez had made the pills accessible and available and continued to make them accessible and available even with the full knowledge that I was taking them. Under the increasing drug regimen, Dr. Gamez had examined me, questioned me, and exploited me in the development of the new drug—all for his personal and professional gain.

In the interest of judicial economy, the court allowed the two civil actions to be heard simultaneously.

Meanwhile, the media gobbled up the story. My parents responded to Dr. Gamez's smear campaign with press conferences of their own. For weeks, gay-rights groups protested at Daley Plaza outside City Hall, supporting my case. They called Dr. Gamez the real criminal—a *NAZI DOC*. They held up signs. *WHERE'S THE RX FOR HOMOPHOBIA?* and *PRESCRIBE LOVE, NOT HATE.*

Anti-gay activists gathered at Daley Plaza too. Their signs said things like *ALL FAGS EVENTUALLY BURN* and *SEND PANSY PYRO UP THE RIVER.* Their hostility toward me was shocking. I began to realize how popular Rehomoline would be if it ever was approved. It was a scary reminder that grownups could be just as homophobic as teenagers.

Because of the amount of damage I had caused, along with the media attention, Dr. Gamez's attorneys made the case that I should be tried as an adult. The judge, who was running for re-election, agreed. Public opinion seemed to be on my side, but that didn't count for squat in the courtroom. The problem was, I didn't have proof. All the damn notes were gone.

Then again, Dr. Gamez didn't have proof that I had intentionally and directly caused the explosion. It turned out there was one room in his fancy lab that did not have a security camera: Dr. Gamez's own office. He couldn't even prove that I trespassed. After all, I had several weeks' worth of school service-hour forms with Dr. Gamez's clear signature.

Due to a lack of compelling evidence, the court determined that I could not be held accountable for the major damages to the laboratory. At the same time, the court could not determine beyond a reasonable doubt whether Dr. Gamez experimented on me as I claimed he did. With the few pills I could produce—shown to the court in the now-famous plastic Army tank—the court could only say for certain that Dr. Gamez had violated an Illinois statute called the

Drug Dealer Liability Act. He had endangered my life by making a dangerous drug accessible and available, and this exposure had caused me pain, suffering, emotional distress, mental anguish, loss of educational potential, and a list of other factors that may or may not have contributed to my alleged behavior on the night of the fire.

It did not take long for the court to reach its decision.

I was awarded one million dollars in civil damages.

A miracle.

The other miracle was that Dr. Gamez didn't appeal the verdict. According to newspapers, he left the country "on business" immediately after the trial.

I gave the money to my parents and grandparents. I figured I owed it to them: payment for the petty cash I'd "borrowed," with plenty of interest.

"Let's all take a fancy vacation to *Mex-i-co!*" my grandmother suggested at our celebratory dinner after the trial.

"*Aloha, amigos,*" my grandfather said, raising his beer.

"A college fund comes first," my mother said.

I nodded. "And I have an idea, too."

———

Several days later, a perky realtor in a too-tight, too-short skirt unlocked the front door of the Bound & Ground and ushered us in. She switched on all the lights, chattering about the "huge potential" of the space. The café had been empty for over a month, chairs stacked on tabletops, but the place looked and smelled remarkably clean. The chrome shelves behind the counter still held rows of gleaming ceramic mugs. I listened for the ghost of Rita and her bracelets.

"It's cute," my mother said. She approached the sleek bar area with its black countertops and industrial lighting. Then she turned and faced the bookcases lining the wall. "It looks like something Julia Roberts would own in a movie."

I almost laughed. "It was a good business. I was in here dozens of times. Every neighborhood needs a place like this."

"But the name...Bound & Ground?" my dad said. "Kind of a downer, right?"

As soon as we bought it, we rechristened it the Island Café. We painted the walls with bright blue skies and palm trees, fixed the wobbliest tables, and added more food to the menu. Comfort foods like meatloaf and pulled pork sandwiches and veggie chili. The day we reopened, a line formed all the way out the door.

———————

In the weeks after the fire, my body returned to normal. I started sleeping again, for one thing, and dreaming. My eyesight improved. Maybe it was being off the drug, or maybe it was just springtime, but I had forgotten how colorful the city can be. Color is everywhere—in the city parks, alley murals, neon signs, even on passing cars. It took some time, but I started noticing boys again, too. Now that the days are warm, I'll be in the café, pouring coffee or clearing dishes, and I'll see the most handsome boys walking by the big window. Guys my age, hanging in groups, or college dudes walking alone, listening to music in their own little world. It makes me smile. It's the most common and ordinary thing, but seeing them makes me feel alive inside.

I had forgotten.

No, I don't have a boyfriend—I don't even want one. Give me a break, I'm only fifteen. I can't even drive. "A teenage boy without a crush isn't a teenage boy," my grandfather still says to encourage me. Well, maybe I do have a crush or two, but I keep them to myself. I don't want to talk about my love life— real or imagined—with my family. Isn't *that* normal?

———————

Wesley's back on his Ritalin, a lower dosage than before. Even he agrees he's better on it than off. After my story made the newspapers, Wesley came right over and said he wanted to hear the whole sordid saga from my own mouth. We sat in my backyard, leaning against the brick wall of the garage to hide from reporters, and I told him everything. I was finally ready.

"Okay then," he said when I finished. "Cool."

"Cool?"

"Yeah, more chickies for me." Turns out Wesley was waiting on the island too, right next to my parents. Now he and I split afternoon shifts at the café, better friends than ever. Wes is saving money to go to college and study medicine. He says he wants to develop better drugs for kids with ADHD. He was the first one who showed me the newspaper article on the FDA's unprecedented decision to preemptively deny approval of Rehomoline for Dr. Gamez's intended purposes, which is awesome. Not so awesome is the fact that Dr. Gamez can still apply to the FDA for approval of Rehomoline if he can show the drug has other benefits—a shady way for the FDA to cover its ass. No doubt, those pills will be available someday for people who want them. But that won't be me.

———————

During the trial, a letter came for me in the mail. Maxwell Tech stationery, with Mr. Covici's name printed above the return address. I opened it eagerly, hoping it might contain some piece of big-picture wisdom like something he'd paint on the wall of the library, but intended especially for me. But it only said,

> *Dear Jamie,*
>
> *Using the club money, we have acquired a beautiful new screen for the auditorium. You must come help us plan the film series. Some suggestions for Halloween, please? We are pleased that you are safe, and we look forward to your return to school.*

Covici's message cheered me, but to be honest, I've had enough of horror movies for now. My old copies can gather dust in my bedroom. If I go back to Maxwell and work on the film series, I want to show something else. Anything else. *Love stories, maybe.*

I miss Celia. I miss exploring the city with her. Even though the café is only a few blocks from her house, I never see her. Maybe they moved away or went to Mexico for the summer. I don't expect to hear from her. She has more than enough reasons to be angry with me for a long time.

————————

But a funny thing happened the other day.

It was a crazy-hot summer afternoon. Ivan and Anella were hanging out at the café, playing cards. They come in a lot when they're not out sailing on Lake Michigan. Tan, their hair the color of the beach under the sun, they both get free drinks from me—for different reasons. The weirdest part? Now that they know I'm gay, it's actually easy for us all to be friends. The old unspoken tensions are gone. We can flirt and tease one another and there's no risk. No expectation. We feel comfortable with each other.

I even taught them to play "Sex or No Sex?" We'll sit at a table near the window like a panel of judges on reality TV, and we speculate about random people walking by. Odds are, we're correct at least fifty percent of the time. We all like playing games we can win.

Anyway, the other day a stranger with a familiar face entered the café. She was dressed professionally in a dark suit, not like a college student anymore. But her mousy hair, nervous mouth, and John Lennon–style eyeglasses were unmistakable.

Anella lowered the cards to her lap and whispered, "No sex."

"You'd be surprised," I said.

I jumped up and went to the register.

The woman gave her order for coffee and I took her money. "Can I ask you something? Is your name ... *Amanda Lynn?*"

She smiled uncertainly. "Do we know each other?"

No joke, it felt almost like meeting a celebrity. "Well," I said, "you may recall that you lost a wallet and a silver bracelet a while back, correct? If you're interested, I know who has them."

"Wait a minute—those things were *stolen* from me."

This was a first: accused of taking something I hadn't actually taken.

"No, my friend just found them ... on the ground." I hesitated, wondering how specific I should be. Was she telling the truth? Maybe she was embarrassed. "She found them on the sidewalk and didn't know how to contact you." I scribbled Celia's name and cell phone number on the back of an old receipt. "She'll be glad to hear from you."

Reading the information, she still seemed suspicious. "Thanks." She moved down the counter, took her coffee, and turned to leave.

"Hey," I called. "If you wouldn't mind, tell her Jamie says hi. *Hi* and *sorry*. Would you remember to do that?"

She nodded and left in a hurry.

It makes me smile to think of Celia getting that phone call.

Maybe, if we both return to Maxwell in September, I'll give her one more flower. But what would I write on the message?

Regrets—This boy regrets not being honest with you
  from the beginning.
Secrets and schemes—This boy has had enough of
  them.
Sex—Nope, not yet. How about you?

In retrospect, the whole thing feels like a mixed-up movie—part romantic comedy, part horror flick—instead of what it was, just weird and confusing normal life.

My life. Maybe it's time to start falling in love with that.

Hey Jamie, you rock!
Love,
Yourself

Author's Note

As far as I know, no drug exists that could change a person's sexual orientation. I made this story up. Never consulted with doctors, never cruised the Internet for information about cutting-edge pharmaceutical news. I just sat down and wrote the story using my imagination.

Moreover, I hope a drug like this *never* exists. I'm gay and—not to brag or tempt fate or anything—my life is pretty dang wonderful just the way it is. My whole perspective would change if I were straight. So would my tastes and my sense of humor, and who knows if I'd even be a writer? More than anything, I love my partner, Mike, and the life we share together.

But here's something I'm not proud of. When I was young, I might have taken a drug like the one in this book. I definitely prayed for the same miracle Jamie prays for. I did not want to be gay. I wanted to be like everyone else. The notion of being gay filled me with a secret terror—a real dread of my future. And I think many gay teenagers feel that way too. That's why I wrote this book. It's normal to want to "feel normal," whatever normal means. Especially in high school.

Over time, I grew up and stopped being afraid. Once the fear was gone, everything in my life changed for the better. It was a miracle. No drug required.

Acknowledgments

The author wishes to thank his family, as well as the following people for their generous contributions to this novel: Brian Farrey and Sandy Sullivan and everyone at Flux, Kate Klise, Mike Kuras, Kristine Huntley, John Carpenter, Sheila Kohler, Jonathan Demme, Anne Brashler, Alfred Hitchcock, Colleen Collins Greene, Mia Farrow, Erin O'Brien, Brian Alesia, Mary Shelley, and students at CICS Northtown Academy in Chicago, who unanimously voted for the best title.